UR
ECTIVE

*A DCI Bryce mystery*

Peter Zander-Howell

Copyright © 2024 Peter Zander-Howell

All rights reserved.

Certain well-known historical persons are mentioned in this work. All other characters and events portrayed in this book are fictitious, and any similarity to real persons, alive or dead, is coincidental and not intended by the author. Real-world locations in this book may have been slightly altered.

No part of this book may be reproduced, or stored in a retrieval system, or transmitted in any form or by any means, electronic, mechanical, photocopying, recording, or otherwise, without the express permission of the publisher.

Cover photograph © Peter Zander-Howell

# INTRODUCTION

In 1950, a death occurs under the uniquely-banded cliffs in Hunstanton. It is soon realised that this is a case of murder, but the Norfolk police inspector runs into difficulties, and Scotland Yard DCI Philip Bryce finds himself back in the county for the second time in a matter of months.

A local amateur detective with a considerable knowledge of murder cases (both real and fictional) is determined to help the police, and comes up with various suggestions. However, initially neither he nor the police seem to be able to pin all the usual key elements – means, motive, and opportunity – on any one person.

Eventually, one person ends up in the dock at the Assizes in Norwich – but the drama still hasn't ended!

# PREFACE

## DETECTIVE CHIEF INSPECTOR BRYCE

Philip Bryce is an unusual policeman. A Cambridge-educated barrister, he joined the Metropolitan Police in 1937 under Lord Trenchard's accelerated promotion scheme.

After distinguished army service in WW2, by 1949 he has become Scotland Yard's youngest Detective Chief Inspector.

His fiancée was killed during the war, but he recently married a woman whom he met on another murder case.

Bryce is something of a polymath, and has a number of outside interests – railways and cricket near the top of the list.

# CONTENTS

Title Page

Copyright

Introduction

Preface

| | |
|---|---:|
| CHAPTER 1 | 1 |
| CHAPTER 2 | 13 |
| CHAPTER 3 | 33 |
| CHAPTER 4 | 50 |
| CHAPTER 5 | 76 |
| CHAPTER 6 | 94 |
| CHAPTER 7 | 106 |
| CHAPTER 8 | 127 |
| CHAPTER 9 | 147 |
| CHAPTER 10 | 162 |
| CHAPTER 11 | 179 |
| CHAPTER 12 | 191 |
| CHAPTER 13 | 212 |

| | |
|---|---|
| CHAPTER 14 | 230 |
| CHAPTER 15 | 248 |
| CHAPTER 16 | 259 |
| CHAPTER 17 | 272 |
| CHAPTER 18 | 286 |
| CHAPTER 19 | 294 |
| CHAPTER 20 | 311 |
| Books By This Author | 329 |

# CHAPTER 1

*Sunday 24<sup>th</sup> April 1950*

The living room in Philip and Veronica Bryce's Brentham Garden Suburb home had a large selection of reading material. Works of history, both military and political, were well-represented, as were the classics and the major eighteenth and nineteenth century novelists. Custom-built bookshelves covering the walls on either side of the fireplace also held the Detective Chief Inspector's law books, and those of his great interest – railways.

Detective stories were a category which the couple both enjoyed, for the pleasure of reading as well as for the discussions about plots and characters which these books afforded. There were two hundred volumes in this genre alone, the combination of their personal collections when they married. The protagonist in many of the books was a police detective. Just three of these policemen – Joseph French, Robert Macdonald, and Roderick Alleyne – accounted for some seventy titles between them. In general,

Veronica and her husband rated the authors of these stories highly, Bryce particularly approving of the manner in which the policemen tackled their cases.

Roughly half of the remainder featured amateur detectives: Wimsey, Dupin, Marple, Brown, *et al*. The rest depicted more-or-less professional private detectives: Marlowe, Campion, Spade, Poirot, and Vance. Bryce enjoyed all of these, but purely as entertainment, because he found the premise and development of most of the stories was too often unrealistic.

Absent from the collection was any book featuring Sherlock Holmes. The couple had read Conan Doyle's novels during their youth – at school, or in holiday hotels – and both would concede that the books were well-written. Controversially, however, the DCI felt this detective was overrated and many of his conclusions absurd. He thought that if the books had been written twenty years later, they would have been viewed as caricatures of the style. Long before he had given up the bar to become a policeman, Bryce had also disliked the contemptuous way Sir Arthur often depicted a Scotland Yard detective.

With extended time to relax on a mild Spring afternoon, he took an old favourite off a shelf and sat by a pair of open French windows. Two comfortable chairs had been positioned here to take advantage of the view of the garden throughout the year, the spot especially enhanced today by the sunshine flooding through the doors.

Veronica appeared at his elbow, ready to go out. Philip gave her a kiss as she leaned forward and wished her "Good luck at your auction, my love," then settled himself to read, a cup of tea on the table beside him.

\*\*\*

Guy Ferris, former colonial tea planter, was similarly about to enjoy a 'cup that cheers'. An avid crime story reader himself he was also, in his own estimation, a talented detective, albeit an amateur one.

Born a little before the turn of the century, he had served as an infantry army officer towards the end of the Great War. In 1919 he started his peacetime career, sailing on the SS Equatorial to India. There, he broke his journey, and spent a few days in Bombay before embarking for Colombo. The final leg of his travels took him into the low-lying part of Ceylon, where he took up his post as assistant to the Under-Manager at a tea plantation.

Barely fifteen months later, he found himself promoted to General Manager of the entire enterprise, Spanish influenza having claimed the lives of many islanders as well as both of the senior men in the chain of command above him. The plantation owner, his own health broken by influenza and now finding the heat quite unbearable, decided to return to England. Guy Ferris was left in sole charge.

Although still relatively inexperienced in the ways and workings of a tropical tea plantation, Ferris found his new position and lifestyle surprisingly agreeable. A major factor in this happy outcome was the realisation that the heat – more than ninety degrees at times – did not trouble him unduly. This was possibly because his compact height and lean frame made lesser demands on his heart and system than that experienced by more corpulent Europeans. Fleshier ex-patriots soon realised that relocation to plantations on higher ground (where temperatures were closer to seventy degrees) was essential, not just for comfort but for their longer-term survival.

His enjoyment of the local food, particularly the dishes which used fish and crustaceans from the waters surrounding the island, provided additional support for his smooth transition into life in the tropics. Back home, he had always been fond of the spices which transformed the basic ingredients of a kedgeree. Pickles – whether onions, beetroot, or red cabbage – had been regular standbys for livening up suppers of cold cuts; and a spoonful of chutney could always be relied upon to help out some tired ham or cheddar in a sandwich. He was therefore delighted to find that the variety of curries, pickles and chutneys available to him in Ceylon perfectly suited his taste, and realised they were Epicurean in comparison to those he had previously enjoyed.

With these advantages, Guy Ferris settled into his new life well. He became increasingly knowledgeable about the processes involved in growing and exporting tea, and managed the long-established business competently. Most notably, he did all of this with more than a little consideration for the workers.

In exchange, he was remunerated very well and very regularly by his repatriated principal, Charles Crowther, each quarter day bringing confirmation that his remittance had been credited to the Overseas & Colonial Bank. Always enclosed with this notification was the necessary business correspondence between the two men, with all the tasks to be accomplished in the coming three months clearly set out. Rather tiresomely, from Ferris's point of view, Crowther was also in the habit of writing on a matter which was not strictly related to the plantation as such.

The topic returned to during those early years was the suggestion that Ferris should give serious thought to *'...marriage, my dear chap'*. Ferris became adept at politely swatting aside recommendations from Crowther of presentable girls who were willing to travel to the island so that they might *'...complete his happiness'.* He correctly suspected that each '*...she's ideal, I do assure you...*' protégée, was more than casually connected to his principal, and intended to be an additional 'plant' in what he increasingly considered to be his plantation.

In truth, Crowther had no need to worry and no need to install a willing spy to report on his General Manager. As time passed, it became clear that Ferris was trustworthy in his dealings. But the offers of '*...a charming gal of my acquaintance...*' didn't finally dry up until old colonial friends brought news back to England that Ferris was most unlikely to avail himself of a long-distance bride. It was an open secret that from 1923 he lived with a rather lovely Sinhalese woman.

His overseas sojourn continued, the passing of the years marked by the death of his companion in 1937 and, to a lesser extent, the war which started two years later. It was only when Independence was achieved in 1948 that Ferris thought he saw the writing on the wall. Approaching fifty years of age, he decided it was sensible to give up his post and return to England himself, to live out his life on the accumulated funds in the Overseas & Colonial.

Having spent almost three decades away from England, he was undecided where to buy a house for his retirement and initially moved in with his aged and infirm parents, both of whom promptly died. Born very late to his parents and an only child, he became sole beneficiary of their estate, which included a seafront property in a Norfolk coastal town. Judging that the house was very suitable for his current and also future needs (his parents had achieved advanced old age in it after all) he abandoned looking elsewhere.

Ferris' background and newly settled status in Hunstanton automatically gave him entrée to the upper echelons, such as they were, of the town. But his time in Ceylon had not really given him the love of socialising – and had also left him woefully out of practice. He could play a perfectly decent hand at whist or bridge and was sought after for this purpose. He attended Matins sporadically, but adroitly managed to escape being roped in for reading the lessons. His over-arching preference was to stay at home reading a detective novel. He could be found enjoying these tales while variously sipping whichever of the beverages best suited the time of day, all brought to him by ElaineTrott, his parents' live-in servant, whom he had kept on with the house.

So it was that Guy Ferris, a capable man in good health (and, arguably, not so very long out of his prime,) but with no close relations and no contact with the friends of his youth and infantry days, simply didn't have enough to do.

This was how, in the eighteen months since his return, he had fallen into the habit of following every major criminal case which had made the national news. Sometimes, where he sensed that a case wasn't adequately reported in the national press, he ordered copies of local newspapers to see if more details were to be discovered from those. As well as his immersion in all of the current reports, he made regular trips to the Reading Room in the British Museum to read about crimes in the preceding eighty or so years, seeking out the notorious cases which had captured national, and often international, attention.

Having taken up this new hobby, it wasn't long before Ferris decided that his own powers of detection would be superior – probably vastly superior – to those of the police detectives in charge. Through the letters pages of the newspapers in which he read about unfolding investigations, he began to offer opinion and instruction on how the police should proceed, even going so far as suggesting a ready-made solution to a current crime.

He wrote frequently, mostly to the editors of the Times, Daily Telegraph, and Manchester Guardian, but occasionally to the News of the World or a local paper. Convinced his former colonial connections ought to distinguish him and enhance his standing as a correspondent, he made a point of signing each letter:

*Yours,*
*Guy Franklyn Alwyn Ferris (lately of British*

*Ceylon)*

To his chagrin and bemusement, these letters were never printed. Undeterred, he took to writing directly to the constabulary involved in a case, enclosing a copy of his unpublished newspaper submissions at the same time. Quite often, this would be Scotland Yard rather than a county or borough force. The Yard was obliged to keep a file of letters from Mr Ferris, including those which had been defaced with scrawled comments from exasperated detectives. These epithets were not appreciative. Typical examples read:

> *'What rubbish!'*
> *'Complete failure to grasp the facts'*
> *'None of this makes sense'*
> *'Utter tosh!'*

Curiously (or perhaps not) no senior detective had ever made contact with Mr Ferris. Occasionally, a detective constable or sergeant was despatched to see whether he might have something of value. Invariably, these emissaries returned to report nothing more than one of two options: either Ferris was proposing a course of action already in train or, alternatively, and being ignorant of facts not released to the public, he had made an erroneous assumption and his suggestion was irrelevant.

Unaccountably, the self-styled detective

failed to see the yawning gaps in his assessment of reality; didn't recognise that he was repeatedly misguided; and, worst of all, had a subconscious tendency to overvalue the importance of his own notions.

These deficiencies aside, Guy Ferris, although not possessed of an exceptional intellect, was not of low intelligence either. In his favour, his extensive reading meant he was almost as familiar with crime fiction as Chief Inspector Bryce. He was aware, for example, that the Marple-style of amateur could really only function in certain situations – generally where some parallel could be drawn with a person or situation within their own milieu. An amateur with experience only of village life could hardly be expected to have the requisite insight and experience to follow the clues in a gangland murder. He knew that other fictional amateurs whom he admired rather more, brought different skills. Wimsey, he reflected, (or in another age, Dupin,) would be in a superior category. He relished the way these upper-class amateurs showed the knuckle-headed professionals how to do their jobs.

Very soon after taking up his interest in crime, Ferris told himself that there was a vacancy – a need, even – for an amateur detective of that type. A modern-day man with both the intellect and the financial freedom to engage with the professionals. An irritating impediment to his ambition which had to be acknowledged, however, was the fact that these fictional heroes naturally had excellent contacts with the police, thus ensuring their involvement. He recognised this as a great advantage, since most of the sleuths were actively sought out and consulted by those in nominal charge. In real life, he had disappointingly found no precedent for such cosy partnerships. He resolved to rectify this.

Bryce had heard various stories about Mr Ferris but had so far managed to avoid his attention. (This may have been because the DCI's clear-up rate was particularly good and none of his cases had ever dragged on for weeks, much less months.) In fact, the pair had narrowly missed meeting each other quite recently. While Bryce had been working in Ferris's hometown of Hunstanton, the amateur detective had been in Bognor Regis, interfering in a Sussex police investigation. Very annoyed at his absence from a sensational murder case in his own territory, he had barely discovered what was happening before it was all over.

Most of Bryce's police work had been within the Metropolitan Police area, and it was only in the last three years – since transferring to Scotland Yard from one of the Divisions – that he had been allocated to cases elsewhere in the country. He had never worked in most of England's counties but, by coincidence, was about to find himself back in Norfolk, in exactly the same area where he had solved a series of murders only a few months earlier.

The paths of the Detective and the Pretender were now destined to cross.

# CHAPTER 2

### *Tuesday 26<sup>th</sup> April 1950*

Adelaide Marner's body was under the cliffs at the northern end of the town. She lay just above the previous high-tide mark. This was where Thomas Wilkins spotted her while taking a leisurely morning constitutional with his dog. The old man had been walking on the firm stretch of sand above the water line – the sensible place to walk for someone of his age. Looking around for another walker to help him, he saw he was completely alone. He faced the cliff and picked his way up towards the base, past the rocks which studded the beach closer to the crags.

    Reaching the woman, he paused only long enough to check that life was extinct, then turned back the way he had come as quickly as he could. At almost eighty years old this was not very fast, but it was his best effort. Thinking that the pier would not be open to visitors at that time of the morning (it wasn't yet seven o'clock) and might not have a telephone anyway, he saved himself some wasted steps and turned straight up the slope towards the main part of the town.

At the Golden Lion Hotel he hesitated for a moment, then pushed the door open and went inside. It was not much further to the small police station in James Street, but he felt at the limit of his exertions. His spaniel, equivalent in age to her master and equally unused to such a burst of speed, dropped to the floor panting heavily.

The old man wheezily explained what he had found as the stunned receptionist lifted the hinged portion of the counter and pulled forward a chair for him. She waited while Wilkins sat and caught his breath a little, before calling the police station and handing the telephone receiver to him.

"There's a poor dead woman under the cliffs!" He repeated everything he had told the receptionist to the officer on duty. "She's above the high-water mark from the last tide. Oi'd say a rock fell on her – or mebbe she went over the top o' the cliff. Howsomever, you do be sure her head's proper bashed in."

The police officer calmed him down further and Wilkins, now in better control of his ragged breathing, was able to answer necessary questions and give a coherent report. He gave his name and address and the approximate position of the body, and was told that he would have to make a statement later.

The Landlord of the Golden Lion had been summoned to reception during this conversation. He knew Wilkins slightly and invited him into his private quarters, arranging some refreshment for the old man and his dog.

The local police quickly moved into action. The station Sergeant who had taken the call consulted a binder of tide tables. The next high tide was hours away, and the tables showed that it was going to be slightly lower than the last – which hadn't reached the foot of the cliffs. There was thus no urgency to move the body before it was washed away. He despatched Constable Booth to stand guard, and then telephoned the police surgeon sixteen miles away in King's Lynn. A second call arranged for an ambulance to transport the body, Sergeant Timmins helpfully warning that it would have to be carried along the beach for a distance.

Booth walked rapidly from the little police station to the seafront and down the steps at the northern end of the promenade. Making his way over the sand and rocks, he was soon beside the body. The woman lay face down on a white chalk slab, her cream-coloured jacket blending with its background, her black skirt making a dramatic contrast. Thick, shoulder length hair, as black as the skirt, was stiff and matted with congealed blood and unmoving in the occasional soft puffs of breeze. No medical expert was needed to see that she had received a heavy blow to the back of the head, exactly as Wilkins had said.

The Constable looked up at the striped wall facing him and shifted back a few yards. It was never a good idea to approach the cliff face too closely because there were frequent rock falls. While these were more common in winter, they could occur at any time, and rocks from the unusually layered cliffs – white chalk, red chalk, and carrstone – were littered all along this section of beach, some of them an immense size like the one the woman now lay on. It was, he knew, not unknown for someone to fall from the top of the cliff. A few previous cases also suggested attempted suicide rather than accident, although the height wasn't really sufficient to guarantee that outcome.

Booth debated with himself whether to turn the body over to see if he recognised the woman but thought better of it. He didn't want to be responsible for disturbing anything which might be useful to a better trained eye than his own. And in any event, his orders were to wait for assistance, so he could hardly go to the nearest telephone box and do anything useful with the knowledge of her identity if he did recognise her. He moved a further few yards back down the beach and sat down on a large boulder to wait.

Over the next hour or so he saw ten people: three couples and four individuals. One of the couples and all of the solitary walkers had at least one dog with them. All were walking from the town towards Old Hunstanton. By making a series of manoeuvres with his arms, and shouting warnings to people as they came into earshot that they must control their dogs, Booth managed to keep the body and its immediate vicinity more or less as he had found them. Even the most curious of the walkers was easily persuaded after a brief conversation that there was no reason to loiter.

Several people had already passed him again on their way back to the town when an excited orange and white pointer arrived far ahead of a new walker, and on a course for the body. Responding curiously to the policeman's loud and diverting command of "Here girl!" the dog bounced up and licked him enthusiastically, before turning again in the dead woman's direction. Booth only just managed to get a hand on the animal's collar and prevent any movement in that direction.

The dog's owner was now closer. The Constable realised that he'd seen the man before but didn't know his name. This gap in his knowledge was soon rectified.

As the walker approached, he saw the body and sized up the situation. Grasping the dog's collar, he clipped on the lead he was carrying and ordered, "Stop pulling, Xanthe! Sit!"

The pointer obeyed and the stranger introduced himself.

"My name is Ferris, officer. What on earth has befallen that woman – suicide is it?" He didn't wait for an answer. "I've made an extensive study of sudden death, you know. I can see even at this distance her head has suffered severe trauma."

"Too early to say what's happened, sir," replied Booth. "The Doc's on his way," he added, hoping that this statement would soon be true. He was struck by the eager tone of this walker, contrasting as it did with earlier and sorrowfully expressed remarks of 'Oh, poor woman!' and 'How absolutely awful!'

Ferris looked up at the cliffs, just as the policeman had done. Abruptly, he thrust the dog's lead against Booth's chest. "Hold her!" he commanded, simultaneously letting go of the leash and striding off towards the bottom of the cliff where the woman lay. Reaching her chalk bier, he peered closely at the surrounding ground.

Having instinctively caught the pointer's leather rein, the constable was now completely wrong-footed. Not wishing to take the dog any closer, he called out, "You shouldn't be there, and you shouldn't stand too near the cliffs anyway, sir. Tha's very dangerous!"

"I'm a resident of this town, officer, and I'm well aware of the dangers. But I do need to see what's what." Ferris spoke with consummate authority.

THE AMATEUR DETECTIVE

Taken aback a second time, Booth mentally reviewed what the word 'need' might imply. Although he had seen the man before, it had never been in a situation where a clue to his job was given. He looked to be in his early fifties which, unless he was very senior, practically eliminated any possibility that he was a police officer. But the constable had never heard of a senior Norfolk officer named Ferris, and why wouldn't he have said so, if he was?

Nor did the Constable believe he was a local doctor. Having said he lived in the town, Booth was sure he would have known him if he was a medic, or at least been aware of his existence. And again, the man would surely have mentioned he was part of the same profession, when told a doctor was coming.

A newspaper man then? No. Booth was familiar with the local press reporters, and all the 'stringers' who picked up the gossip to supply to their editors.

What was left? From his simple process of elimination, the Constable provisionally – and correctly – identified Ferris as a 'nosey parker'. "You must move away from the scene *directly*, sir," he shouted, "and explain to me why it is you need to see what's what!"

Ferris returned down the beach. "I'm something of a detective, Constable; oh yes. I've helped the police to solve serious crimes."

"Tha's as may be, sir, but you must keep

well clear just the same. Not that I'm saying this is a crime, of course. Far too soon to tell."

Ferris was immediately accommodating. Accepting the pointer's lead he said, "I'll not argue with you. But my hound and I will wait nearby until higher authority arrives and I can discuss the matter with them."

He plumped down onto a sea-smoothed piece of carrstone and continued, "Do you know who she is? If not, it may be that I'll be able to help by identifying her for you. I'm well-connected hereabouts, and I can see from her clothing that she's more likely to have moved in my circles than yours, Constable."

This observation with its social one-upmanship was arrogantly delivered, but it was also undeniably true. Booth felt he shouldn't be too hasty to dismiss potentially useful help in the matter of identifying the woman as quickly as possible. Much as he would have like to send Ferris on his way, he was also constrained in that he had no idea whether he had the power to order the man completely off the beach. He contented himself with cautioning that the pointer be kept on the lead, then sat back on his rock to wait for the promised assistance.

"Not the best spot for jumping, you know," remarked Ferris after a while. "More height twenty yards further along. Better chance of success by far over there. No, my money's on accident of some sort."

Given that he was getting bored with the waiting, Booth wasn't averse to talking. "Could be," he replied. "She's very cold, so whatever happened, it didn't happen in daylight this morning."

"Hmmm. People do walk along the green to and from the lighthouse in the evening," said Ferris. "She could have been walking yesterday and went too near the edge. The grass up top has been growing apace now the weather's turned finer. What with the usual April showers, it would only take a slippery tuft underfoot to lose your balance and over you'd go." He made a diving motion with his hand to illustrate.

"Maybe," agreed Booth. "Or she could have been down here walking just before dusk, and a rock fell on her – she just happened to be the last person along here before nightfall, so no one saw anything."

"I'd agree that's another possibility," said Ferris, pleased to be of one mind with even this lowliest representative of the law. He looked past Booth's shoulder. "I can see a group of people approaching – and no dog. Perhaps the doctor is among them."

A pair of walkers who had passed earlier heading north were now retracing their steps. Their mongrel barked excitedly at Xanthe and received a wagged tail of recognition in return, the pointer otherwise lying subdued and obedient on the patch of sand beside her master's rock. The new arrivals looked inquisitively again towards the body but didn't speak as they continued back towards the town.

The little group was close enough for individuals to be distinguishable. In the lead was a tall, slim man, wearing a tweed jacket and twill trousers. This was Dr Daniel Bartlett, walking beside an equally tall but heavier uniformed police sergeant. A little way behind were two comparatively short ambulance men, struggling along the rough beach with a stretcher.

"'Morning Booth," said the doctor as he arrived. He had met the constable on a couple of previous occasions and never forgot a name.

"'Morning sir. 'Morning Sarge," replied the officer, on his feet beside his rock to greet his superior and the medic.

Sergeant Timmins, not at all pleased to see a member of the public, rounded on the spectator. "And who might you be then, sir?"

Ferris explained.

Timmins, sharing Booth's conclusion that help in identifying the deceased would be useful, changed his attitude. "I suppose now you're here you'd better wait where you are. You can come forward if we can't identify her and see if you can. But after that, there's nothing else for you to do here."

The three professional men advanced towards the body.

"Nasty," muttered Bartlett to himself, as

he crouched down beside the dead woman and began his preliminary assessment. "Lend a hand to turn her over now, Constable," the medic said presently.

Between them they carefully turned the woman so that her dark brown eyes faced the slow-moving clouds overhead. She appeared to be in her early thirties, and had evidently fallen on top of a slim leather bag – the sort that had a large flap instead of a clasp to close it, and without a frame or handles because it was carried under the arm. This was now exposed, together with a gold powder compact and a handkerchief embroidered in one corner with small French knots. Both these items had apparently fallen out of the bag. The woman's left hand was also visible now. Two rings adorned her wedding finger, and a small cameo ring on her little finger matched the large cameo brooch on her jacket lapel.

None of the men recognised her.

Timmins picked up the bag and replaced the wayward contents, searching the interior at the same time for an identity card. He found nothing except a purse and a gold lipstick case, which matched the compact. Both the cosmetic cases weighed heavily in his hand, identically and beautifully engraved with wavy lines. These were not inferior, gold-plated items; nor was the woman's jewellery of the costume variety. Thinking that the bag had already demonstrated its unreliability as far as security of its contents were concerned, he undid the brooch from her lapel and pushed the pin deeply into the lining of the bag. Asking Bartlett if he would remove the rings, Timmins slipped them into the purse alongside a tight fold of notes and three florins. He called to Ferris.

"You can step forward now, sir!"

Ferris moved with alacrity. "Dear me, dear me," he tutted as he gazed down at the woman. "It's Adelaide Marner, gentlemen. She lives on Cliff Parade, not very far along from me. We often play a rubber of bridge together."

The two policemen nodded. "Marner," said Timmins, "the name's familiar. Her husband has some sort of business in King's Lynn, I believe."

"That's right, Sergeant, and not just in Lynn. His firm is East Coast Shippers & Freight Forwarders. Seymour Marner is the grandson of the founder. It's a sizeable company of coasters, with a growing fleet of lorries now, too. You've maybe seen some of them on the road – very distinctive livery. He's an odd sort of cove, though. Never plays bridge with his wife because he's either out, or in his study. I've only seen him a couple of times."

Doctor Bartlett had risen from beside the body and was now examining the various pieces of rock in the immediate vicinity. He moved around, stooping to inspect the areas of shingle and rock. Straightening up he said, "Well,

Sergeant, I'm not altogether happy. First, I'm pretty certain that this woman didn't go over the cliff because I don't believe there are any broken bones. Maybe I'll find contusions under her clothing later, but again, the damage to her stockings is trivial, and there's no damage to her skirt or jacket, which would be consistent with a fall from the top."

The Doctor spelled out his next reservation. "Also, if she'd been killed by falling backwards onto this rock, not only would she still be lying on it as she is now – and not face down the way she was found – but there would be evidence on the chalk where her head struck it. The position of her bag beneath her is also inconsistent with a fall. I don't believe it would have landed anywhere near her, never mind beneath her as we found it, had she fallen."

Bartlett rotated and made another sweeping visual scan of the area around Adelaide Marner's body. "Equally, I can't see any piece of rock which could have fallen on her and caused her injury." Looking up at the cliff face, he applied some simple trigonometry. "In fact, I'd say she's definitely too far from the base to have been struck by a natural rockfall of the stones around her." He waved at the area he had just examined, "All of these are embedded and have undisturbed sand around them.

"That said, her injury was almost certainly caused by a heavy bit of rock, and since I can't see anything nearby which might conceivably have inflicted it by accident, I must assume that this was a deliberate blow. Murder, in other words." He looked towards the Wash. "The rock in question has probably been thrown into the sea.

"You'd best get your CID boys out, Sergeant. Meantime, we'll get her to Lynn, and I'll do the PM. Provisionally, she's been dead between twelve hours and fourteen hours, but I'll try to get a more accurate estimate when I've got her in the mortuary."

Bartlett signalled to the waiting ambulance crew. With help from the doctor, the men zig-zagged with the loaded stretcher around the rocks and down towards easier walking on the sand, then made their way to the promenade.

Sergeant Timmins had a decision to make. He didn't need to open the bag again to assess its contents. The presence of the cash, the gold items and the jewellery, he felt, lent some weight to the suggestion that Mrs Marner had accidentally slipped to her death, because she certainly didn't appear to have been killed for what she was carrying. That said, he couldn't argue against Dr Bartlett's reasoning regarding the way the woman had been found face down, which – given the wound was in the back of the head – appeared to eliminate a fall.

Knowing, in principle, that the scene must be preserved intact as far as possible, Timmins considered the area beyond where Bartlett had inspected, and whether it would be possible for detectives to discern any useful clues from that further expanse. Although the rocks and seaweed wouldn't show footprints, the sandy patches leading towards the body above the tide line, might. Even as he turned this over in his mind, he realised that the most crucial area of the beach was already badly compromised, the world and his dog having walked over in both directions, according to Booth.

The Sergeant reconsidered Dr Bartlett's opinion: that the rock was now in the water and added another possibility of his own – that it was, instead, lying washed clean on the beach with countless others. Either way, there was no advantage in this speculation as it amounted to the same thing – the rock used in the fatal assault on Adelaide Marner was undiscoverable.

Dissatisfied with these conclusions, Timmins wondered if there was a chance, however slight, that the murderer might have carried the rock a distance and then just discarded it on the beach, thinking it would be the equivalent of the proverbial needle in a haystack for any investigator to subsequently find. If so, there might also be footprints nearby.

Timmins decided that however remote the chance, he should prioritise this last thought. He apologised to his colleague, "Sorry Booth, no time to explain my thinking to you, but you'll have to stay a little longer and carry on keeping everyone well away from here. The tide isn't coming in very high today, so you won't get wet feet, and no doubt the CID will be here long before next high water anyway. If I've not heard that someone's been despatched within a couple of hours, I'll arrange for you to be relieved."

Constable Booth knew that 'no time to explain my thinking' simply meant that Timmins wasn't going to speak freely in front of a member of the public. He acknowledged his orders with the standard "Yes, Sarge," response.

"Mr Ferris, you come with me, please," said Timmins. "You can maybe help us a bit more with information about the victim."

The two men and the dog walked off towards the town.

Constable Booth resigned himself to another hour or two of boredom, but consoled himself that there would certainly be a few more beach-walkers with whom he could at least have brief, albeit shouted, conversations.

Reaching the tiny police station in James Street, Timmins put Ferris in the room used for interviews and went to the telephone. He spoke to the Superintendent at King's Lynn and explained the situation.

Superintendent Reeves suffered from digestive problems, which sometimes caused his temper to flare and expletives to flow. This was one of his 'good' days, but he didn't hold back his anger at the news.

"We've only just sorted out a triple murder and now the Doc says there's another? I'm beginning to think he must be paid by the ruddy body!"

He fidgeted with a treasury tag, one end of its green string almost hanging out of the crimped metal end. "Our DI missed the last show because he was in Scotland. Now he's here but our DS is away and…".

Realising that none of this information was helping the situation, and that the string would never be reinserted, he threw the tag into the bin and cut himself short. "Oh Lord. All right, Timmins, you carry on. I'll get Inspector Cordy on the case. Do what you can for a bit longer – find and inform the next of kin for a start."

He put down the telephone. Rather than try to contact his detective inspector using the same device, he made a petty display of his authority by shouting for his assistant, a uniformed constable working at his desk in the adjoining room. The man arrived in seconds.

Reeves, fishing in a drawer for something new to fidget with, looked up and growled. "We've got another murder on our hands. Go and see if DI Cordy is in the building, Palmer. If he is, tell him I needed him in here ten minutes ago!"

Alan Cordy arrived promptly. A perpetually worried man in his late forties, he had held his present office for only two years. Surprised to be promoted at the time, he suspected his appointment was linked to his masonic activities and that he would never progress further, even with that association to champion him. Far from enjoying his new rank, for the last year he had often considered resigning from the force and taking up an offer to join his brother, Roger, in his business. A smallholder in Acle, the younger Cordy had taken early notice of the success that a man called Matthews was having with turkey farming. He had started a similar venture himself and his early results were promising, but now he needed help to expand.

With a plentiful supply of self-doubt about his ability as a detective, Cordy had experienced mixed feelings about missing the county's big case a few months earlier. It was, he thought, probably better to have been away from the outset, than to have failed after a couple of weeks and had the humiliation of Scotland Yard being called in over his head. Hearing Palmer pass on the news of another murder as he issued the summons from Reeves, Cordy felt a test of his ability was now inescapable.

Meetings with his superior were always tense occasions for the DI, and the demand for his presence this morning didn't bode well. But the conventions had to be followed. He knocked on the Super's door and entered, just as his boss was depositing a handful of rubber bands on his desk.

"You sent for me, sir?"

"I did, Cordy. Another murder in our patch, according to Dan Bartlett." The Superintendent passed on everything supplied by Sergeant Timmins, his fingers in perpetual motion as he stretched the flexible brown rings over a growing ball of the fasteners.

"The body's been removed, but a constable is guarding the scene. Dan thinks the weapon was probably chucked into the sea, but you'd better scour the immediate area. Gray's away, so it's all down to you and Malan. Gray's not as bright as Malan anyway, so I doubt you'll feel too short-handed."

A long band was wound and looped three times over the ball. "And in any case, I've been thinking Malan deserves some recognition for his work in the last murder case, so I'm making him up to Acting DS until this case is over. You can tell him, Cordy, and I'll get the paperwork done today. Make sure you emphasise it's only temporary, though; we don't have the budget for two permanent detective sergeants."

The Superintendent looked up, steely-eyed. "And you can take it from me we're not calling in the Yard this time. This show's all down to you and Malan, Cordy."

A thick rubber ring stretched to breaking point and snapped in Reeves fingers, one end whipping sharply against the back of his hand.

"Well, what are you waiting for? Clear off and get to it then, man!" he barked.

The DI left the Super's office even more worried than when he entered. He had noted the Superintendent's remarks about Malan, and fully agreed that Malan's intelligence was higher than that of Sergeant Gray's. He knew he was lucky that the DC was on his team. However, given that he privately believed that Gray was also brighter than he was himself, and was pretty sure that Reeves thought the same, his boss's assessment didn't help very much with his self-esteem. Unconsciously slumping his shoulders as he returned to his office, he considered what he should do first.

# CHAPTER 3

Detective Constable Malan, occupied in drafting a statement relating to a burglary, was awaiting the DI's return with interest. It wasn't every day that his leader was called upstairs. The Superintendent's angry shout for his Constable had been heard in their office, but such bellows weren't unusual and until Palmer appeared they weren't aware that the CID was to be involved.

Arriving back in the room he shared with his two subordinates, Cordy threw himself into his chair and looked at Malan.

"Good news and not-so-good news," he announced. "First, we have what looks like a murder to investigate." He passed on what he knew. "Given there's only you and me, and the Chief absolutely doesn't want the Yard back this time, that's perhaps not so good. You, though, are being made up to acting sergeant, just for the duration of this case, mind."

Malan thought that both bits of news were excellent, but he had seen enough to suspect that his boss was insecure in his own role, so he tried not to look too happy.

"I'll do my best to live up to the rank while I still have it. And I'm sure you'll soon get this murder sorted, sir," said Malan loyally.

Cordy, despite his worried mien was a realist. Although he would not normally admit to his limitations, he liked and trusted Malan, believing that the young detective would never try to take advantage. "Look," he said, "You've had recent experience with a top Yard man and his juniors. As you know, I've never seen a murder. There may or may not be parallels between that case and this one, but, frankly, I'm looking to you for ideas anyway."

Malan nodded. He knew he was being primed to take a more onerous role in the investigation. He also recognised that an opportunity was opening up before him, and that he should always grab these whenever they presented themselves. This positive attitude was in contrast to that of Cordy, who mostly functioned in fear of failure.

The DI continued. "For kick-off, we'd best get to Huns'ton and look at the scene." He stood up.

Malan stayed seated. "Before we go, sir, perhaps we should find out when Dr Bartlett is doing the PM? One of us should probably attend."

"Good point, yes. You sort that out."

Malan picked up the telephone, and with some difficulty obtained the information required. "He's doing it in the hospital mortuary at a quarter to three this afternoon, sir. I've left a message to say we'd like to observe."

Cordy, who had never witnessed a postmortem examination, and wasn't keen to break his duck, merely grunted in acknowledgement and suggested they could now get going.

The detectives left their office, Cordy pausing in the foyer to let the duty officer know where they were going and why. Outside, he took the wheel of the department's pride and joy, a fairly new Wolseley, and drove up to the only East coast seaside resort which faces West.

The DI was not a great conversationalist, and much of the journey passed in silence. "Can't help hoping the local boys have informed the next of kin," he said at one point. "Not a job I care for at all." He changed down to second gear and negotiated the bend in Snettisham.

Five minutes later, as the car climbed the long Redgate Hill approach to Hunstanton, Cordy spoke again. "We'll call in at the police station first and pick up any new information before we go down to the beach."

After the extraordinary start to the day, the James Street outpost of policing in Norfolk had reverted to normal – not much was happening. They found Timmins and listened to his recount.

"She was lying on top of this, sir," the

Sergeant told them, tapping the bag. "Money and other valuables still in it. Easy enough to pull it from under her body if that's what someone was after, so I doubt this was robbery.

"She's been identified as Adelaide Marner. We've been to her address, but we only found a couple of maids there. The deceased's husband is away in Birmingham for a few days, on business, but they told us of a sister and brother-in-law, Frances and Henry Ayers, who live in the town. They were at home, and both very upset to hear the news. In the absence of Mr Marner, the sister has agreed to go and make a formal identification of the body before the PM is started. Her husband will support her.

"Constable Booth is still on the beach, sir, waiting to show you where the body was found. Doc Bartlett thinks she died around dusk last night, and the rock which killed her probably thrown in the sea, but we thought you'd want to check the area yourself. When you've had a look, I'd be grateful if you'd send Booth back here.

"I've spoken to Mr Marner's personal assistant in Lynn. He's going to try and locate Marner in Birmingham. He'll let me know if he's successful – and of course he'll get Marner to telephone here as well. I've also jotted down the various names and addresses that will be helpful to you, sir." A sheet of foolscap was offered.

"Thanks," said Cordy, taking the paper and reading it. "Wilkins found the body and reported it, but who's this man Ferris that you've noted as being present?"

"He's the local who identified the deceased and said he knew her from playing cards with her sometimes. Came along with his dog before the Doc arrived, and hung around. Says he's a private detective. Reckons he helps various constabularies with their cases."

Cordy grunted and looked at Malan to see if he had any questions. Malan shook his head.

"By the way, Timmins, you should know that Peter here has been made Acting Detective Sergeant – so don't try bossing him about!"

Timmins, who had known Malan for several years, grinned and congratulated him.

"Only temporary, Eric, alas," said the new DS. "Was the body nearer to the promenade end of the cliffs, or to the access from the Old Hunstanton end?"

"Not much in it. It was just on the town side of the bend in the cliffs, so I'd say the prom's the best way to go. We all went that way earlier."

Cordy was suddenly feeling decisive. It seemed obvious what needed to be done next. "We'll have a quick look at the handbag, then take the car down to the pier and walk from there."

He emptied out the bag on Timmins' desk. The gold of the lipstick case and compact gleamed with the deep lustre of twenty-four carat quality. He opened the purse and released the rings and cash. Spreading out the notes and coins he said, "We're definitely eliminating robbery as a motive. If there's no evidence of sexual assault at the PM we'll be looking for her killer among all the people she knew."

Thanking Timmins, the DI signalled to Malan that it was time to go.

Reaching the northern end of the promenade, the two detectives could make out the figure of the Constable in the distance. Descending the steps, they made their way towards him. Several people passed them, and they could see more ahead walking in the same direction they were. As they neared Booth, they noted a man perched on a boulder a few yards away. The Constable, who had met both the detectives before and had spotted them almost from the moment they stepped onto the beach, sprang to attention as they reached him.

"All right, Booth, stand easy," ordered Cordy. "Report, if you please."

Booth explained that since the body had been removed, his only job had been to ensure that no one trod on the area surrounding where Mrs Marner had lain, and to answer questions from members of the public as to why a uniformed policeman was hanging around on the beach without obvious purpose. He gestured over his shoulder towards the man on the rock.

"That's Mr Ferris, sir." The Constable correctly assumed he had no need to add any further detail, because Sergeant Timmins would already have done so. "He's come back for a chat."

"Has he now," muttered Cordy.

Ferris had risen and moved nearer to the detectives. "Inspector, I assume?" he asked, extending his hand to the older man. "I have some experience in criminal cases and I'm sure I can be of help to you."

"We'll talk to you in a minute, sir," said Cordy. "First, Booth, show us exactly where the body lay, and then we'll look around ourselves."

The Constable pointed out the chalk slab. Like all the others who had visited the scene, Cordy and Malan looked up at the cliff. Being the end of April, the fulmars' breeding season was close, and already a few birds were circling, each probably looking for the nesting site it had used with its partner in previous years. Neither man could see anything of significance, and so turned their attention to the beach instead.

Here, much of the rock was deeply embedded in the sand, and not of a size which could be manipulated by a human at all without a lifting device or machinery. Nearer the cliff there were lumps, mainly of the white chalk, which had broken off in earlier rockfalls, and had not yet been washed away or eroded by the tides. But these examples were also mostly too large to use as weapons. Expanding their search beyond the area looked over by Dr Bartlett, Cordy and Malan examined each of the few possible rocks within twenty feet of where Adelaide Marner had lain. There were very few pieces of suitable size; almost everything else was either far too large or small shingle. Without evidence of blood or hair, none of the intermediate examples were considered a possible murder weapon. Eventually, the men stood upright again, and each silently indicated to the other his negative result.

"The Constable here wouldn't let me do what you've just done, gentlemen," said Ferris, "but I scanned every square foot over a bigger area beyond where you've just looked and could see nothing useful. I rather think the Doctor was right. Our rock – whether chalk or sandstone – is in the sea."

Cordy grunted again. (He did this quite often, in acknowledgement of some comment, when he thought speaking was unnecessary. There were several different grunts, and those who knew him well could deduce shades of meaning from the various sounds.)

"How was the woman dressed, Booth?" asked Malan.

"Light woollen cream jacket and black skirt, with a cream bow-tie blouse beneath, and what my missus calls 'sensible' shoes. No coat or hat, but then it was unseasonably warm again last night."

"All right, Booth, you get back to the station," said the DI.

The Constable turned quickly and walked away, being quite keen to visit the public conveniences which he would pass on the road back to the police station.

"You, Mr Ferris, might walk with us, if you will. This is Sergeant Malan, by the way. Where is your dog?"

"I took Xanthe home after I'd assisted Sergeant Timmins with names and addresses. She'd had a good walk already, and if I brought her down again she'd only want to go and sniff around where the poor woman was lying."

Malan was curious. "You say you have experience in this sort of case, sir. How has that come about?"

"Oh, I've interested myself in many cases, Sergeant. The only reason I missed the recent murders here was because I was down in Sussex helping the police there. And I've given advice to various other constabularies – and of course to Scotland Yard. I'm very much at your service and disposal, gentlemen!"

Neither Cordy nor Malan was immediately sure what to say to this. Malan's instinct was to apply a different meaning to the 'disposal' part of Ferris' offer and send him permanently packing. As the junior in the little team, however, he said nothing.

Cordy was far more hesitant. If what the man said was true, he might be useful. The Inspector knew in his heart that he would welcome assistance from any source, and it couldn't be denied that Ferris had already helped by identifying the body, perhaps saving hours of work.

The three men talked over various other matters – the tides, the cliff formations, and the nasty spitting habits of the fulmars – as they walked back towards the town.

"What are you going to do now?" asked Ferris as they reached the police car.

Cordy was not obliged to make more than a non-committal response to this question, but he saw no harm in saying, "We'll go and interview Mrs Marner's servants. They're most likely to have some knowledge of her movements."

"A very sound first step, Inspector!" approved Ferris condescendingly, before boasting, "but I can save you that bother because I've already spoken to them. They know nothing."

The detectives barely had time to register this gratuitous assumption of their own responsibilities by Ferris before he added some advice of the egg-sucking variety.

"You'll have to check everyone's alibis as well, you know. Everyone with any possible connection or motive must be found and closely questioned." He pushed on, completely insensitive to the boundaries he was crossing. "I can tell you now that I took Xanthe for a walk soon after lunch yesterday, towards Heacham for a change, so not even in this direction. I got home about half past three and didn't go out again. That's the sort of information you'll need to gather from other people."

Failing to register the expressions on the policemen's faces, Ferris delivered more 'pearls'. "You should check out Adelaide's husband immediately, and thoroughly test his alibi. He's allegedly away on business in Birmingham. Your contacts in the Midlands are better than mine, of course, so I think it's best I leave that job to you. Closer to home, you should probably concentrate your efforts on the brother-in-law, Henry Ayers. If it wasn't Seymour, my finger's pointing at him. Shifty individual. Very shifty indeed!"

Seeing that his boss looked lost under the weight of these pronunciations and the high-handed manner in which they were delivered, Malan decided it was time to step in.

"Our decisions, Mr Ferris, not yours," he said. "Murder enquiries must be carried out meticulously, and procedures followed to the letter. The place to start is the deceased's household, as the Inspector has mentioned, after which *we* will arrange *our* priorities as we see fit."

Cordy nodded. He was content, at least for the moment, to let his temporary Sergeant take control. Ferris made no reply, but Malan's subtle emphases had not escaped him. There was a scowl on his face as the officers climbed into the

Wolseley and drove away.

"Quite right, Sergeant; thank you," said the DI from behind the wheel. "However much he might like to direct our investigation, we can't really allow it."

Being addressed for the first time as 'Sergeant' made Malan very happy, although he reminded himself that this pleasure would be short-lived.

The two officers went up the steps to the front door of a house in one of the grand terraces on Cliff Parade. It had hardly been worthwhile starting the car to travel this short distance, but Cordy had decided it was the easiest way to detach Ferris. Malan rang the bell, and a red-eyed maid came to the door. With a sad little sniff she acknowledged the officers' warrant cards and took them to a charming sitting room off the hallway.

"Is anyone else in the house?" enquired Cordy.

"Just me and Faith, sir. I'm Elsie Long," replied the girl. "We haven't taken in all this awful news yet."

"No, that's very understandable," said Cordy kindly. "Tell us about the household to begin with. Who lives here, and who regularly comes and goes?"

"Apart from the Master and Mistress, only Ruby the cook lives in, but she's had permission to visit her sick mother for a few days. There aren't any children. Me and Faith, we come in six days – Saturday or Sunday off alternately, so there's always one of us here at weekends. We don't always do the same hours, though. If the Mistress has a card evening, or people are coming to supper, at least one of us works late." The girl gave an involuntary shudder and looked thoroughly miserable.

"Perhaps it would be a good idea if you fetch Faith now, Elsie," suggested Malan. "We can talk to you both together and save time."

The maid gave a bob and went out. Within a minute she was back, followed closely by another girl. Both were of much the same age – still in their teens, the officers thought, and of similar height, but they were quite different in appearance. Where Elsie had brown hair and was big-boned, Faith's hair was mousey and she appeared delicate beside her larger friend.

"Sit down," instructed the DI. The two perched side by side on a sofa. "I'd like you to think about yesterday afternoon. What time did each of you go home?"

They had left together at six o'clock.

"And was Mrs Marner in the house when you went?"

Both maids were sure that she was. Further questioning extracted the fact that nobody else had been present at that time. Apart from a couple of tradesmen making deliveries, there had been no visitors – certainly not between the time the maids arrived at half past seven and when they left. Nor, as far as they knew, had there been any telephone calls. Mr Marner, the officers learned, had walked to the railway station on the Monday morning. They understood he was going first to London, and then on to Birmingham. He was expected back home late on Thursday.

"Tell us about other people now, the ones who visit the house from time to time," said Malan, pencil and notebook at the ready.

"I dunno, sir," began Elsie. "There's two sorts of those, really."

Faith nodded. "There's the ones who the Master invites to supper, mainly people he does business with I think, rather than friends," she said. "Usually, it's just one or two men – I don't remember a wife ever coming. The Mistress always eats with them, but afterwards she leaves them with the port and goes to the upper drawing room while the men sit and talk. Then the Master takes them to his study, and they talk some more. She never joins them."

Elsie agreed with all of this. "The other sort are the ones who are friends with the Mistress. They come in for an evening of supper and bridge, or sometimes just bridge. That's all much more lively and jolly. The Master never plays cards himself. He shuts himself away in his study on those evenings and we take him something on a tray."

Cordy and Malan considered all this.

"Would it be fair to say that your Master and Mistress didn't share the same interests? Perhaps they didn't really get on that well together?" asked Malan. The girls looked at each other again. Faith spoke up.

"I think that must be right, sir. I've been here about three years, and in all that time I hardly ever saw the two of them talking together. Even at breakfast or lunch when there was just the two of them, whenever I arrived in the dining room I never felt I was interrupting a conversation.

"'Course, she was the best part of twenty years younger than him. Maybe they didn't get on, but I've never heard a row or anything." She turned to her friend, "Did you ever?"

Elsie shook her head. "No. Not even a half-raised voice from either one of them."

"You told a policeman earlier about your Mistress's sister," said Cordy. "We'll see her shortly, but in the meantime, do you know if either Mr or Mrs Marner has any other relatives, not necessarily living around here?"

"I never heard any talk of the Master's family," said Faith. "The Mistress's Mother used to come and stay when I first worked here – I think she lived in Southampton. But she's in a nursing home now. Mrs Marner used to visit her once a month, and always came back more upset than when she set off. Her sister, Mrs Ayers, is a very nice lady; she'll be no end upset when she hears what's happened." Elsie nodded along to all of this, and both girls had to wipe their eyes.

"We know this is difficult for you," said Malan, "but we do need more help. Can you give us all the visitors' names, please."

Neither girl was really clear about the identities of the businessmen. Obviously, these guests were not introduced to the servants by name, and some only came to the house once. Even those who visited more frequently remained, as far as the maids were concerned, anonymous. All they could say between them was that Marner had been heard to address one man as 'Davies' or 'Davis', and another as 'Linley'.

However, eleven names were known from the second group. Three married couples, and five single men. Another young man sometimes came for the bridge, but neither maid knew his name.

The Ayers were among this group. Mr Ferris was also a regular. The detectives recognised the names of five more, as these were members of the top stratum of society in the little town, and were known over a far wider area. They were a retired rear admiral; a retired brigadier; a doctor who was also a serving magistrate; a well-known author and an even-better-known artist.

"Well done", said Cordy when the list appeared complete. "If you think of any more information, or anything happens which we should know about, you contact the Lynn police station at once and ask for me or Sergeant Malan." He handed a card to the nearer maid and the policemen stood to leave.

# CHAPTER 4

Outside the house, the officers sat in their car for a few minutes. "I have a feeling we're going to be stymied now, sir," said Malan. "Chances are the sister has gone to Lynn already to do the identification."

"Yes. Well, let's ask at her house anyway. If she isn't there, someone might know roughly what time she's expected back."

As they were already in the car, Cordy drove the two hundred yards further up Cliff Parade to the next address. The maid opening the door explained that Mr and Mrs Ayers had left ten minutes earlier, going to King's Lynn. She had no idea when they would return. Malan asked her to inform Mrs Ayers that he and the Inspector would come back to see her later in the day.

"It's half past twelve," announced Cordy as they returned to the car. "Time to sort out the inner man. Your choice Sergeant – fish and chips, or something in the Golden Lion?"

Malan happened to have had fish and chips

the previous evening. He explained this to the DI, and opted for the pub.

The hotel Landlord had seen both men in his bar on odd occasions in the past, but never together. Now, however, he correctly placed them. "Ah, gentlemen, you'll be looking into this death on the beach, I take it? What can I get you?"

When orders had been placed for two pints of bitter shandy and two helpings of lamb hotpot and carrots, the Landlord continued.

"Henry Wilkins came puffing in earlier to use the telephone, and we just thought there'd been an accident. But now I hear someone hit the poor woman on the head!"

"Where did you hear that?" asked Cordy.

"Mr Ferris dropped in for a drink about a quarter hour ago – he told me. Only stayed ten minutes, then shot off again. He's by way of being a detective himself, I hear."

"No doubt you heard that from his own lips, and not from anyone else's," remarked Malan with some acidity.

As the landlord moved away to attend to new customers Malan quietly added for the DI's ears only, "I expect he's shot off to go and spread his gossip elsewhere in the town, sir."

"I daresay. But we could hardly force him to keep his mouth shut," replied Cordy.

The officers opted to eat in the bar and took their drinks to a quiet table. The DI had been building up to pass on a decision he had made. He waited for Malan to take a good swig from his jar and said, "Look here, there's no point in both of us watching the PM. You take the car and go to see Doc Bartlett do his stuff. I'll stay in Hunst'on. I can easily walk everywhere I need to go from here. I'll try two or three of the names the Marner's maids gave us, and then go back to the Ayers again – I'm banking on the fact that she'll come straight home after the ordeal of identifying her sister."

Cordy took a long pull from his own glass. "When you get back, go to the Ayers' house. If I'm not there, and they are, you go in and make a start without me. We have to check out if there's anything in what Ferris said about Mr Ayers, so make a point of getting a feeling about him if you can, and definitely get all his movements at the relevant time. If I see the car outside I'll know you've arrived and I'll join you."

Given the DI's earlier lack of enthusiasm about witnessing the *post mortem*, Malan wasn't surprised that he had found an excuse to avoid it. There were not many unexplained deaths in West Norfolk, and it was doubtful if Cordy had ever had the opportunity to see one. Malan wondered if the DI assumed that he himself had observed one in the triple murder case – he hadn't, as each PM had been carried out before anyone had anticipated that the death might involve homicide.

However, it was undeniably true that for

both officers to attend today would be a waste of time for one of them. And although Malan had mixed feelings about watching, he felt that it would be a useful, if distasteful, experience.

The hotpot arrived and the two men prepared to tuck in. Cordy, lifting the shingles of sliced potato on top of his portion to inspect the meat below, pronounced himself more than happy with the quantity. "They say Welsh mutton is wonderful, but as far as I know I've never sampled anything other than Norfolk," he told his colleague as he loaded up his fork with meat. "I don't for one minute believe it's better than this, though," he said, jabbing at his plate with his knife, completely satisfied with the excellent quality of his first mouthful.

While easting, the two officers discussed what questions should be put to the various people whose names they had been given.

"With Mrs Marner's valuables intact as far as we can see, we have nothing in the way of a motive to pursue," said Cordy.

"No, sir. Nor do we have any idea why she was down on the beach. No mention of her having a dog, incidentally. Maybe she often went out along there for a walk. Hopefully the PM will give a more accurate time – 'around dusk' isn't that helpful."

"True, although even without the Doc's first impression, I don't believe anyone would go wandering down there with the intention of returning in the dark. Far too many obstacles to trip on, even with a moon out. No, I reckon she went down while there was still reasonable light, and with enough time left to come back in daylight. Anyway, that's one question to put to everyone for a start: was she in the habit of walking under the cliffs in the evening – and who might have known that?"

"Pity the cook is away, sir. She might have been able to say when Mrs Marner went out – and perhaps what she was intending to do. And another thing. The maids painted a picture of two people who didn't seem united. The wife is still young, and the husband doesn't even want to play cards with her. I think we'd better ask delicately if anyone knows of an extra-marital interest."

Malan's suggestion produced another of Cordy's grunts, this time accompanied with a nod.

Lunch concluded, the DI said he intended to return to the police station first. It had occurred to him that at least some of those to be visited would be on the telephone and he wanted to see if he could make some appointments.

Malan set off towards King's Lynn. As he drove, his thoughts turned to Ferris, and in particular the man's remark about helping other constabularies in the past. He wasn't happy about such external 'help' in this case. He also sensed that Ferris would do his best to intervene as much as he was allowed to. He found it hard to believe that the man had any standing with Scotland Yard but would have like to know for sure. He remembered the parting remarks made by the Yard officer who had handled the triple murder case. DCI Bryce had wished him well in his career and told him that he was welcome to call him for advice in the future.

With some spare time before the *post mortem*, he decided to call into his office and see if he could make contact and avail himself of the offer. Rather to his surprise, the Yard switchboard connected him with Detective Chief Inspector Philip Bryce straight away. Malan explained who he was and was pleased as well as relieved when he heard:

"This is an unexpected pleasure! How are you getting on, Malan?"

The young detective explained his temporary promotion.

"Well done! I'm sure you'll get the rank permanently soon. What can I do for you?"

After outlining Adelaide Marner's murder, Malan broached the subject of an amateur detective named Ferris.

"First, good luck with your investigation," said Bryce, "West Norfolk seems to be descending into lawlessness these days. As for your self-styled sleuth, I assume this is Guy Ferris. I haven't met him myself, but I've seen a file of his letters here." Bryce gave his opinion bluntly, "He doesn't seem to have been any help on any case in which the Yard has been involved. Rather the reverse, in fact, and the detectives concerned – to a man – are uncomplimentary about Mr Ferris."

Malan was happy that his instinct had been correct.

The DCI continued. "My advice to you is this: keep him away from everything. Don't even keep him up to date with what you're doing beyond anything that you're sharing more widely – with the press and so forth. Obviously, you'll have to listen if he says he has information for you, but don't treat what he gives you with anything other than caution. Oh, and be warned. He doesn't only try to interfere with the officers in a case directly – he also writes to the newspapers undermining the detectives with criticisms. Get the picture?"

"Yes, thank you very much, sir. It's what I thought, but I'm glad to have your confirmation."

Delighted that he had made the call, Malan left his car at the police station and walked the few hundred yards to the hospital. He was directed to the mortuary, and found it tucked well away from the public areas. Just outside the building's entrance was a cheerful-looking man leaning against the wall, smoking a cigarette and enjoying the Spring sunshine.

Malan introduced himself.

"Afternoon," responded James Williams. "I'm the mortuary attendant. Doc Bartlett is due soon." He waggled his cigarette, "You've got time for one yourself, if you want. People find it steadies the nerves."

Malan declined but joined Williams' in leaning against the wall – upwind of the drifting smoke – and facing the sun.

"The Hunst'on woman, isn't it? Bit of a mess she's in, Sergeant. Have you seen a PM before?"

Malan admitted he had not.

"Here's what you need to know then. You feel ill, you run outside double-quick. Dan Bartlett can stand all the horrible smells we get in here, but he can't abide anyone being sick. Just one of those things," said Williams philosophically, taking a final drag on his cigarette before dropping the butt and grinding it out with his boot. "Anyway, here comes the man himself."

Doctor Bartlett joined them by the door. "Afternoon, Jim," he greeted his assistant. To the detective he said, "I saw you at the inquests of the last few murdered people here, officer – Malan, isn't it? I expect I'll be seeing you again at the trial in a few weeks."

He opened the outer mortuary door and enquired, "Are we all set, Jim?" as he led the way into a corridor.

Williams nodded. "All laid out ready for

you, Doc. I've bagged up her clothes."

Entering a fully tiled inner room, Bartlett and his attendant both donned gowns and gloves. "You just stay a few feet away on that side, officer," directed the surgeon. "You'll be able to see everything. You don't need a gown."

Williams drew the sheet off the body on the mortuary slab. Mrs Marner was face down in preparation for the first part of the procedure.

"Take her temperature, Jim, then make all the usual notes as we go along."

With his attendant engaged on that task, Bartlett did a visual examination of Adelaide Marner's head. "You can shave around the wound, now Jim," he instructed.

Williams stropped a razor while Bartlett moved around the table, taking each limb in turn to carefully examine. "Arms and legs not broken," he said presently, "and no contusions of any sort on this side of her body either."

The attendant, his work completed, stood aside from Adelaide Marner's head, making way for the doctor to take his place.

"Jar please, Jim."

Bartlett used a pair of forceps to gather several specimens of material from the wound, each of which he dropped into the ceramic pot held by Williams. "Carrstone, I'm almost certain," he said. "Be able to see properly under the microscope. Did you search the beach this morning, officer?"

"Yes," replied Malan, "but we couldn't see anything useful."

"No, I didn't think you would. I was pretty sure it was a lump of sandstone and not chalk this morning – and although there were some chunks of chalk there didn't seem to be anything suitable in the way of sandstone.

"Zero chance of finding a weapon to fit the wound, of course; gone forever, I fear." Bartlett moved aside and told Williams, "Better take some pictures, Jim, and then I'll get on."

Malan had primed himself as best he could beforehand, reasoning that Adelaide Marner would surely want every scrap of evidence assembled which might lead to a conviction of her killer. As the procedure progressed, he found this thought uppermost in his mind. Somehow, the necessity of what he was seeing done mitigated the sheer unpleasantness of the exercise.

Bartlett kept up a running commentary throughout the surgical aspects of the examination. At last, he was finished. "Okay, Jim, you can sew up, please."

He crossed the room to a sink, where he rinsed his gloves before removing them and his gown, which he simply dropped on the floor before washing his hands thoroughly.

"Right, Malan. I'll get the report to Superintendent Reeves first thing in the morning, and a copy to the Coroner as well. But

I can tell you everything is very straightforward. Death occurred between six and eight last night. Cause was undoubtedly a very heavy blow to the head with a lump of carrstone. There are no other injuries of any description, so nothing whatsoever to indicate a fall from height – voluntary or involuntary. No indication of a sexual assault, either.

"Nor is there any indication that the body was moved after death. Her clothes weren't disarranged at the scene, as you'd expect had she been carried or dragged. She was killed where she was found, and was otherwise in perfect health. No signs of diseased organs. It's probably not relevant, but she had never borne a child. What's more significant for you, I think, is that the likely mass of the rock used means the assailant could have been male or female."

Williams had begun sluicing down the slab and Bartlett indicated that they should move into the corridor.

"What I tell you next isn't part of my official report. It's just an opinion and you can make of it what you will. In my view she was too far out from the base of the cliff for the injury to be caused by a naturally falling rock. Apart from the distance, I don't believe the sandstone stratum is high enough for a falling lump to cause the injury she sustained."

Malan noted this down in his pocketbook.

"No doubt you'll consider the possibility

of someone throwing a rock from the top of the cliff – a stupid and reckless thing to do at the best of times, but I'm afraid there's no shortage of stupid and reckless people around. I dare say that the kinetic energy in a rock carelessly hurled down might be enough to cause such damage to the skull, although I don't propose to run experiments to find out! But for that scenario, the rock should still be beside the body."

Thank you, doctor," said Malan, grateful for this additional detail. "I'd best get back to my Inspector and report."

\*\*\*

Malan returned to Lynn police station to collect his car and drove back to Hunstanton, wondering where he would most likely find his boss. Turning the car towards Cliff Parade, he spotted Cordy walking up the slope, and pulled in beside him.

"Go and park up by the lighthouse for a few minutes, Sergeant," instructed the DI as he slammed the Wolseley's front passenger door shut. "We'd better exchange information before we try the Ayers.

"Right," he continued, after Malan had stopped again and turned off the ignition. "What have you got?"

Malan relayed Bartlett's findings and thoughts on the manner of Adelaide Marner's death.

"Well, that seems pretty clear. Anything else?"

"Mr Ferris," said Malan. "I took the liberty of talking to the Scotland Yard DCI who was here for the other murders. He'd said I was always welcome to consult him."

Cordy looked surprised, and Malan thought he was about to be rebuked for his initiative. The DI just grunted.

"I thought if Ferris was genuinely involved in serious cases so often, as he told us, that he must have worked with the Yard. So I asked Chief Inspector Bryce. He knew all about him." Malan passed on Bryce's dismissal of Ferris as nothing more than a nuisance, and to be avoided as far as possible.

Malan expected another grunt from his superior, but this didn't come. Instead, after a few seconds Cordy nodded. "Useful information, Sergeant. Good thinking to ask someone in the know. Next time you're by a telephone, get on to the Sussex boys. Try to speak to someone involved with the case Ferris talked about, the one which was going on at the same time as the big case here. Find out what they thought of him.

"As for my information – there isn't much of it. First, I've seen Mr & Mrs Webster. Nice couple, in their early sixties, I'd guess. No question they were shocked to hear their friend has been murdered.

"The Websters confirmed a lot of what the maids told us. They'd been for supper once, and found Marner so odd – 'distant' was the word Mrs Webster used – that they've avoided dining there ever since. They reckon they've been playing bridge with Mrs Marner for the five years since they moved here, but they've only seen him three or four times. Both felt sorry that she didn't have a happier marriage.

"I asked – delicately – about whether Mrs Marner had any particular male friends. Mrs Webster reckoned every man who knew Adelaide was a bit in love with her. She pointed at her husband, 'ask him!' she said. He agreed. But neither of them knew of any particular liaison – they didn't think she was 'that sort'. Both of them said they were at home last night, and never went out at all. Said at least one of their staff could confirm that, if need be.

"Next, I saw the author chap, David Prentice. He hadn't heard about the murder. Said he'd been in Lynn library all day doing some research for his next book. I imagine that's why Ferris didn't buttonhole him earlier in the day to tell him. Seemed knocked sideways when I told him – could hardly believe it. Very bright young man, I think. Have to say I liked him. Never read any of his books myself; romances mostly, and a couple of thrillers, I gather. He described the card evenings as being just as Ferris and the Websters said. Agreed that most men adored Adelaide

Marner, but hadn't heard of any lovers. Went so far as to admit that if she'd been free he'd have pursued her himself. He's a bachelor, and close to her age."

Cordy shifted in his seat. "He implied that we need look no further than the husband – obviously didn't know Marner was away. Claimed he was in his study writing all evening, but no witness to that. Another one with a live-in maid, but it was her evening off. Last snippet of interest is that Prentice served in the navy during the war, coming for a time under Admiral Wynterflood who I saw next.

"By the time I got to him he'd been told about the murder by Ferris. The interview started badly – he implied that there should be a far more senior man in charge of investigating the death of his friend. He's probably got a point, but we are where we are. Anyway, after a couple of large G&Ts he thawed considerably and was quite apologetic."

Cordy paused, thinking back over this particular encounter. He nodded his head slowly. "There's no doubt that he also had a soft spot for the deceased. He's a widower, so he's single, but he must be twenty-five years older than her – older even than her husband. Refused to believe that she would have been having any sort of affair. He more or less said straight out that we should arrest Seymour Marner; didn't even wrap it up like Prentice did. Seems he wasn't aware Marner was away either. Incidentally, he confirmed that Prentice served under him for a time, and was decorated for bravery. 'Pity Adelaide couldn't have married a decent man like that, instead of someone who doesn't appreciate her and who can't even play bridge', was his opinion.

"He walks his dogs on the beach every day, and said he'd never seen Mrs Marner on his outings. Said he'd gone to Old Hunstanton that afternoon. Played a round of golf, and stayed in the nineteenth hole until about ten o'clock, when by his own admission he staggered home. Told me the Club staff would confirm that."

Malan had never heard the DI make such a long speech before. He wondered if his boss had consumed a couple of large G&Ts as well. There was of course a convention that officers on duty shouldn't accept alcoholic hospitality, but his boss appeared perfectly sober and his words were not in the least slurred.

"So, Ferris is starting to spread the word, sir."

"Seems so, yes." Cordy checked his watch. "Let's see if the Ayers are back yet. Ferris obviously didn't need to inform them, but in the absence of his first choice of Seymour Marner, perhaps he's contacted them to suggest Mr Ayers gives himself up at once!"

Malan grinned. He wondered if his promotion, albeit temporary, had led to his boss's new attitude. Perhaps sergeants could be treated in a friendlier manner and taken into a DI's confidence more than a mere constable could. Or perhaps it was only the effect of the gin.

Both alternatives were wrong. The fact was that Cordy was frightened of failure, and simply needed to talk. To do him justice, it could easily have been that his nervousness translated into becoming tetchy and abrupt with his subordinate; but the reverse happened.

Malan turned the car back from the lighthouse and drove the short distance to stop outside the Ayers' house. The doorbell was answered by Henry Ayers himself. Cordy performed the introductions, apologising for intruding at a difficult time.

"Can't be helped, Inspector." Ayers stepped aside for the detectives to pass into the hallway. "Sooner you catch the culprit, the better. Anything we can do to help we will, obviously, although I'm know you'll bear in mind that Frances is in a fragile state at the moment." He pushed open a sitting room door. "Let's sit down. I'm sure you'd like a cup of tea?" He pressed a bell push before waiting for acceptance and sat down opposite the officers.

A tap on the door preceded a sad-faced middle-aged woman. Although she wasn't dressed as a maid, that was clearly her function. "Tea for four, and some cake, please Trudy. And see if my wife is ready to come and talk to the police."

"Quite an ordeal for Frances, having to identify her sister's body," he said. "Not something a woman should have to see, and I can tell you it upset me badly, too. But with Seymour away…have you spoken to him yet?"

"Not yet, sir," replied Malan. "We understand he's in Birmingham. His secretary's trying to make contact with him there."

Ayers nodded. "Well, were he not safely miles away, I'm afraid I'd be pointing to him as the culprit. Terrible thing to say about my own brother-in-law I know, but he's an unusually cold and strange man."

Mrs Ayers entered the room and her husband introduced the two detectives, who had politely risen.

"I heard your last comment, Henry," she said as she sat beside her husband, "and I can't disagree with what you say. It's best that we're all completely open about all this. Seymour is undeniably strange."

She paused for a moment to use a small handkerchief, embroidered with the same French knots as the one her sister had been carrying. She squashed the little square of white lawn between her hands and let them rest in her lap. Malan sensed her unwillingness to expand her comment about her brother-in-law and sought to help her out.

"We've heard from a few other people

about how Mr Marner behaved, ma'am. Not joining in for cards and supper; being distant with guests coming to dinner; removing himself to his study as soon as he could whenever he did take part."

"Yes, that's exactly right," said Mrs Ayers. "You've put that well, Sergeant. There was no overt unpleasantness as such in his conduct, you understand. No shouting or outbursts when company was in the house. But of course, one never really knows what goes on in a marriage behind closed doors."

"Would it be fair to say that your sister and her husband didn't have a close relationship?" asked Cordy.

"Very fair," replied Mrs Ayers. "As far as I could make out, they rarely spoke to one another on anything beyond the running of the house. As for the card evenings, it's not that he can't play the game, it's just that he had no time for either his wife or her friends."

The crushed handkerchief was produced again. Eyes and nostrils were dabbed. "She never complained, you know. Not once. She never said that Seymour was a brute, or that she found life with him unbearable and needed to escape." Frances Ayers swallowed hard. "But then again, I never asked her."

Complete stillness and silence fell over the room, the bereaved woman's utter misery and self-reproach hanging above them all.

Henry Ayers stirred first to pat his wife's arm consolingly. Watching this gesture and the expression on Ayer's face, Malan felt that Adelaide Marner's brother-in-law also believed himself to be responsible for not rescuing her. The detectives and their hosts remained silent as the tea trolley was brought into the room.

When the maid had gone, Henry Ayers opened the conversation again. "I hope you'll do a thorough check on Seymour's alibi, gentlemen. It's hard to think of another soul who might have killed poor Addy."

"We'll check everything, sir, and we'll do it thoroughly," Malan assured him. "At the moment, it doesn't seem likely that a stranger is involved. But assuming Mr Marner is in the clear, what other men friends might Mrs Marner have had?"

The Ayers clearly understood the thrust of his question.

"You mean Addy was down on the beach with someone she knew, Sergeant? Yes, I think that must be so. She wouldn't go there at that time by herself," agreed Mrs Ayers.

"Do we assume she was killed on the spot – not carried there?" enquired her husband.

"There's no indication that she'd been moved, sir," replied Cordy.

Husband and wife looked at each other.

"You answer, Henry, while I deal with the tea."

Ayers looked down at the carpet, and then up at the ceiling, before switching his gaze to the DI.

"Everyone – male or female – loved Addy. And everyone who knew her domestic circumstances pitied her. Every unattached male in our circle would have taken her away if he could. However, most of our friends are either happily married, or too old. You've probably spoke to the Marners' servants, and obtained names?"

Both officers nodded.

"Good. Well, let me say straight away that we know of no attachment between Addy and any of the men of our mutual acquaintance. That said, let me tell you about those who are notionally available, and you can make up your own minds.

"There's Rear Admiral Patrick Wynterflood. A widower, but old enough to be Addy's father. Thoroughly decent fellow.

"David Prentice, the author. Another ex-naval officer – very correct and straitlaced chap. He's a suitable age, and certainly very fond of Addy.

"Then there's Connor Proudlove; daubs and dabbles in oils."

Ayers caught his wife's reproving glance and adjusted his remark. "No, I'm putting it unkindly, he's a Royal Academician. Undeniable oddball, though."

"How so?" enquired Malan, immediately anticipating a motive might be forthcoming.

"Prone to exhibiting his emotions far more than the rest of us," said Ayers with disdain. "The whole gamut. Anything from rigid anger because one of his paintings was rejected by the Academy; to slush and tears because the stray cat he was feeding had run away. His mood swings are politely attributed to 'artistic temperament'. As far as I'm concerned, it's just as likely to be the dodgy substances he mixes into his paints. Can't do you any good can it, officers, breathing in fumes all day?" asked Ayers rhetorically."

Ayers broke off to accept a cup of tea from his wife. "He's years older than Addy," he continued, "but younger than Seymour. There are salacious rumours that Proudlove has had a string of mistresses over the years, all prancing around in the buff in his studio – you're bound to hear about that. But there's never been the slightest whiff of anything untoward between him and Addy. She sat for him, but always fully clothed. Incidentally, the Academy didn't reject the painting he did of Adelaide; I have to say it was rather wonderful."

Mrs Ayers nodded and dabbed her eyes again. She now looked extremely tired as well as forlorn.

Ayers scratched his forehead with his thumbnail, thinking who else he hadn't so far mentioned. "Oh, Guy Ferris. About ten years older than I am, I should think, so he must be twenty years older than Addy, give or take. Appeared to worship at her feet, but another eccentric. He's been overseas for a very long time, so it's probably prolonged and unwise exposure to heat in his case, not solvents." He looked at his wife to check her approval of this description.

She nodded. "Perfectly true, Henry; I can't argue with that, either."

Ayers took his wife's hand. "Who've I forgotten, old girl?" he asked affectionately.

"Bertie."

"Ah, that's right. Brigadier Bertie Pullen. Again, getting on in years, and if anything, even more prim than Prentice. Never been married, as far as anyone knows. Very nice fellow all the same."

Ayers spread his hands. "All the others in our set are married. Happily, we believe. Although as Frances mentioned, who really knows what goes on behind closed doors, eh?"

His wife nodded again. With a need to be active, she rose and started refilling teacups.

"I think we understand what you mean about 'artistic temperament' in Mr Proudlove, sir," said Malan, picking up the last crumbs of seed cake from his plate. "But what sort of odd behaviour does Mr Ferris display? We have met him, by the way."

Ayers gave a humourless smile and a semi-snort. "If you've met him, I'm surprised you need to ask! The man's a self-declared detective. He regales us – *ad nauseam* – I might say, with his alleged triumphs helping the police. He was absolutely livid last year because he was down south when the murders happened up here. He also holds himself out as an expert on historical murders. And he apparently owns a copy of just about every crime novel ever written, although I've never actually been inside his house to see them."

"One last question, sir," said Cordy, "we have to ask everyone this: can you tell us where you were between six and nine o'clock yesterday evening?"

"Yes," replied Mrs Ayers. We'd arranged to go with friends to the last showing of *'Kind Hearts and Coronets'* at the Pilot, with dinner at the Duke's Head beforehand. We'd seen the film last week, but it's such an entertaining picture. We got home a little before eleven o'clock. We can give you the names of our friends. It's hideous to think," she added with a sob, "that we might have been laughing at a film about eight murders while my sister was herself defenceless and being murdered."

Frances Ayers buried herself in her husband's arms, weeping a torrent of tears. The officers could think of nothing to say and wordlessly agreed it was time to leave.

"Thank you both for your help and hospitality," said the DI. "Our condolences again on your loss."

"We'll keep you informed of progress," added Malan, "and you can telephone your friends' details to James Street as soon as you like."

Back in the car, both men were reflective.

"I didn't see anything to back up Ferris's remark about Ayers being a shifty sort of man," remarked Cordy. "If anything, a very straightforward chap. Told us everything the way he sees it and no side to him, I'd say."

"Same here, sir," said Malan. "And if they were watching that film fifteen miles away, and in the company of friends throughout the evening, he couldn't have been killing his sister-in-law on the beach here."

"Correct," agreed the DI. "Take us back to James Street, Sergeant. Perhaps there's some news for us."

\*\*\*

At the police station they learned that Seymour Marner had been located in Birmingham and informed of his wife's death. He was unable to return that evening, but would travel back by the first possible train in the morning.

Cordy let out one of his grunts.

Malan had been thinking. "Mr Ayers is right, sir. Marner seems like the most likely suspect. We'll need to check wherever he says he was and find reliable witnesses to back everything up."

"Yes, but we can't do any more about it this evening. I'll drop you at your digs and pick you up again on my way back here in the morning. Might as well work out of Huns'ton rather than Lynn for the time being."

# CHAPTER 5

*Wednesday 27th April 1950*

The DI, who lived in King's Lynn, collected Malan from Snettisham as agreed the following morning. Conversation on the way to the coast was limited to a brief remark about the weather forecast, which promised another fine Spring day.

Cordy pulled up in front of the police station and the detectives were soon standing at Constable Booth's desk, where Cordy told his colleague "You take a look at the railway timetables between here and Birmingham, while I get the latest griff, if any, from Sergeant Timmins. We'll meet back at the car as soon as we're both done."

Booth handed Malan the station's copy of Bradshaw's Guide. The DS spent ten minutes perusing the dense tables and making notes. Passing the book back to the Constable, he went to wait outside.

Cordy reappeared soon after.

"As far as I can see, sir, it's not easy to come

from Birmingham to Huns'ton across country," said Malan as they climbed back into the car. "I think it would take three changes just to get to Lynn. So it's almost certain Marner will come via London. If he takes the express at seven thirty, he'd be in Euston about ten. Allowing an hour to get to Liverpool Street, he could catch a train and get here about three o'clock. I can't see how he could do it any quicker, unless he took a milk train or something overnight – or hopped onto one of his lorries."

The DI shared what he had learned. "Timmins says that Ferris has been here already this morning. Reckons he has some important information and wants one or both of us to go and see him as soon as possible.

"I'll call on him. You can try the artist first, Malan, then the army chap. And we'll have to put off seeing Marner until late afternoon, from what you say. I suppose we could make an assumption about which train he'll be on, wait at the station, and invite him in here for a chat. We've no grounds to detain him, of course."

Malan wasn't sure if the DI was joking but thought he'd better scupper this idea, just in case he wasn't. "Problem is, sir, not only do we not know which train, we wouldn't know Marner from Adam. We'd be wasting our time."

Cordy grunted but said nothing. Malan would never know whether his boss was serious, or not.

"Tell you what, though, Sergeant. I'll be passing the Marners' house, so I'll call in and tell the maids to ask Marner to contact the police station when he gets in, and set up a time for us to go and see him.

"Oh, and if you get back before I do, talk to the Sussex police."

"Will do, sir."

Since both of Malan's interviewees lived in the same part of town as the Marner home, the detectives walked together until Cordy reached his destination and peeled off.

Malan continued on and reached Connor Proudlove's house. This was another of the typical double-fronted five storey properties. Easily room enough for the artist to house two or three mistresses if he so chose, thought Malan, who knew the size of these terraced properties from his previous murder case. Trotting up the front steps, he pulled the bell knob and automatically straightened his already neat tie as he waited. A faint jangling confirmed his arrival would be heard.

A fair-haired young woman opened the door and leaned against the jamb, one arm tucked behind her into the small of her back, the other outstretched and holding the edge of the door.

"Yes?" she asked.

She was not a classic beauty; her cheekbones were not quite high enough to cross that exacting threshold and her nose was a fraction too short. But her skin was flawless, and the perfect pale complement to her reddish blonde hair. Malan, always happy to appreciate a pretty girl, thought there wouldn't be many men who didn't find her alluring. He assessed her age as early twenties, and wondered whether she was perhaps a relative of the artist – she had certainly not opened the door in the manner of a maid or housekeeper. There was nothing in her ordinary if colourful clothing or her monosyllabic question to help him decide.

"I'm Detective Sergeant Malan, from King's Lynn, Miss. I'd like to speak to Mr Proudlove, if he's available. It's about the death of Adelaide Marner yesterday."

"Oh, we know all about it," replied the girl. "We heard it from Guy Ferris last night."

She dropped the arm holding the door and tucked it behind her back to join its twin, the action throwing her bosom forward as she allowed Malan to come past her. Closing the front door behind him, she moved down the hallway and told him over her shoulder, "Come in and take a seat."

Swishing ahead of him with a snake-hipped gait, she led him into a living room. "Ghastly business. Murder, according to Guy," she said, at the same time pointing towards a leather Chesterfield. "Make yourself at home and I'll go and check if Con is fit to be seen. I'm Maisie

Lawrence, by the way."

Malan settled himself at one end of the large couch, using its conveniently broad arm to position his notebook and pencil in readiness. He assumed from the girl's use of both men's Christian names and her educated-sounding voice, that his first impression was correct – Maisie was no servant. Although it was always possible, he supposed, that in a Bohemian type of household the roles and status of the occupants might either be undefined or very flexible, with a less hierarchical and a more communal structure.

He gave his head a small shake, still unsure of her status, but very sure indeed that he had just been treated to some sort of performance. The girl's movements had struck him as poses in a seductive sequence, choreographed for his masculine approval. He hoped that his approval hadn't been obvious to her.

A few minutes later a large man of perhaps forty waltzed (there was no other word for his arrival) into the room, Maisie returning with him. Malan had never, to his knowledge, met an artist before, but this man certainly conformed to the visual image he had subconsciously held. Proudlove was tall and large, with a bushy brown beard and, as far as could be seen from the flowing locks visible, plenty of hair above. He didn't have spectacles, but wore the French impressionist uniform of dirty knee length smock and a black velvet beret. The artist stuck out his hand – freshly washed and paint-free.

"Sit yourself down again," he instructed when the handshakes were exchanged. "Maisie my angel, I don't suppose the Sergeant will imbibe on duty so just bring us whatever you feel like making, please."

The girl swished off to do his bidding and the artist dropped himself into a chair, fastening shrewd eyes on his visitor. "Ferris says poor Addy was murdered. Is that really true, or one of his absurd embellishments?"

"Very true, I'm afraid, sir. I attended the *post mortem* examination myself yesterday."

"To think of that beautiful woman in such a vile and bleak setting breaks me, Sergeant. It completely breaks me." The artist flicked up his smock, fished in a trouser pocket for a handkerchief and blew his nose. "Down under the cliffs, was it?"

"That's right," said Malan, noting that genuine tears had sprung into the artist's eyes. "We're puzzled as to why she would be walking there not long before dusk."

"You aren't the only ones puzzled, Sergeant. I've never even seen her on the promenade, never mind that part of the beach. You can put your money on one thing though: she wouldn't have gone there by herself, let alone at that sort of time. She was killed by someone who went there with her – or who had arranged to meet her there. Not a stranger, in other words."

Malan was surprised at this categorical statement, and wondered whether Proudlove, who had struck him immediately as an attention-seeker, was attempting to snatch Ferris' homemade 'Hunstanton Detective-in-Residence' crown for himself.

The artist smiled grimly. "You think I'm jumping to conclusions? Well, I don't think I am, and I'll tell you this: Addy was a very nervous woman. Outside her house and even inside it, sometimes. She always behaved as though who knows who was after her. There's no chance she'd have been down there without someone she knew to act as her escort and – as she must have thought – her protector, God help her."

"Any ideas who that might be, sir?"

"For heaven's sake, stop addressing me as 'sir'! I really can't be doing with it. Call me Connor or Con; or Mr Proudlove if you have to be more formal, although as a detective you must have worked out that this isn't a formal household," laughed the artist.

"To return to your question, no, I can't say for sure. I was, as you obviously know, a member of a circle which included Addy Marner. I suppose I've known her since she and Seymour moved here, newly married; must have been twelve years ago.

"This isn't a huge place, Sergeant, and the

number of people of what used to be called 'the quality' can be numbered on two hands and as many toes. Most of those who were resident here when I arrived have died." He held his hands up and made a gesture of surrender. "Although I completely deny any suggestion that I scandalised them to death with my doings!" He laughed again.

Malan was struck by the accuracy of Henry Ayer's comment. Proudlove was certainly prone to rapid swings of mood, having already veered from tears to laughter in no time at all. He wondered if he would see a display of anger before he left the house.

"If I wasn't closely related to various members of the House of Lords," continued the artist, "I'd probably have been excommunicated or something. Anyway, since the departure of the dear old fuddy-duddies, the Huns'ton set has been recharged by the arrival of a few welcome additions. You'll have been told about most of them. My point is this, Sergeant. I don't think Addy had any friends, or even social acquaintances, outside our little set. She was a reclusive little waif in many ways."

Maisie returned with coffee. She poured and handed the cups out efficiently and then sat down on the Chesterfield, far too close to Malan for his comfort, positioned as he was against the arm of the sofa and with nowhere to shift to. His expression must have involuntarily registered this, because Proudlove gave her a mild reproof.

"Now, now Maisie, you little minx! Put away your wiles and let the Sergeant do his duty without distraction; we owe it to Addy."

The girl made a moue at the detective and slid to the other end of the sofa.

"I can see you're curious about Maisie – and why wouldn't you be!" Although he was speaking to the detective, Proudlove was gazing at the girl as he spoke, his voice caressing. "She's my current muse amongst muses. My artistic fulfilment and inspiration, at least for the time being. Unlike almost all of those I've had in the past, Maisie has a very keen brain. A good bridge player too, when the fancy takes her."

Maisie preened under the fulsomeness of this praise, tossing back her titian locks for the benefit of her admirer.

Proudlove turned back to Malan and continued. "I don't know whether you've come across the portrait of Adelaide that I did in 1938. I painted it in my old studio in Boston Square; absolutely marvellous north light in that house. She was twenty-one at the time, and not long married. It was her portrait that ultimately got me elected to the Royal Academy. I'm working on a painting of Maisie right now, and I guarantee that it will get even better reviews."

Malan returned the conversation to the only portrait subject he was interested in. "Someone else mentioned your painting of Mrs

Marner. Where can I see it?"

"You can't, it wasn't a commission. I simply asked Addy if she would sit for me, and the darling girl agreed. Her husband knew, of course. Given the reputation I already had by then, it's perhaps surprising that he raised no objections. She never became my mistress, incidentally, and not for want of trying on my part."

As Proudlove picked up his coffee and drank, Malan was struck by the potential significance of the artist's last comment. Maybe there was a crime of passion to be uncovered. Perhaps Proudlove had made a renewed attempt at intimacy with Adelaide Marner and lost all control when rejection was his only reward – possibly after years of similar failures. He made a note.

The artist put down his cup and continued. "Before I moved to this house, I could have shown you the Academy catalogue. You could at least have seen a photograph of Adelaide's portrait that way. All wrong of course. Monochrome, and tiny in comparison to the real thing. Damn fool removal company lost two boxes of my books when I moved to this house, the catalogue in one of them." The coffee cup was back in his hand. "Naturally, I gave Marner first refusal on the canvas. He wasn't interested, which tells you something about the man, I feel."

"How did you portray Mrs Marner,

then?" asked Malan. If there was something in Proudlove's depiction of his subject which Seymour Marner had found objectionable, the detective wanted to know about it.

"I'd been toying with the idea of creating a new canvas entitled *'Ariadne'* for quite some time before I met Adelaide. As soon as I met her, I knew she'd be perfect, and I immediately asked if she would sit for me. She told me she liked the idea very much because Ariadne was her middle name. I expect she thought I intended a rendition of the ball of string story."

He threw back his head and gave a huge laugh, his eyes looking up at the ceiling rose as he recalled his true intention. "I didn't at all, of course. I wanted to depict her in one of the final aspects of the myth; you know, wearing as near-to-nothing of some flowing fabric as I could persuade her to.

"But I knew she would never agree to sit semi-nude. In any case, that's all been done before, both in paintings and in sculpture. I also realised it would be horribly wrong to pose Adelaide that way. Her loveliness was heartbreakingly real, and I was desperate to capture it.

"So I told her the portrait would be contemporary, and asked her to wear whatever she felt comfortable in, certain that inspiration would come to me on the day. She turned up in a beige gown, with only that cameo brooch she always wore for adornment, her raven hair swept up. Any other woman would have looked drained or drab at best – severe even. Not Adelaide. She looked quite wonderful. Perfect.

"I stood her with one hand resting on a table with a copy of Homer's Odyssey on it, the other holding a red twisted yarn bookmark. She was looking towards a window at an ocean beyond, the edge of a distant island just visible. All of that was for the benefit of anyone who was familiar with the myth and wanted to pick up on the allusion; and all of that you have to understand was *subtle* – she alone was the focus."

Proudlove paused and Malan opened his mouth to speak, stopping himself only just in time when he sensed that the artist hadn't finished his recollections.

"She was exquisite, Sergeant. Exactly the right degree of abandoned tragedy in her expression – as befitted the ending to the tale that she had supposedly been reading. I realised it was by far my best work and knew I had to submit it to the Academy for the next Summer Exhibition. It was accepted, and its value soared almost automatically, of course. Praise was absolutely heaped upon it. 'Comparable with Singer Sargent's portrait of Madame X' said one of the reviews.

"I spoke to Marner again before the hanging, gave him another chance. But he still wouldn't take it, not even at the original low price I'd suggested. It went on the open market and was snapped up by Duveen. An American collector beat off other offers and *'Ariadne'* now hangs in a great mansion in New York State. Not on view to the public, alas.

"These days I'm rich enough, and my reputation high enough, to be able to ensure that Maisie's portrait will stay in this country, hanging in a gallery where the public can enjoy it." He looked adoringly at his latest 'artistic fulfilment and inspiration'.

"But you don't want to hear about art, Sergeant. You want to know, as do we all, who murdered one of the loveliest women you could ever meet. You asked for my ideas on that. As I said, I have no evidence, only an assemblage of what I've witnessed over the years, and my own conclusion drawn from those scraps.

"Top of my list is Marner himself. A strange and easily disliked man. He presents as having almost no social skills, which is absurd, as he comes from a long line of county gentlemen. We almost never saw him, even if he was present in the house. Addy never mentioned him. Even thinking back twelve years, I don't believe she ever mentioned him spontaneously then. But who knows about others' private relationships. Unless they're as open as mine, they're unknowable to outsiders. I'm sure I shan't be alone in assuming that theirs was not a happy and contented union. Have you spoken to

Seymour yet?"

"No. He's been away in Birmingham on business. He returns later today."

Proudlove grunted. This was not the non-committal grunt of DI Cordy. It was a noise which quite clearly expressed disbelief. Malan thought it best to ignore the implication that Marner wouldn't show up and changed the subject. "You mentioned Mr Ferris, earlier, Connor," the Sergeant used the name diffidently, "you suggested he might have embellished the story."

This time, Maisie, who had sat silently throughout her patron's eulogy for Adelaide Marner and the recital of his own brilliance, replied. "Oh yes, we're a pair of cynics. We take a lot of what he says about his own doings with a cellar of salt. 'Embellished' is spot-on."

"That said," added Proudlove, "he does have a tremendous knowledge about old crimes."

Again, Malan thought it prudent not to comment.

"What about admirers?"

"Of Ferris?" Proudlove looked askance at the detective before realising his mistake. "Oh, of Adelaide. Every man who ever met her. No question. Frances, her sister, is a charming lady, but Addy put her in the shade. Not in pleasantness, there's nothing to choose between the two of them there, but Addy possessed something quite indescribable."

"That's true, Sergeant, interjected Maisie. "Even as a female, I could see that."

"But you want to know who else might have lured her onto the beach and killed her. Is it right what Ferris said – that she was hit on the head with a rock?" asked Proudlove.

"I'm afraid so, yes."

"Appalling thing to murder anyone. And beyond appalling to do it to such a woman; not to mention the brutality of the method. I'll happily volunteer to hang the culprit myself when you catch him."

The artist's handkerchief came out again. "No, there really isn't anyone else. Admirers, as I said, aplenty. Ones reasonably close to her age though, very few. And you needn't count me in that latter cohort, although naturally I still think of myself as young."

"And you act like it, Con," laughed Maisie.

Proudlove smiled, cupped his hands and mouthed an exaggerated kiss into them, then opened his palms and blew it towards the girl. "There's really only a couple of prospects," he said. "Young Prentice, first. Worshipped Addy, no doubt of that. But I can't conceive he'd make a move on her any more than he would if he bumped into our recently-married young Princess at Sandringham. A very upright man; definitely not a killer. Have you met him yet?"

"I haven't, but my Inspector has interviewed him."

"Well, you have to consider everyone, I understand that. I expect you'll waste some time looking at our two local military types as well. Both enthralled by Addy, despite the difference in ages. Mind you, I suppose it has to be acknowledged that, in common with young Prentice, they're no strangers to professional slaughter. Unlike the rest of us."

"You didn't serve yourself then, Connor?"

"No. I had legitimate ill-health grounds." He patted his chest but didn't explain whether he was indicating his heart or lungs. "You'll want to know my movements too, no doubt."

"Yes, if you could say where you were on Monday evening, say from six o'clock?"

"Certainly. Maisie and I were here until about six. I finished painting her about five, and it takes a bit of time to get cleaned up. We walked to the Le Strange Arms soon after six, had a few drinks followed by dinner. Back here at, I suppose, half past nine. We were together all evening, and indeed through the night."

Malan made a note. "You said there were a couple of younger prospects, but only told me about Mr Prentice. Who else?"

"Ah, yes, I'd almost forgotten. Arthur Trevelyan. A callow youth, really, must be a dozen years younger than Addy and only indirectly part of our circle. His parents are John and Pippa Trevelyan. They're both medics, although she only does a bit of locum work, standing in for our GP occasionally. Sits on the local bench as well. He's a general surgeon in Lynn. Both good bridge players. Arthur is their son; he joins the group occasionally, when he's home from university and we're short of a player. His parents have taught him well.

"Transfixed by Addy, always gazed at her with cow's eyes. But I'm not sure what conclusions you could draw from that; he fixes on Maisie with even more longing!"

"Too true! He's asked me several times to go dancing at the KitKat. One day I might say 'yes', although he must be three years younger than I am."

"You'd better not, if you know what's good for you," snorted Proudlove, but he was laughing.

With nothing further to learn Malan was relieved to say goodbye and make his exit. Paradoxically, he had found the Proudlove household far from liberating, feeling instead almost smothered by the exhibitions of 'openness'.

He looked at his list to check the address for Brigadier Pullen. It was in the same part of the town but set back from the seafront. The house was not as imposing as the others visited, but was still an attractive terraced property, built to a good standard, and probably had a good sideways view of The Wash from the oriel window on the upper floor.

He knocked at the door. There was no answer. He tried again, harder. A man appeared in the garden of the neighbouring house, and called across the fence:

"If you're after the Brigadier, he's away."

Malan stepped nearer and identified himself. "Do you know when he left and when he'll be back?" he asked.

"He left on Saturday, Sergeant. Gave his housekeeper a few days off. She'll be back on Friday, and he returns on Saturday. He's gone to Biarritz; goes around this time every year. If it's urgent, you could reach him at his hotel – the Edouard Sept. Quite a modest place, I understand, but I imagine it has a telephone."

Thanking him, Malan returned to the road and started walking back towards the sea. The DI had only told him to visit the artist and the soldier, but there was still the Trevelyans on the list – now with the addition of their son.

He decided to use his initiative and call on them. Checking his list again, he found that this time he would have to go to a different quarter of the town, just off the King's Lynn Road. The house was only a couple of hundred yards from the police station, and as he had to pass it on the way he called in and left a message for DI Cordy, to explain where he had gone.

# CHAPTER 6

The Trevelyan's house was another carrstone structure, probably built in the 1920s, and so some forty years younger than the Cliff Parade properties. A young man came to the door in response to the bell and Malan explained the purpose of his visit.

"Yes, we heard about that. It's terrible!" exclaimed the lad, looking very worked up. "My parents are both at work, and neither will be back before six or six-thirty."

"I see," said Malan, "either I or my Inspector will probably come back this evening to see them. But I have some questions for you as well."

"Me? I don't know anything about it!"

"I doubt your parents do, either, but we must talk to everyone who knew Mrs Marner. Can I come in?"

Trevelyan nodded and showed Malan into a sitting room.

"You would be Arthur Trevelyan, is that right?" asked Malan, as he turned up a fresh page in his pocketbook.

The lad nodded again. He seemed to have lost the power of speech.

Malan decided to test the information Proudlove had given him. "You liked her a lot, didn't you?"

Trevelyan became more emotional. "Yes, I did. Very much. She was about the best lady I've ever met – after my Mother, of course. Beautiful, kind, understanding; but married. And in any case, she would never have looked at me that way."

"What 'way' is that?"

"You know," replied the youth, turning very red.

"Do I? Do you mean she wouldn't have looked at you with any amorous thoughts?"

"Yes."

"I see. But *you* looked at *her* that way – lustfully?"

With his eyes fixed on the floor, Trevelyan looked abjectly miserable as he mumbled his response. "I couldn't help it. I'm not really used to females, much as I'd like to be."

"But I hear that you also look at Maisie Lawrence that way. What about her?"

Trevelyan was now on the verge of tears. "Yes, all right, I'll admit I think Maisie is very lovely too, although in a different way."

"You've asked her to go out with you, haven't you?"

At last Trevelyan showed a bit of spark. "Yes, I have!" he retorted. "And what's so wrong with that?"

"Nothing. Did you ask Adelaide Marner out?"

"No, of course not," the youth snapped, his eyes on the floor again. "I told you; she was married."

"What did you know of her marriage?"

"Only what my parents said from time to time. That she wasn't happy with her husband. I've never met him, though, so I never saw them together."

"All right," said Malan. "We're asking everyone this question. Where were you yesterday evening from about five o'clock?"

Trevelyan didn't answer immediately. "I was here in my room. I have a lot of work to do before I go back to university next week."

"You didn't go out at all?"

"I think I went for a short walk, about seven, perhaps. Just down to the pier and back."

Malan's expression was disbelieving and his tone hammered home the fact. "You *'think'*? It was only yesterday; you must *know*. Did you see anyone you recognised?" Malan left unspoken the crucial corollary to his question: 'and who might have seen you and recognised you, if we ask them'.

Trevelyan gave another miserable shake of his head.

"Will your parents be able to confirm that you were mainly here – and for how long you were out?"

"No. They were both out that evening. But I'm telling you the truth. You think it was me who killed her, but I didn't. I really didn't!"

"How did you hear about the murder?"

This change of tack surprised Trevelyan. "Mr Ferris came round this morning. He told Mother and me all about what had happened; Father was at work. We were both shocked. Mother liked Mrs Marner a lot."

Malan sat and observed the young man for a while. "All right," he said, "I think I've heard enough. Someone will come back to talk to your parents this evening. I think it's likely that the Inspector will want to talk to you too."

At the front door, Trevelyan had something more to say. "I realise you don't believe me, Sergeant, but I honestly had nothing to do with this. I couldn't have harmed a hair on her head. I think I loved her. I don't mind admitting that now."

"I think perhaps you'd better not admit that to Maisie, Mr Trevelyan – I don't think it would help your cause there!" said Malan with a half-smile. "And you're wrong. I'm actually inclined to believe you. Goodbye."

As Malan shut the front gate and made his way back to James Street, Trevelyan stared after him for several seconds, before a smile spread over his face, and he turned and went back into the house.

Chaos met Malan at the police station. Four reporters were besieging the desk, where Sergeant Timmins was valiantly but fruitlessly trying to ignore them.

Seeing the DS arrive, the single local reporter recognised him and began to ask a question. The others, now realising that Malan was a detective and not a member of the public coming in to make a report, immediately turned to him too. As all spoke together, the questions quite incoherent.

Malan held up his hand. "Look, gentlemen. I'm only a humble Acting Sergeant, and I can't tell you very much. You'll have to wait until Detective Inspector Cordy comes back. He's out interviewing people at present. I'm surprised it's taken so long for you lot to get here."

"Give us something, Sergeant, at least," called one of the journalists. Malan hesitated, but thought he couldn't be criticised for giving a little basic information.

"Mrs Adelaide Marner was killed on Monday evening, on the beach below the cliffs he in Hunstanton. She received a blow to the head from a piece of carrstone. Accident and suicide have been ruled out. The matter has been reported to the Coroner, who will no doubt convene an inquest shortly. The police are presently engaged in interviewing people who knew the deceased lady. That's all I can say."

The clamour started up again. "It's no use, gentlemen; I'm not answering questions. I will ask you one, though. How did you all hear of Mrs Marner's death?"

"Mr Ferris, your local private detective – he gave us the tip, said one reporter." The others all nodded.

"And he says he's pointed you towards the murderer, and that you'll soon be making an arrest," interjected another. "Is that right?"

Privately flabbergasted, Malan managed to keep his face expressionless. "No comment at this stage," he replied. "Now please go away."

He turned to go through to the back of the police station, and found the DI in the corridor, leaning against the wall only a few feet from the entrance foyer. Cordy was not smiling, and for a moment Malan thought he was in trouble for speaking to the press.

In the room they had commandeered as their operations centre, the DI closed the door. "You handled that very well, Sergeant," he said to Malan's surprise. "I got back just in time to hear you. But I was angry before I came into the station – and bloody furious a minute later!"

"You mean about Ferris, sir?"

"Yes. I wish now I'd let you loose on him, to be as rude as you liked. He was certainly rude to me. 'Condescending' might be a fairer word. Suggested – like Wynterflood – that I was too junior and inexperienced to be taking charge of a murder. But unlike the Admiral, Ferris didn't get out the gin and start to mellow. He cast doubt on Marner's alibi, and then repeated his remark about Mr Ayers. Ranted on for ages about his own expertise in these matters. Says he's going to write to the newspapers, and to the Chief Constable.

"Now we hear he's already tipped off the Press. Can't complain about that, of course – but I do object when he makes unwarranted comments about an imminent arrest."

"I'll get onto Sussex in a minute, sir, and see what they have to say. But I don't think we can do anything about the arrest thing. He would claim that he'd given us a tip, and that he naturally assumed we'd act on it. The fact that the tip was probably useless doesn't enter into it."

Cordy produced one of his grunts. "All right. What have you been doing?"

Malan gave a précis of his visit to Proudlove, and explained the existence of Miss Lawrence. He reported what he had been told about Brigadier Pullen, and suggested that they would have to check with his passport to verify the man's absence from the country.

He explained how he had heard about Arthur Trevelyan, and what he had been told by the young man.

"Interesting; he sounds like our best bet up

to now. But do I get the impression that you don't think so, Sergeant?"

"I don't, sir, no. Initially I wondered if there was a twisted half-parallel with the Thompson and Bywaters case – you know, an unhappy married woman takes up with a man a lot younger than herself. But of course it was the husband that was murdered in that case – not the older married woman. And apart from that vague comparison popping into my mind, I got absolutely no impression of criminal guilt from Trevelyan – just huge embarrassment. I think he's in the grips of his hormones, but it was all looking and lusting after her. Incidentally, I said one of us would return to interview his parents this evening' they should be back after half past six. The Trevelyans are the last ones on our list, by the way, assuming Pullen is genuinely in France."

Cordy thought for a moment. "Yes, all right. We'll both go this evening. I'm distracted by this Ferris thing, though. I hate to think what the Chief will say if he gets a letter from the man.

"But are we right to concentrate only on the people we are? Suppose Mrs Marner did go for a walk along the beach, and just encountered some homicidal maniac?"

Malan shook his head. "Problem is that we've heard nothing from anyone to suggest that she ever did go walking alone – quite the reverse, in fact. She seems to have been of a nervous disposition, possibly neurotic. I really think we can forget that idea, sir."

The DI's grunted response seemed to express doubt rather than acceptance, Malan thought. Cordy announced that he was 'paying a visit', and Malan decided he would use the time to telephone Sussex and see what they could tell him about Ferris. The call took a few minutes to connect, but Malan was soon speaking to the detective in charge of the case in which Ferris had claimed involvement. He listened to Chief Inspector Burvill's castigation and caution.

"He's a blithering, blathering windbag! But don't let that fool you for one minute into underestimating how much of a menace he is. You've no idea how badly I wanted to bring a charge of wasting police time against him. But be warned, he's clever at keeping everything just on the right side of that line. At the point where I thought I might have enough to make the charge stick, he finally left off pushing his oar in and stirring the pot. Didn't stop him sending another letter to the Chief Constable though, telling him that I deserved to be disciplined for dereliction of my duty and, would you believe – harassing him!"

The resentment and grievance in Burvill's voice told Malan as much as his words did. He thanked the Sussex officer and hung up.

When the DI returned a few minutes later he was still looking gloomy. He sloughed off his jacket and hung it on the back of his chair then sat down heavily.

Malan tried to lift his boss' spirits by relaying his conversation with DCI Burvill, but it didn't seem to make any difference.

Cordy made an effort to shake off his despondency. "Let's press on and review our suspects, Sergeant, assuming you're correct about no stranger being involved, number one must be the husband and I have to admit that Ferris is right to cast doubt on the alibi. We'll have to really go into that when we find out what it is.

"Then I suppose we must look more closely at the two younger men – Prentice and Trevelyan. But based on what we've seen of them, I don't think Prentice is involved, and you don't think Trevelyan is.

"What about the artist chap? He's not all that much older than Mrs Marner. What did you really think of him, Malan?"

"He's everything Ayers said about him, sir, and I can't say I exactly took to his lifestyle. But I got no impression of anything other than genuine regret at Mrs Marner's death, and absolutely no sign of guilt at all, or that he was trying to hide anything from me.

"I do think Maisie Lawrence should be added to the list, though. She's in some sort of relationship with Proudlove, but there was no way of telling from the bit of billing and cooing that I saw going on whether it extends beyond the verbal and superficial.

"If she's genuinely infatuated with the artist herself, and thought he was involved with Adelaide Marner in some way, then maybe she would want her rival out of the way. We've gravitated towards our suspect being a man, but the Doc suggested a woman could equally well have picked up a bit of rock and done the deed."

Cordy nodded. "Good point. I'd like to meet the young lady."

Malan felt obliged to prepare his boss before such an encounter. "She's very attractive; and very provocative in the 'come hither' department. But…" Malan looked back at his time with Proudlove and his muse, "I have to say I got no sense at all that she's a wrong-un."

"Between us, we seem to be eliminating everyone, Sergeant, which won't do at all. Who's left?"

"Most of the others are at least twenty years older than the deceased, sir. Whatever Ferris suggests, Henry Ayers simply doesn't seem to have a motive to kill his sister-in law – and nor do any of the others, as far as we know."

"No. We still have to the older Trevelyans to see, of course, but who's your money on so far?"

"I wouldn't put my money anywhere yet, sir," said Malan without hesitation. "The husband may have the best motive, if the reports of their marriage are correct. But he's not poor, and he could get a divorce or annulment if the two of them couldn't carry on. Why risk the gallows? It doesn't make sense."

"Can't argue with your logic there, Sergeant. Let's go and find something to eat. My turn to choose today, so it's fish and chips."

# CHAPTER 7

The detectives ate their lunch sitting on a bench on the promenade, the Inspector silent throughout. Standing up to take his chip papers to a nearby wastepaper basket, Cordy announced he was going for a walk.

"I'll go by myself, Sergeant. No offence to you, but I want to get my head clear. I'll see you back at the station in half an hour." He set off towards Heacham.

Malan decided he would also benefit from a walk and turned the opposite way to his boss. Passing the pier, he reached the northern end of the prom a few minutes later. Having decided that he would take the steps up to the top of the cliff and walk towards the lighthouse, he found himself being pulled down to the beach again instead. It was about two hours before high tide, and although he didn't know where high water would reach, he knew he could get to the murder scene and back comfortably enough.

He met several other walkers, and exchanged a few 'good afternoons'. There was of course nothing new to be learned at the scene, but he sat down on a boulder for a minute, hoping that something enlightening would happen. It didn't.

He was just getting up from the uncomfortable rock, when he saw a man and dog a few yards away, approaching from behind him. With sinking heart, he recognised Ferris. At low tide, it was possible for walkers to pass so far apart that they could hardly even shout to each other, but the water was now high enough that the ground available to walk on meant that he couldn't avoid speaking.

Xanthe, off her lead, was running on ahead, darting in and out of each tiny wavelet as it ran across the sandy bits of the beach. Her master accosted the detective.

"Looking for inspiration, Sergeant? Your dull-as-ditchwater Inspector could certainly do with it," he said rudely. "I gave him some first-rate advice this morning, but he didn't seem inclined to listen properly. More fool him! As a consequence of that discourtesy he's in line for an almighty jolt in the morning, I can tell you. I've written to the Chief Constable."

Malan, being aware of Cordy's lack of self-confidence, was already sorry for his leader. He felt it was time to prick this overbearing man's ego.

"Your privilege, of course," he said, starting to walk back, Ferris falling into step beside him. "But there's something you should know. I've made enquiries about you. At Scotland Yard, and at Sussex Police headquarters. When I tell you that neither establishment gave a good report of you, I'm putting what I was told very politely indeed. Very!"

Malan didn't bother to look at Ferris as he spoke and couldn't see the furious scowl on his face.

"Professional jealousy!" came the retort. "To be expected when an amateur could be more successful than they were. And that lot in Sussex – absolute shower."

The Sergeant wondered if he could produce a grunt like his boss to illustrate how he felt, but instantly decided that this would require some practice. He said nothing and continued to stride along, quickening his pace and hoping to shake off the nuisance beside him.

Ferris, not remotely struggling to keep up with the detective (who was half his age) hadn't finished. "I've taken note of your attitude too, Sergeant. I'm considering raising your name at police headquarters. I'm giving you a chance to redeem yourself, though. I told you about Henry Ayers before. Well, I happen to know that he and his wife have rowed about his relationship with her sister. That means he needed to get rid of Adelaide before she could tell any tales.

"Of course, Seymour is still a possibility – I can't deny that – but in some ways it's too obvious. And why would he take her down on the beach to do it? No. If you've checked out Seymour's alibi, then Ayers is your man. You'd be very unwise not to listen to me," he added meaningfully.

Malan bore in mind the advice from DCI Bryce: to take notice of whatever it was Ferris wanted to say on the off chance that he did know something useful.

"I shall pass all that on to the Inspector."

"I should think so too, Sergeant. If you persuade your man to arrest Ayers there may be hope for you yet."

"We'll be seeing Mr Marner later today, but I think you'd better come along with me now and make a formal statement regarding what you know about Mr Ayers," said Malan. "Obviously we can't arrest him without more to go on."

Ferris was dismissive. "Oh, I don't know about that, Sergeant," he said airily. "I deduce from my observations. I have no need to put something down in black and white, with exact times and all of that. My job – my *modus operandi* if you like – is to give the police the ideas. Following which they must get a move on, do their job, and come up with the necessary proof."

Malan could feel his eyes widening in surprise as he listened to this remarkable statement, but he didn't bother to reply. He resolved to revisit the point later, deciding that for the moment he should push a bit more and see what else might be offered.

"There are other suspects, Mr Ferris, of course. What do you think about Mr Prentice, for example, or young Arthur Trevelyan?"

"No, absolutely not. No doubt they both desired Adelaide – what red-blooded man didn't? But they aren't killers. Or at least, Prentice stopped killing people after the war. No; if not Marner, Ayers is your man."

"What about Mr Proudlove, though?"

"Him I've considered very carefully. And also his 'muse', as he calls her. He's a philanderer, of course – mistress after mistress over the years, apparently. And maybe his latest wouldn't be too pleased if she found that Adelaide was one of her predecessors, and still on the scene, as it were."

This at least tied in with Malan's earlier thinking, and he began to pay closer attention to his irritating companion.

"But Maisie Lawrence is far from stupid," continued Ferris. "She knows very well that she's only a passing fancy, and she plays him along exactly the same way he plays her along. She'll be discarded soon enough and paid to go off without a fuss, so there's nothing for her to gain by killing Adelaide. As for him, he couldn't care less what anybody says or thinks about him. If Addy threatened to tell everyone about their relationship, he'd see it as a feather in his cap and broadcast the fact himself. No, it wasn't Proudlove and it wasn't his strumpet!"

Although there was nothing helpful in Ferris's elimination of the two younger men, Malan admitted to himself that the argument about Proudlove and Maisie seemed sound.

They had reached the steps up to the promenade, Xanthe joining them of her own volition to have her lead attached.

"I trust I'll see Ayers under arrest by tomorrow, Sergeant. In the meantime, I'll wish you a good afternoon," said Ferris, and went with his dog up the nearest steps.

Malan walked on a further fifty yards, before he turned to the left by the pier, and walked up into the town.

He found Cordy chatting to Sergeant Timmins at the front desk. "Don't want to annoy you any more, sir, but I've just bumped into Mr Ferris again."

The DI groaned, and motioned him to come along to their room. "Tell me the worst, Sergeant."

Malan reported his conversation pretty well verbatim. This elicited a particularly expressive grunt.

Cordy closed his eyes and sighed deeply. "I'll just have to see what tomorrow brings. Nothing to be done about it now. Good idea of yours to ask him to make a statement, though. Pin the beggar down a bit.

"As for Ayers, we'll have to talk to him and his wife again, I suppose. We'll leave that until tomorrow, though. Goes against the grain, doing something because this so-called detective tells us to."

"How about telephoning to Marner's house, sir, and asking a maid to get him to call us here as soon as he arrives? I know you left a message before, but just to reinforce it."

"Yes; do that, Sergeant." Cordy sat morosely while Malan made the call.

The two officers had just begun to talk about Prentice, when the telephone rang with an incoming call. Malan, still nearer to the instrument, picked it up.

"Yes, he's here, sir. One moment. Superintendent Reeves for you, sir," he said, passing the handset to his boss.

There followed a largely one-sided conversation. All Malan could catch were a few examples of "yes, sir", and "of course, sir". There was also an "he's an extremely difficult man with a poor reputation with other forces". The call ended with Cordy saying "I'll certainly explain all that in my written report, sir".

The DI's expression as he replaced the receiver was even less happy that it had been ten minutes earlier. "Well, you probably heard all that, Sergeant. It seems that Ferris, whether or not he's written to the Chief Constable, has managed to get through to the Super. I'm not in anyone's good books, it seems. Damn the man."

Malan was unclear which man was being

damned but thought it really didn't matter. The two sat in silence again, Cordy seeming to have lost interest in going through Ferris's logic regarding the other suspects.

A tap on the door produced a constable's head, poked into the room. "Visitor for you, sir – a Mr Marner."

Cordy came out of his reverie. "Excellent – show him in here, Packer."

The two officers stood as Seymour Marner came into the room. An undistinguished man apart from his height, thought Malan, which was a good six foot. He had closely cropped dark hair with streaks of grey here and there. He wore neither beard nor moustache, but his facial hair was already creating a black shadow and obviously of the vigorous sort that needed to be shaved twice a day. He took the seat offered and regarded each officer in turn, alert dark eyes beneath the bushy dark eyebrows.

Malan made the introductions and expressed condolences for the man's loss.

"Thank you for coming in, Mr Marner," said Cordy; "your maid gave you the message, then?"

Marner shook his head. "I haven't been home yet. Yesterday in Birmingham I received a message from my assistant, telling me what has happened. I telephoned two or three times in the evening to speak to my cook – she's the only servant who lives in – but there was no reply even at eleven o'clock. I thought it odd, as Tuesday isn't her evening off, but I had to get to bed in order to catch an early train today."

"We understand she's gone to see her sick mother, sir – went away lunchtime Monday with your wife's permission; one of your maids told us."

"Ah, that explains it. Now, what can you tell me about this awful thing?"

Cordy nodded to Malan.

"There's no nice way of putting this, sir. On Monday evening, your wife was on the beach under the cliffs, where she was struck on the head with a piece of rock. There's no question of suicide or accident. It's a case of murder. The Coroner has been informed, and no doubt he will open an inquest soon.

"At this stage we've been talking to Mrs Marner's local family and friends."

Marner looked at Malan, disbelief on his face.

"Murder! I was only told she'd been killed – I assumed an accident. This is dreadful. But under the cliffs? Why would she go down there – and surely it must have been getting dark? She didn't go out like that at any time. Are you sure this wasn't a rockfall – they happen frequently along there, as you must know."

Both detectives thought Marner looked and sounded genuinely distraught.

"We're quite sure, Mr Marner," said Cordy.

"But, as you say, it seems very unlikely that she would be wandering by herself along that part of the beach at that time. Her bag and valuables weren't taken, so it's not a robbery gone wrong. We're working on the assumption that she'd either walked down there with someone she knew well; or she met someone there whom she knew well.

"But before we talk about her friends and acquaintances, we need to ask you the same question that everyone else is being asked: where were you on Monday evening between five and nine?"

Marner gave the DI a nasty look. "Are you seriously suggesting I'm a suspect, Inspector?"

Malan took over. "Everyone is treated equally, Mr Marner. In your case, you tell us you were in Birmingham – but we only have your word for that until we get corroboration. And you should know that we have various reports on the state of your marriage. Now, perhaps you would answer the question – in detail?"

The nasty look was transferred to the DS.

"I see. Investigating the murder of my wife when I'm many miles away justifies poking your nose into my private affairs, eh?"

For whatever reason, Malan felt he had reached his limit for the day of being criticised and lectured by a member of the public. He looked back defiantly at Marner. "Private affairs cease to be private if they impinge on a murder investigation, sir. That would be especially true if the 'affairs' mentioned mean relationships outside business ones. We're waiting, Mr Marner."

Marner seemed to fold up a little in his seat. "All right then, I went to London on business early on Monday and then on to Birmingham later the same day. My assistant, Bennett, can vouch for the fact that he contacted me there yesterday."

"Where did you stay?"

"I decline to say."

"Very well," said Cordy. "Anyone told about this conversation might well think it strange that you don't want to do everything you can to help the police. We'll get the number that Mr Bennett, called, and see whether it's a company or a private number. We can find out who it belongs to. Then we'll work out from the railway timetables whether it was possible for you to be here on Monday evening and back wherever it is by Tuesday, when Bennett found you. You can be very sure that we'll find out where you were, eventually. I don't say I think you murdered your wife at this stage, but you're certainly acting very suspiciously."

"All you have to do is say who you were with on Monday during the day," added Malan. "Since it would take you at least five hours to get here, if you were in a business meeting – or with any other credible witness – in Birmingham after say three o'clock that afternoon, you'd be in the clear, and we could move on."

There was a silence. Eventually, Marner stirred. "Very well. I suppose it really doesn't matter now Adelaide has gone – and from what you say, people have been talking about my marriage anyway. I had a perfectly genuine business meeting in Birmingham on Tuesday morning. But the rest of the time I was with a friend. I went straight to her house after I arrived in the city on Monday afternoon, and stayed with her that night. I went to my meeting on Tuesday morning, and returned to my friend at lunch time. I was there until early this morning. It was her number that I'd given Bennett in case my firm needed to talk to me. I hadn't envisaged this as a reason for his doing so, of course. I'll give you her name, address, and telephone number. She will verify what I say."

He pulled out a small notebook, scribbled on it, then tore out the page and pushed it across to Malan. Cordy signalled to him to leave the room and make the call immediately.

"Now, having got that sorted, would you care to tell us about your wife's acquaintances. All the people she was perhaps sufficiently friendly with to have gone for an evening walk with them?"

Marner shrugged. "I suppose so. As no doubt you've discovered, Adelaide and I were not close – we never were. I went my way, and she hers. We just happened to live in the same house. Really, the only acquaintances I'm aware of are the people she played bridge with. Her sister and brother-in-law too. I'll jot down a few names, but I can't guarantee it's complete; she didn't confide in me so there could be others."

He wrote again. After a couple of minutes he put away his pen, tore off another sheet, and handed it over. Cordy scanned it quickly, and saw that it was identical to the list produced the day before by the maids. Like theirs, the name of Arthur Trevelyan didn't appear.

"Have you already talked to any of these people?" Marner enquired.

"Most of them, yes. We know about the others, just haven't got around to them yet.

"If you were to pick one person on this list as being someone your wife might have gone for a walk with, who would it be?"

"Just a feeling, you understand – with no evidence whatsoever. And I'll deny I ever said it if you mention it in public. The only candidate as far as I can see is Connor Proudlove. The man has had a series of consorts – or 'muses' as he euphemistically calls them – for as long as I've known him. He did a painting of Adelaide, years ago. Whether they were lovers as well, I really don't know, although I rather think it would be a break with precedent on his part if they weren't. I didn't much care even then, you see. But whether they were or not, my guess is that

Proudlove would be close enough to her for her to accompany him for a walk.

"I really can't see either of our retired military gentlemen making such a suggestion. And I'm pretty sure that she wouldn't have been attracted to a young chap like Prentice, even though he, like every other man in Hunstanton, was attracted to her. I was myself, of course, for a short time." The bitterness in Marner's voice was unmistakeable.

Cordy would have liked to know why that 'short time' had come to an end but could think of no reason to ask. There was nothing to suggest that it would be a legitimate line of enquiry.

Malan came back into the room. "The lady-friend, Mrs Reynolds, was a bit reluctant to start with, sir, but eventually she confirmed what we've just been told. Specifically regarding Monday – Mr Marner was with her from about two o'clock, and they went out for a meal in the evening. I've warned her that we might need a signed statement, and she was perfectly obliging. She hopes you're all right, by the way, Mr Marner, and asks you to telephone when you can."

"Do you want to ask us anything, Mr Marner? asked the DI.

"Not really. I assume Frances has been told of her sister's death?"

Both officers nodded. "And I also assume we can't begin to make funeral arrangements just yet?"

"That's right – it should be sorted out when the inquest is held. You'll be notified of that, of course."

Marner stood up. "Well, if you aren't going to arrest me, I'd like to go home. I'll not be hypocritical and say I need time to grieve, but I've had a shock all the same, and should like some time to recover from that and to think."

Malan showed him out. At the police station door, Marner turned and looked at the Sergeant. "I apologise for being difficult earlier. I don't doubt you and a lot of other people think I've been a very poor husband, and perhaps even an unpleasant one. I really can't argue against either description. All I'd say is, I never harmed a hair of Adelaide's head, and I sincerely hope you soon find whoever did this and hang him."

Malan returned to find the Inspector with his elbows on his desk and his head cupped in his hands. He focused on Malan. "What did you think, Sergeant?"

"Not guilty, sir. Unless he'd coached his lady friend in what to say, I'm convinced she told me the truth. Everything fitted in. He apologised just now, by the way."

"So he should have done. I didn't like him, but I agree with you. I wonder how often he goes to Birmingham. Hell of a long way to go to visit your mistress."

"I'm asking myself whether Mrs Marner

was aware of his infidelity; and if she was, to what extent it affected her own behaviour," said Malan. "All this distance between them that people refer to – did his behaviour cause that; or was it something she did that drove him to a mistress?"

"Don't suppose we'll ever know," said Cordy, "one of those chicken-and-egg posers."

The ringing of the telephone interrupted them again. The DI answered it this time. "Right, thank you madam. We'll come straight away."

"Dr Trevelyan," he said to the Sergeant. "Apparently she and her husband got home much earlier than expected, and Arthur passed on the message that we wanted to speak to them. We can walk there now."

Within five minutes the two detectives were at the Trevelyan's front door, which opened before they could ring the bell. A man, formally dressed in charcoal grey suit and dark blue tie, motioned them inside. "I'm John Trevelyan," he said when Cordy identified Malan and himself.

"Come and meet my wife. I understand you've already met our son, Sergeant." He ushered the two officers into a pleasant drawing room. Dr Trevelyan was sitting by French windows, with a newspaper in her hands. Arthur was sitting nearby, he stood up as the three men entered.

"My dear, this is Detective Inspector Cordy and Sergeant Malan – gentlemen, my wife

Philippa. Inspector, this is our son Arthur. Now, please take a seat," he continued after hands had been shaken.

"Would it be in order to offer refreshments?" Both officers shook their heads with muttered thanks.

"Well, it's obvious why you're here We understand you've given Arthur the third degree, and now it's our turn. Let me say at once, that in the last half hour Arthur has been totally frank with us about his feelings were for Adelaide; we were just too stupid to realise earlier. Anyway, hopefully you can eliminate him from your list of suspects."

"John should really have started off by saying that we are all quite devastated by what happened to Addy," said Dr Trevelyan. Actually, it's fair to say that none of us quite believed it when Guy Ferris gave us the news. We still thought he must have made a mistake, and that it was an accident. Your presence means he was right, unfortunately. Anyway, how can we help?"

"Quite possibly you can't, ma'am," said Cordy. "We're working on the assumption that Mrs Marner went down on the beach under the cliffs with another person. We don't believe she would have gone alone. And we think, from what we've learned about the lady, that this person could only be someone she knew well. So that would seem to reduce greatly – perhaps eliminate – the possibility that the assailant was a stranger. She was neither robbed nor assaulted.

"We need to hear from you who that companion might have been."

"I saw Dan Bartlett in the staff canteen at the hospital this morning," said the surgeon. I spoke to him, knowing that he does the PMs in cases of unexplained deaths. Probably shouldn't have done that. From my interest, he realised that I knew Adelaide, although he could reasonably have assumed that anyway, knowing where I live and that the social circle in this town is not extensive. He was very tight-lipped – no doubt he rightly assumes that I am a suspect. All he would say was that the murder could just as well have been carried out by a woman as a man."

Neither policeman spoke.

"Well," Trevelyan continued, "I have no ideas as to who the killer might be. But whereas, stretching disbelief beyond breaking point, one could say that any of her male acquaintances might have done it, I can honestly say that I can't suggest even one of the females."

"We've been told that Mr Marner was away – has that been confirmed?" asked Arthur, speaking for the first time.

"It has, yes," replied Malan. "We'll need to get a formal statement from Birmingham, but it seems he was exactly where he said he was."

This information appeared to depress the three Trevelyans. Mr Trevelyan laughed in some embarrassment. "Sorry; this looks bad, gentlemen. Truth is, I suppose, we'd prefer it to have been him rather than anyone else." His wife nodded sadly.

"Understandable, from what we've seen and heard," remarked Cordy somewhat improperly. "Anyway, can you provide a few names for us, please, in case there may be someone we haven't heard of yet. You see, Mr Trevelyan," he said looking at the young man, "Your name didn't appear on the original list we were given. Maybe there are others still unknown to us."

The three Trevelyans called out names, but their joint efforts amounted to the same names as the list already held.

"We need to talk about alibis," said Malan. "We're asking everyone, of course. Where were you on Monday evening?"

"I wasn't working that day, Sergeant," said Philippa Trevelyan. "I was here until about half past five. I took my car – we have to have two because of the way we work – and drove to Lynn. Arthur was here when I left, incidentally. I met John in the hospital car park at about six. We left my car there, and he drove us to our friends in Downham Market for dinner. We wanted to save petrol, of course. We picked up my car on the way back. That would be about half past ten."

Dr Trevelyan provided the details of their Downham friends.

"Good, thank you," said Malan. "You, sir,"

he nodded towards the surgeon, say you have no ideas. But, with respect, neither of you," he looked towards mother and son, "have answered the Inspector's question about whether you have any ideas. Off the record, and not to be quoted, of course."

A glance was exchanged. "You hinted to Arthur that perhaps it is more likely that a younger man would have been with Addy," said Philippa, "and I suppose that is logical. David Prentice would be the most likely to fit the bill. He certainly looked at her as much as he possibly could – just as it now seems Arthur did. I make no moral judgement, but everyone knows that Connor Proudfoot doesn't believe in abstinence outside of marriage. He was close to Addy, long after he had finished painting her. But I emphasise that I don't see either of them as murderers."

Cordy looked at Malan with eyebrows raised to see if he had another question. Receiving a shake of the head, he stood up to leave, the Sergeant following suit.

"Thank you all," said the DI. "I doubt you'll be called to give evidence at the inquest, but that's out of our hands."

Walking back to the police station, Cordy seemed very tired, and didn't speak. At the entrance he stopped, and turned to face Malan.

"You'll become a very good detective, Sergeant, and one day you'll make a far better DI than I can ever be."

Malan looked at his boss in astonishment, suddenly feeling that something momentous was about to follow this preliminary.

Cordy continued, "You take the car tonight, and come back tomorrow to check out the story about Henry Ayers. I'm going back home on the train now, and I'll be going straight into our office in the morning. I rather fancy I'll be summoned there sometime tomorrow anyway. I'd like to get my resignation in first."

"No, no, sir! that's not necessary, surely? Whatever Ferris says can easily be shot down. Don't let someone like him drive you out of your job – it's just wrong!" Malan felt very forcefully that this was true.

Cordy gave a half-smile. "No arguments, lad. I'm still your superior officer, so just do as I say. It's not just Ferris anyway. I've been thinking about this for over a year. And if I don't see you tomorrow, best wishes for your future."

He shook Malan's hand, and walked off. The Sergeant decided against going inside the police station. He climbed into the Wolsesley and sat very still, thinking through the consequences of Cordy's intended action and feeling even less well disposed towards Guy Ferris than before.

# CHAPTER 8

*Thursday 28th April 1950*

After his breakfast, which his landlady had done pretty well that morning, Malan drove to Hunstanton. He was perfectly happy to go by himself to see the Ayers if they were available, but he thought half past eight might be a little early.

That point, whilst valid, was not really uppermost in his mind, however. If the DI had resigned, then it was inevitable that the Superintendent would want to contact him – this was a murder enquiry, after all, and an acting Sergeant could hardly be left in charge of it. He decided to wait in the James Street police station for a while, to see what happened. He chatted with Sergeant Timmins for a few minutes, without saying anything about the DI, then settled himself in the little interview room to start compiling his report.

A little after ten o'clock he was thinking that he would have to move, when the telephone rang. It was Constable Palmer at Lynn.

"The Super wants to see you at eleven, on the dot," said Reeves' assistant. "Don't ask me why, because I don't know. But he's hopping up and down and the Chief Constable's been on the phone."

Malan drove slowly back to King's Lynn, half dreading what he was going to be told. If Cordy had really resigned, as now seemed probable, presumably a senior officer that he didn't know would be sent over from Norwich.

Going into the police station via the back door, he managed to get to his desk without seeing anyone. As he expected, there was nobody else in the CID office. Looking at Cordy's desk, he could see at once that the few personal items that had been on it, including a photograph of his grandchildren, had gone. He sat down heavily. Mechanically, he looked through the few notes left on his desk.

The top one read: 'Goodbye and good luck!'

Malan idled at his desk for twenty minutes, before moving towards the door. On his way up to the Superintendent's room he met a couple of officers. When both greeted him quite normally he supposed that news about the DI had not yet reached the grapevine.

Checking his watch, he tapped on the Super's door at exactly eleven o'clock. He had only been in this office twice before, and wasn't aware that the call of 'come in' was today several decibels lower than the Superintendent's usual bellow. Inside, he was surprised to see a second officer, standing by Reeves' desk. This man was also in uniform, but displaying even more silver badging than the Superintendent. This was the Chief Constable, and Malan automatically snapped even more to attention than he would have done for the Super.

"Easy, Malan, and take a seat," said the Chief, sitting down himself beside the desk, and looking hard at the acting Sergeant.

"Are you aware that Inspector Cordy has resigned?"

"He told me last night that he intended to do so, sir. I tried to talk him out of it."

"Well, you were unsuccessful, and perhaps that's for the best. Are you also aware that this man Ferris has written to me about your Hunstanton case?"

"Yes, sir, he mentioned it yesterday. But he's a very unreliable character. I made enquiries about him at Scotland Yard and with the Sussex police – he claimed to have been instrumental in solving some of their cases. I spoke to two chief inspectors, and they both said it was all fantasy on his part."

"I see. Interesting. Well, in his letter he claims to have told you and Cody who did it, and says the two of you haven't taken him and his expertise seriously. In fact he's very rude about Cordy. When I received that letter, and almost simultaneously heard from Mr Reeves that Cordy has resigned, I drove over from Norwich at once.

"Anyway, regardless of the letter, the fact is that your DI has resigned with immediate effect. He hasn't given formal notice, and although that would normally count against him, I'm inclined to ignore it in the circumstances, and treat him as though he'd followed procedure properly.

"Putting all that to one side, are you anywhere near finding out who did this murder?"

"No, sir. We've had to make certain assumptions – in particular that the lady would never have gone along that beach unless she was with someone she knew. So we've been looking at her friends and acquaintances. We've uncovered nothing so far to point to any particular person. The husband, whom people think is the most likely killer, seems to have a good alibi."

"So, we have a murder case with no senior officer," summarised the Chief Constable. "It seems that CID elsewhere in the county are fully occupied. I could divert someone off another case, but there's a more practical alternative. I've asked Scotland Yard for help. I'm not happy – nor is Mr Reeves – that we're having to go cap in hand to the Yard twice in a matter of months, but that's just unfortunate. We're going to have to beef up the CID establishment this side of the county – especially if we're entering a new era and this murder rate is going to be sustained.

"Anyway, I spoke to the Assistant Commissioner an hour ago. He says that DCI Bryce, who came here last year, is available. I spoke to Mr Bryce. He told me his usual bagman is away on another case. However, he reminds me that in his report on the last case he commended you highly, and suggests that the two of you could work together on this one." He gave a tight smile. "Saves us money if they only send one officer, of course.

"Mr Reeves also rates you highly, and tells me that he has temporarily made you up to Sergeant. Well, I'm making that rank permanent, as from now."

Malan stammered out his thanks, which the Chief waved away.

"Mr Bryce will have left London now and will go straight to Hunstanton." The CC addressed the Super, "If the Sandringham Hotel is still closed, Reeves, arrange a room for him at the Glebe again." To Malan he said, "You go back and carry on with whatever you were doing, Malan, and be at Hunstanton police station to meet Mr Bryce when he arrives – about two o'clock, I imagine. Any questions?"

Malan shook his head.

"On your way, then."

Happy with his new substantive rank and the prospect of working with DCI Bryce again, Malan made his return journey to Hunstanton in much better spirits. It was now a little before midday, and he decided to try the Ayers before going back to the station. Parking as close to the house as he could, he walked up to the front door. He was in luck. Frances Ayers answered the door, and invited him in before he could even speak.

"Come and sit down, Sergeant. Henry is on the telephone, but I'll fetch him in a minute. We were just about to have a belated mid-morning coffee – I'm sure you would like one too?"

Malan accepted with thanks and sat looking out at The Wash through the huge windows until Mr Ayers joined him a few minutes later. Greetings had just been exchanged when Frances Ayers returned with a tray of coffee and opened the conversation. "Too much to hope that you've come to tell us who killed my sister, I suppose?"

"I'm afraid not, ma'am I have some news of a different sort, but first I have a question. It's delicate. Probably I should be asking it of each of you separately, but still.

"Mr Ayers, we've been told that you and your wife had a row over your relationship with your sister-in-law. Is that true?"

Malan had positioned himself to watch both the Ayers as he asked the question. The couple instantly displayed the same shocked expression.

"No, it most certainly is not true," they both exclaimed almost in synchronism.

"Wherever on Earth did you get that idea?"

asked Mrs Ayers.

"Sorry, madam, I can't tell you that. Are you both saying that there's nothing in it?"

"Nothing whatsoever," growled Ayers, " and if I ever catch up with the muck-spreader who told you that they'll get a damn fine tongue-lashing, I can tell you!"

"Just a second, Henry," intervened his wife as she reached out and placed a hand on her husband's arm. "Something's coming to mind. Do you recall a bridge evening two or three months ago – I think we were at the Websters' house. You were partnering Addy, and I think I was with David Prentice. You had just revoked, badly, and I said something like "You'd better divorce me and marry Addy. She never shouts at you when you make an error!"

Henry Ayers nodded. "Yes...that's right. And you went on to say that she was probably a better cook, too. Addy laughed and said, 'I may not shout at people revoking, but please don't endow me with skills that I don't possess.'"

Ayers turned away from his wife to face Malan. "But what manner of a complete cretin could have misunderstood that fond exchange for anything other than affectionate family banter?"

Frances Ayers was also looking at Malan. "That, Sergeant, is the only possible thing that your spiteful sneak could be dredging up," said Mrs Ayers. "Unlike poor Addy, we have a very good marriage. Henry has been a solid brother-in-law to her, and nothing more. Tell your source to get his or her ears syringed, or to acquire a sense of humour!"

Malan felt everything he had heard had the ring of truth to it. "Can you remember who was present that evening?" he asked.

The Ayers looked at each other.

"I'm pretty sure we had three tables that night. I don't think Arthur would have been home from Oxford, so probably Maisie would have been playing," said Frances. "I hope we've convinced you that this story has no foundation, Sergeant?"

"Oh, I'm happy enough for the moment, ma'am. But let me pass on my news, such as it is. Inspector Cordy unexpectedly resigned from the force this morning. "He's done nothing wrong, by the way, and he'd been thinking about leaving the force for some time. Between you and me, perhaps the workload was getting a bit much. Anyway, the Chief Constable has called in Scotland Yard. I'm very pleased to tell you that Detective Chief Inspector Bryce has been assigned to this case. He's on his way already and should arrive in a couple of hours. You'll remember the triple murder case here a few months ago – well, Mr Bryce was the man who solved that. Working with him again will be a pleasure for me – detectives don't come any better."

"I remember the name; well, it's good that he's coming," said Ayers.

Malan stood up to go, but Mrs Ayers shot another question at him. "What about Seymour?"

Malan hesitated. He really shouldn't pass on information of this sort to anyone, especially not people who technically remained suspects. However, taking into account that Mrs Ayers was the sister of the murdered woman, and Seymour her brother-in-law, he thought he might say something.

"Mr Marner was certainly in Birmingham between Monday afternoon and Wednesday morning, madam. Without a time machine, it would have been impossible for him to have been on Hunstanton beach on Monday evening."

"Just bear in mind that he could have hired someone to do the job, Sergeant, and fixed an alibi for himself. I certainly wouldn't put it past him!"

"You'll gather that my wife doesn't think too highly of her brother-in-law, Sergeant. Nor indeed do I."

Malan acknowledged the suggestion and gave his 'goodbye' to the Ayers without explaining what he saw as the overriding objection to the involvement of a hitman: Adelaide Marner agreeing to walk on the beach with a stranger. He resolved to mention the matter to the DCI, but in his own mind decided it was a non-starter.

The decision on where to eat lunch was now his alone. He didn't feel ravenously hungry, so he parked back at the police station, and walked down to the Wash and Tope, where he ordered half a pint of mild and a cheese sandwich. These he took to a table, where he sat by himself, thinking.

The first thing he considered was what the Chief might have meant about 'beefing up' the Lynn CID. With Cordy gone, that left DS Gray and himself. Nobody promoted to sergeant one day would be moved up to inspector the next, so that let him out. He didn't think that Gray would get promoted either, but if the offer was made he would almost certainly turn it down. (Gray, like Malan, was well aware of Cordy's regret at taking the post.)

Presumably a DS from elsewhere in the county would get the job. Malan didn't know everyone, of course, but he hadn't heard of any up-and-coming men who would fit the bill. There was, however, a youngish DI in Great Yarmouth who was tipped for the top. But surely he wouldn't be too keen to move out to Lynn on a level transfer? Ah, but the Chief had said 'beef up'. Perhaps the team would be led by a competent chief inspector – and that would accommodate the two sergeants and one or two new DCs.

Malan couldn't know it yet, but his thought process was exactly the same as that of the Chief Constable.

As he swallowed the last of his sandwich he turned his thoughts to the case. It was a pity that Sergeant Haig couldn't come with his leader – Malan had really liked the DCI's Scottish colleague. On the other hand, this new arrangement meant that he himself would fill the role of 'bagman'.

As the last drop of beer disappeared, he decided he was very happy with life. He returned to the police station, where he informed Timmins about his own confirmed promotion, and about the forthcoming arrival of the senior officer from Scotland Yard. He then retired to the little interview room and started to write up the key points of the case, which he would need to pass on to the Chief Inspector.

Nearly an hour later, Malan put down his pencil, and stood up to have a stretch. As if he had signalled, there was a tap on the door and DCI Bryce walked in. He smiled warmly, and reached over the table to shake the Sergeant's hand.

"West Norfolk will soon get a reputation as the murder centre of East Anglia," he remarked, motioning Malan to sit down again.

"Yes; a bit depressing, sir."

"Quite. Well, all I know about this is what your Chief Constable told me. A name, the location, the cause of death. So start right at the beginning, please, and talk me through what happened, and what you have so far. I've been told about Inspector Cordy, by the way."

Malan, who had been expecting to have to make a report, was ready. He spoke solidly for ten minutes, without any interruptions from the DCI, who just made an occasional note.

Bryce was reflective for a while when the précis was finished, then smiled at his new subordinate. "Very well explained, Sergeant. Your Chief told me he was going to promote you immediately – I hope that's happened?"

Grinning, Malan nodded.

"Let me just clarify a few points. You yourself haven't seen Mr Prentice or Admiral Wynterflood – Mr Cordy interviewed them?"

Malan confirmed this was the case.

"And it hasn't been possible to see Brigadier Pullen, but you're reasonably satisfied he was away?"

Another nod.

"This artist chap, and his companion. What did you think?"

"Physically, Proudlove is a big strong chap; but I got no impression that he would ever be violent – he was more or less described as a crybaby by Henry Ayers. As for Maisie Lawrence, Doc Bartlett said the job could have been done by a woman but again, there was nothing about her to make me feel she would be a killer."

Malan explained the argument put forward by Mr Ferris as to why these two must be innocent.

"Ah yes, Ferris. The Chief Constable read me the letter he'd received. Have you been told the contents?"

"No, sir; but Ferris indicated to me yesterday what he intended to say."

"Well, leaving aside the malicious remarks about your former DI, he stated that Henry Ayers is guilty. In fact, if Ferris broadcast that beyond the police, he could be liable for a large sum in damages. Not the first time he's veered towards libel and defamation, incidentally. We have a similar letter at the Yard maligning an innocent man. No offence committed because communications to the police have qualified privilege, but we know it was also copied to the press. Unpublished by them, of course, but any number of people could have seen it from the post room all the way up to the editor's office and then the legal department."

Bryce sighed. "Nevertheless, he can't be completely discounted for the moment.

"I completely agree with your decision to assume Mrs Marner knew her killer. Frankly, if that's wrong and it was a stranger, we'll probably never find him.

"Here's what we'll do next. Neither of us has seen Prentice, so a visit to him should be a priority. As you've suggested, a younger man would be more likely if there is a romantic link. We'll see if we think there's any evidence for that.

"If we don't find anything to suggest it's Prentice, we'll look much more closely at all the older men. Someone old enough to be her father would be an equally suitable escort to the beach.

"As a matter of courtesy, I should meet Marner and the sister and explain that I've taken over from DI Cordy. I must see the sister's husband too, given that he's Ferris's preferred nominee and we clearly need to beware of that man's wrath! Does he know I'm here, by the way?"

"I've only told Mr and Mrs Ayers. I suppose they could have told anybody."

"You say Prentice is an author – so presumably he works from home. Can we go on foot?"

"Oh yes, sir, it's no distance."

The detectives left the police station. As they walked, they discussed the forthcoming murder trial arising from their previous case, until Bryce paused the conversation to ask a question about the present murder.

"You mentioned that the Marner's only live-in servant was away. Do we know when she left?"

"The maids told me it was midday on Monday, sir."

"We need to speak to her as well. Unlikely that she knew of her mistress's assignation later that day, but I'd like to hear if she has anything to say about Mrs Marner's strolling habits in general.

"We'll drop in to see Seymour Marner after we're done here," said the DCI as he took hold of the brass whale on the author's front door and gave it a good bang.

Prentice answered the knock. The DCI explained who they were, and that he had taken over from Inspector Cordy. The author immediately invited them to in. They were shown into a room which, although furnished with the usual sofas and easy chairs, also had two large tables. On one, a 'Batwing' typewriter sat surrounded by short piles of papers; on the other, a huge upright Imperial 55 rose above the bundles of papers around it. It was clear that this was both living room and workroom.

Prentice invited them to be seated. Seeing the DCI looking at the smaller typewriter, he volunteered some information about the machine.

"An Oliver 15," he said. "Built in England, but basically the American 11 model. Designed by a vicar, I believe, the idea of the two wings being that the user could always see the platten while typing. When invented it became known as the 'visible writer'. I tend to use that one mostly, but when I have an amanuensis here to produce a fair copy, she invariably uses the Imperial."

Bryce broached the reason for the visit. "Don't read more into this that is intended, Mr

Prentice, but everyone who was friendly with Mrs Marner is inevitably a suspect. We two are the only remaining detectives on the case, and since neither of us had met you that was something we needed to rectify."

"I understand completely, and I'm happy to help in any way I can. As I told the Inspector, I'd have chased after Addy myself if she'd been free. But I'm not one to break up a marriage, not even if it was already in pieces and beyond repair long before I arrived on the scene."

Prentice sighed dejectedly and closed his eyes for a moment against a painful memory. "I never did understand why Addy didn't just get up and go. Make the break herself and leave Seymour. It's not as if the Ayers' would have slammed their door in her face; they loved her unconditionally, I'm sure. And she must have known that my door would be permanently open to her." This last remark was an unhappy sounding near whisper.

"You were here on Monday afternoon and evening, Mr Prentice?" asked Bryce, feeling it was time to change the focus of the conversation.

"Yes; and unfortunately I have no witness to that. My maid has Monday afternoons and evenings off."

"Give us an idea of these bridge evenings, please."

"The formula doesn't vary much, Chief Inspector. We have three tables when we can.

There are eleven of us, with two occasional reserves. Young Arthur Trevelyan joins us sometimes if we're one short and he happens to be down from university. For the last few months Connor Proudlove's new guest has done the same when Arthur's away. Don't be misled by Maisie if you meet her, gentlemen – she's far more than just a model or mistress or muse. She's a highly intelligent girl.

"We don't always have three tables though – sometimes it's only two. We move between, let me see…seven different houses. Neither Pullen nor Ferris ever acts as host; not quite sure why. Sometimes we just gather for a rubber or two after our own evening meal, sometimes the invitation is for a bit of supper as well – but we single men with limited or no staff aren't expected to offer that. I suppose we have a session twice a month. Perhaps a bit more frequently; I don't keep a diary.

"We draw for partners each time, so the composition of the tables is constantly changing and over a period everyone plays with everyone. That evens out any advantage that a better player might have. However, and I say this with due modesty, the standard of play in our group is uniformly high. Even young Arthur is a very competent player, as is Maisie.

"We also get along very well together. Occasionally Frances Ayers will chastise her partner if he or she makes a mistake, but it remains good-humoured, and nobody ever takes offence."

"You've described your own relationship with Adelaide Marner very frankly. How would you describe other people's?"

The author considered the question. "I don't know who you've seen so far, but I can't believe that anyone, male or female, would deny that they had great affection for her. Arthur was the one who behaved most noticeably like a love-sick swain around her; but he probably does with any attractive woman though, it's his age. I'm pretty sure I embarrassed myself in the same way in my younger days, so I don't think you should read anything into that.

"All of the other men, old and young, were much the same.

"As far as our female members are concerned, I think you have to appreciate that Addy never presented as a threat to any of them. She never made overtures to someone's husband, despite the inadequacies and boorishness of her own. Nor, in fairness, were any of the husbands – Ayers, Webster, or Trevelyan – the sort of men to approach her. So, I think you can certainly assume that the wives loved her too. And Frances was especially close to her sister.

"You're obviously assuming that Addy went along the beach with someone she knew well. I'm quite sure that you're right – but that someone wasn't me. I've been racking my brains, but I really can't think who it could have been. Frankly, and I've not spoken of this to anyone else, I'd imagine everyone thinks it must have been Seymour. Probably hopes it was."

"It seems he was safely elsewhere, Mr Prentice."

"Yes, well that wouldn't hold in one of my novels. Either his alibi would prove to be false, or else he handed over a grubby envelope containing used notes to a seedy man in a public house – the down payment for a contract 'hit'."

It was the first glimmer of liveliness in the author and Bryce gave him a half smile. "You aren't the first to suggest those possibilities, Mr Prentice. But if your stories have any realism, you'll know that we shall thoroughly check out the first option, and the second one has a self-evident flaw."

Prentice nodded. "Yes, I quite see that Addy would never agree to walk alone with some mysterious assassin. But Marner might have paid someone like Wynterflood to do it, of course."

"I think you'd better stick to the novel-writing, Mr Prentice," said the DCI. "In real life you're veering perilously close to making slanderous remarks!"

He looked at Malan with raised eyebrows. "Just one last question, sir," said the Sergeant. "Did you ever hear any quarrel, or even just a casual remark, between Mr and Mrs Ayers, regarding Henry Ayer's relationship with his sister-in-law?"

Prentice looked at him in astonishment, and seemed about to say something, when he evidently changed his mind. He looked at Bryce, and then back at Malan.

"I was going to say that's utterly ridiculous," he said. "Henry's relationship was as a good brother-in-law, nothing else, I'm sure. But obviously someone has given you the idea that there was something more. And now I remember a humorous incident from some time ago, when Frances suggested to Henry that he'd be better off if he married Addy. It was to do with criticism when playing cards, I think, but she threw in something about Addy being a better cook, too. If that's the sort of thing you mean, well, it's ridiculous. It was a joke, for God's sake!"

"Yes, you're confirming what we heard about that incident; thank you."

Both officers stood up to go. "If anything more comes to mind, do contact us via the local police station," was Bryce's parting remark.

Outside, the DCI enquired how close Marner's house was.

"Two minutes at most, sir," replied Malan. He led his new boss along Cliff Parade, and up the steps to the Marner residence.

# CHAPTER 9

Elsie came to the door as before. She recognised the Sergeant, who introduced the Chief Inspector.

"Two things, Elsie. Is Mr Marner in; and has Mrs Waddell returned from her Mother's yet? If so, we'd like to speak to her first."

"Mr Marner's stepped out for a bit; but Cook's been back an hour. I'll show you down, if you follow me."

The girl led them through the entrance hall and down to the lower ground floor where she opened a door into the kitchen. A middle-aged woman was working pastry at a table, rolling pin and flour dredger to hand. She looked up enquiringly.

"It's the police to see you, Ruby," announced Elsie across the table, and supplied the detectives' names and ranks.

"Ah – thought you'd be coming," said the Cook. She turned to rinse her hands at the sink, dried them on a nearby roller towel then said with a smile, "Better find yourselves a perch if this is going to take any time." She pulled a stool out from under her side of the table and the detectives followed her example.

"Must have been a shock when you heard the news about Mrs Marner," suggested Bryce.

"Oh, completely sir. My old Mother doesn't take a paper, but I learn now it couldn't have been in Tuesday's Lynn News anyway. So I knew nothing 'til I got back here and the girls told me. A horrible, horrible thing. But life must go on, I always say."

"Yes, indeed. We understand that you left the house on Monday morning to visit your Mother. How is she, by the way?"

"Much improved," replied Mrs Waddell, "and thank you for asking. She's getting on in years and lives alone now, so when she took a heavy cold with a bit of fever, she didn't feel like fending for herself. Her neighbour's very good – went to the telephone box and called me here. The mistress took the call and said I must go and stay for a few days, until Ma was better. Her own mother is in a poorly state, so she was very understanding."

"Mrs Marner sounds like a good employer," said Bryce.

"Oooh she was, sir; she really was. Not many better, I'd say. I don't see myself staying now she's gone."

"Likewise," said Elsie, who had remained in the kitchen; "Faith won't, neither."

"What conclusion should we draw from that," asked Bryce looking from one to the other. The two hesitated, Elsie dropping her eyes to look at her feet.

The Cook spoke. "I don't mind saying it. Anyone would do anything for her, she had such a pleasant manner. He's not nice, though. Wasn't nice to her either. I couldn't work for him, not if he doubled my wages, which he's not likely to do. I haven't seen him since I got back, and out of respect I won't p'raps say anything to him 'til after the funeral; but then I shall give notice."

"'Sright," agreed Elsie. It's not like he's tried to interfere with me and Faith, or anything, but he just treats us like dirt. The mistress, now, she was particular, but like Ruby says, always nice and pleasant about it."

"We understand," said Bryce. "Mrs Waddell, do you happen to know if Mrs Marner was intending to go out later on Monday?"

"No idea about that, sir. And I have to say I was surprised when the girls told me that she had. She wasn't one for going outside much, except when she went to a friend for cards and such. Or when she went to Lynn or Norwich to shop for clothes and things. She sometimes went for a walk along the promenade with Mrs Ayers – that's her sister – but I never heard they went down under the cliffs."

A shadow passed across the window.

"That's the master going up to the front

door," said Elsie. "He usually lets himself in."

"Good," said the DCI as he thanked Cook for her time. "We need a quick chat with him too. Go up ahead of us now, Elsie, and ask him if he can spare us five minutes."

The maid sped off and the detectives climbed the stairs to the upper ground floor more slowly, meeting Elsie in the main hallway just as she was coming down from the floor above. She took them straight upstairs and showed them into another of the rooms common to many of the properties in this road, with floor-to-ceiling windows overlooking the water.

Marner, who was standing in the centre of the large bay, turned as the officers came in. He made no move to shake hands, and just waved the detectives towards chairs before taking a seat himself.

"I'm pleased to see it's been decided to call in Scotland Yard," he said. "No disrespect to you, Sergeant, but I wasn't impressed by your local inspector. What progress can you tell me about today?"

"Not much as yet, Mr Marner, but we'll get there," said Bryce. "I'm starting off by meeting people, looking at statements, and so on, however, I've only been here an hour, so I'm hardly underway.

"We've talked to Mrs Waddell downstairs. I'm afraid she didn't have anything to tell us which might help with finding your wife's killer."

"No, well that doesn't surprise me," said Marner. "Adelaide would hardly have taken the servants into her confidence about who she was meeting on the night she died.

"I don't doubt you've been told by various people that our marriage was effectively 'in name only', and your Sergeant has already heard that I have a lady friend elsewhere. We moved here a year or so before the war, within a few months of our marriage, and I don't recall walking on the beach with Adelaide even then. I can only assume she went with someone very persuasive – or very special."

"For part of the time you were being interviewed yesterday, sir," said Malan, "I was out of the room checking on your alibi. But I understand you told Mr Cordy that Connor Proudlove was the most likely to be close enough to your wife to get her to walk with him. Other than her sister, of course."

"Correct. It's a widely held belief that artists are intimate with their models. Perhaps not a truism, but no doubt it does happen. Adelaide sat for her portrait many times before it was completed. I didn't interfere then, because I didn't care whether or not they had an affair. I still don't know if they did, and I still don't care," said Marner, with indifference. "But they've certainly been close friends ever since. If it wasn't a complete stranger, Proudlove must remain the most likely suspect."

"I gather you didn't buy your wife's portrait," said Bryce.

"No. Proudlove pressed hard me a couple of times, but I wasn't interested. I never even saw it."

"A pity," said the DCI. "Regardless of what you felt for your wife, the painting would have been a first-class investment. People said that it was a good as anything Singer Sargent had ever done. I saw it in the year it went into the Summer Exhibition at the Academy and I would absolutely agree it deserved all the praise that was heaped on it. You can't be unaware that it was snapped up very quickly by a top dealer who recognised its merit and sold it overseas. If it ever comes to the market again, it'll fetch many tens of thousands of dollars, without a doubt. Your loss – and this country's, come to that."

Marner crossed his legs and made a sweeping gesture with one hand over his thigh before folding his arms over his chest, the two motions were unmistakeably dismissive. He made no reply, but looked back at the DCI with what Malan thought was contempt.

Bryce stood up to leave, Malan following.

***

Outside, the detectives walked to a bench in the nearby public gardens.

Malan was feeling frustrated after his

second encounter with Seymour Marner. "Have you ever met a situation like this before, sir – where the husband is so obnoxious but alive, and the wife so well-liked but murdered? I'm beginning to wonder if it's a case of mistaken identity!"

Bryce smiled and shook his head. "Marner certainly isn't an endearing character. But his alibi puts him well out of the running to be the murderer.

"Since nothing worthwhile in the way of a lead has come to light, I think we must cast our enquiry net further afield." He checked his watch. "It's a little after four, now. I didn't see anything in the Times this morning, but has the press got hold of it all by now?"

Malan confirmed his encounter with various reporters.

"I seem to remember that the local paper is published on Tuesdays and Fridays," said the DCI. "Presumably tomorrow's edition will carry the story, but if we're not too late I'd like to get a 'stop press' notice in alongside that and try an appeal. You know the sort of thing: '*did any reader see this woman, alone or accompanied*', etc, etc. Perhaps not surprising given the state of the marriage, but I didn't see any photographs of Adelaide Marner just now. Your next job is to cut back to the Ayers and see if the sister can produce one. Tell them I'll come to see them myself tomorrow."

"Even if we're too late for the Lynn News, sir, the Eastern Daily Press might do it, on Saturday if not tomorrow," suggested Malan.

"Yes, that will have to be our fallback position. While you're at the Ayers, I'll go back to the station and start drafting some wording, and see what the Editor says about his printing deadlines."

The detectives parted to carry out their respective tasks.

The DCI was surprised to find an old acquaintance in James Street. This was a crime reporter from a national paper, waiting to find someone on the case. He was equally surprised to see Bryce.

"If you wait, Danny, I'll talk to you, but I must do something else first."

Addressing Booth, who was on desk duty, he asked, "Is this station manned twenty-four hours a day?"

On hearing that it wasn't, he instructed the Constable to find him the telephone numbers for the King's Lynn police station, and the Lynn News.

Given these on a scrap of paper, Bryce shut himself away in the office and used the telephone. He managed to contact the newspaper's Editor, whom he found most amenable. He learned that the story of the murder was already front-page news, but was assured that things could be rearranged in order to make space for a photograph and an appeal for witnesses. The caveat was that time was very short; the paper would need the photograph within an hour if it was to be included. Bryce promised to get it delivered.

Next, he drafted the wording he wanted. He had hardly finished this to his satisfaction when Malan returned, brandishing a photograph.

"Got quite a good one, sir! Better than that, it's so recent that Mrs Ayers even had the negatives to hand, and she's given me those too."

Bryce held out a sheet of paper. "Well done, Sergeant. Take what you have and my draft wording here and get everything to the Lynn News office as fast as you can. Tell the front desk that it's a stop-press item and that the Editor himself is waiting for it. When you come back, go to the Glebe Hotel. I'll meet you there for dinner, if you'll join me."

Malan, already standing by the door again for a quick exit, wordlessly thumbed his thanks, turned, and ran out.

The DCI picked up the telephone and gave the King's Lynn police station number to the operator. Superintendent Reeves had left the building, but Bryce was told that a message would be put in front of him first thing in the morning, if the Chief Inspector would like to dictate. The DCI began by apologising for any inconvenience and explained that the King's

Lynn station number would appear in the press, requesting that every response should be passed on to him or Sergeant Malan without delay, at James Street or the Glebe Hotel.

Satisfied he had done as much as he could for the moment, he put his head outside the door and called to the reporter to join him. "Take a seat, Danny, and we'll have a little chat."

"I must be slipping," said the journalist, "I didn't know the Yard had been called in. I saw an Inspector Cordy before."

"I only arrived today. I assume you haven't come to bring me any useful information?"

Danny Hobson laughed. "No, it's the usual arrangement. I'm here to extract what I can from you!"

"Well, I can't tell you much – I'm not up to speed myself yet. But I do want some publicity: '*Did you see this woman…?*', and so on. The local paper will publish a photograph and an appeal for witnesses tomorrow.

"But I'm wondering about another angle. Just before the war, a local artist did a superb portrait of the murdered woman. The painting was exhibited in the Royal Academy. How do you feel about getting one of your cubs to go to Burlington House and see if they'll let him have access to the original photograph which they would have taken for the exhibition catalogue? I saw the picture at the time, and it's striking, to say the least. Even in black-and-white, if you put that on your front page it's just possible that more people would look at that rather than at a run-of-mill snapshot, and the local papers could follow your lead and roll it out in their editions."

"I can't guarantee it'll go in, but I'll certainly see if we can get the picture for you to use up here. What do I get in return?"

"Very little at the moment, Danny. I can tell you that the police are working on the assumption that Mrs Marner wouldn't have gone out by herself along a lonely beach, and that it's almost certain she knew her killer."

"Hmm. How many suspects do you have?"

"I'd prefer not to use that term in this case. We're talking to a dozen or so people who knew or were related to Mrs Marner. There's nothing yet to suggest that any one of them has any connection with the murder."

"Semantics, Philip, come on! Every case has such a list of people, and all but one are innocent – sometimes all of them – but you still call them 'suspects'!"

Bryce grinned. "Have it your own way, then. But if you publish any names, I strongly recommend that you avoid the term."

"Why have you been called in? Cordy had hardly started on the case, surely?" asked the reporter.

"I'm not going into that; you'll have to ask the Norfolk Chief Constable. All I will say is that Cordy has done nothing wrong."

"All right; let's get down to something more interesting then," said Hobson. "My paper has had a communication from an amateur detective called Guy Ferris. We've had several letters from him before, as a matter of fact, and he lives here in Hunstanton. He tells us that he knows who did this, and that the police won't act on the information. Have you talked to him?"

The DCI briefly turned over a conflict in his mind: whether to say what he would like to say, or to restrict himself to what might be more politically sound to say.

"Inspector Cordy spoke to Mr Ferris," he said. "DS Malan, who is now working with me, has also talked to him. I haven't yet had the opportunity myself, but the Yard, like a few other police forces, has had contact with Mr Ferris in the past, and I have heard of his…reputation. We have, of course, given careful consideration to his suggestion."

The reporter roared with laughter. "Very delicately put. What you really mean is that you don't trust anything he says. We've certainly never printed any of his letters for the same reason. What he's said in the past is either unprintable, or incapable of verification, or both. But he must have an advantage in this case; he's local after all, and he says he was a friend of the dead woman."

"Local, yes. A friend, apparently also yes. Further than that I couldn't go. Have you met him?"

"Not here. I met him about six months ago on a case up in Yorkshire. He came across as being more than a little obsessive. Blinkered might be a better word. I have an appointment to see him at six o'clock today, so I'll be making a further assessment then."

"Good luck to you. I don't mind if you tell him that the Yard has been called in, but please don't mention that you've actually spoken to me. No doubt he'll find me tomorrow anyway," said Bryce to the reporter, at the same time thinking to himself that he might fairly have said 'no doubt he'll hound me tomorrow' instead.

With Danny Hobson gone, Bryce sat looking at the notes which Sergeant Malan had left on the table. He considered Seymour Marner. The popular favourite for the role of murderer and, according to his servants and others, not a nice man. He would get Malan to contact the Birmingham police tomorrow and double-check that Marner's alibi really was sound.

His mind moved on to Henry Ayers. He was Ferris's suspect, but neither Cordy nor Malan supported this. Bryce decided he would try to see Ferris before he visited Ayers.

He sighed. That still left the Websters, the Trevelyans, the two retired officers, and the artist. He would have to see them all personally. However competent Malan was, the newly appointed Sergeant shouldn't carry the weight of assessing the witnesses alone.

It might also be that there were other people whom Mrs Marner had befriended – quite possibly unknown to the bridge set. He wished he had added a bit extra to the appeal he had written. Picking up the telephone, he called the newspaper office again. He was fortunate. It seemed that Sergeant Malan was still in the reception area, and could be brought to the telephone.

Bryce explained what he wanted, and dictated two more sentences to be added to the original. He sat back, satisfied.

He was just about to go to his hotel, when another thought occurred to him. Rather than wait until he saw Mrs Ayers the next day, he might extract some information from her now, via the telephone.

Going out to the front desk again, he borrowed the station's telephone directory to get the Ayers' number. Returning to the office, he asked the operator to connect him. Frances Ayers answered and Bryce introduced himself. He apologised for disturbing her, passed on his condolences, and thanked her for the photograph.

"I'd like to come and see you tomorrow, Mrs Ayers, but I'm just wondering if you can help me a little sooner. Do you know of any friends your sister might have had, other than those included in the list of bridge players?"

"I see what you're getting at, Chief Inspector, but I can't think of any off the top of my head. The fact is, I'm afraid, that Addy rarely went out at all. She didn't have children and she didn't really have a husband in anything but name.

"Many women in that situation might have been active in the Women's Institute, the WVS, a knitting circle, or the golf club. Anything at all by way of carving out a bit of a life for themselves. But she never joined any group that I know of. In fact, it was only after Henry and I and the Websters started the bridge circle that we persuaded her to join that. She certainly enjoyed it, but as far as I know it never encouraged her to try anything else where she might meet new people.

"Sorry I can't be more helpful, Chief Inspector. But I'll talk to Henry when he comes in. I can't think he'll know any more, but still. We'll both be at home all morning, so do come whenever is convenient for you."

It was provisionally agreed that Bryce and Malan would call at ten o'clock.

# CHAPTER 10

The DCI retrieved his car and drove the short distance to the hotel. He checked in and was shown to the same room he had occupied on his previous visit. After tidying himself up, he went downstairs and spent a quarter of an hour on the telephone to Veronica. He warned her that he was unlikely to be home at the weekend.

When the conversation was affectionately concluded, he moved to the bar. Remembering what Malan drank, he ordered two pints of bitter. The landlord was serving and, recalling the reason for Bryce's previous stay, correctly deduced what he was doing in the town. They chatted for a few minutes, but the man had no information to impart. The DCI took the beers and a dinner menu to a quiet table in the far corner of the room and sat down facing the door. Malan appeared shortly afterwards, and Bryce pushed his glass across to him.

"Thanks, sir – cheers," said the Sergeant, enjoying a large gulp of ale as he sat back.

"We'll choose our food first, and then

have a maximum ten minutes of work-related conversation," said Bryce. After that, we go informal."

The two men made their selections from the menu and Bryce went back to the bar to pass on the order.

"Tell me what they said at the Lynn News," he said when he returned.

"They're going to run the appeal prominently alongside the murder story. The Editor said their circulation was good in Hunstanton, so I'm feeling hopeful."

"I've left a message for your Super, warning him there could be some calls coming his way. I've also spoken to Mrs Ayers, on the same lines as the extra bit I telephoned through to you at the paper. We're seeing them tomorrow at ten."

Bryce explained his intention to see Ferris in the morning, and went on to describe the interview with the crime reporter.

"Something else. When I called Mrs Ayers, I realised that your local exchange here is still a manual one. We must check with the exchange tomorrow, and see if they have a record of either an incoming call to the Marner's house some time on Monday, or an outgoing one."

"I should have thought of that, sir – I'll get on to it first thing in the morning."

"Good. Okay, Peter, that's enough for the day; we're off duty now. Tell me about what you think might happen with your department, with your DI disappearing."

The two men talked comfortably together for the next two hours, first in the bar, then in the dining room, and finally in the lounge over coffee. The DCI deemed a discussion of the progress of the previous case to be not 'work', so that was included for a time. "It's taken an awful while to get this to court, but it looks like I'll be seeing you again at the summer assizes."

"I'm looking forward to seeing a big case all the way through a trial, guv, although I'm not sure what to expect."

"Go and watch a few other cases – spend a day in Cambridge or Bury St Edmunds when the assizes are being held there. There's a lot more formality and flummery, but essentially giving evidence there is no different to doing it before magistrates or even at quarter sessions."

Driving home to Snettisham after coffee, Malan thought how fortunate Sergeant Haig was, working with this DCI. He wondered what his own incoming boss would be like.

\*\*\*

As before, Bryce had invited Malan to join him for breakfast. On Friday morning, the Sergeant presented himself in the hotel dining room on the dot of eight o'clock. He beat the DCI by half a minute. The two officers enjoyed a decent meal, and their conversation avoided any mention of the current case.

"All right," Bryce said with satisfaction as they both finished, "that'll keep us going until lunchtime at least. We'll look into James Street first, and then find Ferris."

At the police station they were given two written messages.

"I hadn't expected anything yet," remarked the DCI as he rapidly read, "and I doubt if either of these will be of much use anyway. One is from a bank manager, who says that he knows Mrs Marner. He doesn't claim to know her socially, though – only as one of his bank's clients; and he doesn't say that he saw her on the day we're interested in." Bryce sighed, "Perhaps I didn't word the appeal quite well enough to weed out extraneous contacts like that.

"The other is from a librarian in King's Lynn. He also says he knows her and suggests we might care to speak to him. Unhelpfully cryptic; whoever took that message should have asked for more information. We'll leave that for the moment and go and find Mr Ferris."

They didn't have to go far. As they left the little police station, Malan recognised Ferris coming towards them only twenty yards away and advancing fast. He alerted Bryce to the fact. The amateur detective was in fact coming to the police station to see them, and they waited until he arrived beside them.

"Good morning, Sergeant – and who is

this?"

Malan introduced the DCI by name and rank only, without mentioning Scotland Yard, and was surprised when his temporary boss extended his hand and shook Ferris's warmly.

"Let's go inside and have a chat," suggested Bryce.

Back in the little office the three men sat at the table, the two professionals facing the amateur. It was immediately clear that Ferris had recognised Bryce's name, as his first remark was "They've called in the Yard, then. What's happened to Cordy? Has the Chief Constable acted on my advice already?"

"We'll come back to that in a minute, Mr Ferris. What brings you to see us today?" asked Bryce, his voice encouraging to the point of friendly.

Ferris lapped up this treatment, feeling it was nothing less than his due. Correspondingly, his manner became more insufferable. "I was wondering if you were keeping on your toes. I know you haven't put Henry Ayers under lock and key yet and I can't understand why not. I've read all the reports on your cases, Bryce, and you'd be unwise to drag your heels on this one. Very unwise indeed. No one's too big to have their feet held to the fire!"

Malan was staggered by this explicit threat.

Bryce, on the other hand, proceeded as

though he hadn't heard it. "We can't just arrest people without some evidence, Mr Ferris. I understand you say there were rows between Mr and Mrs Ayers, regarding his relationship with his sister-in-law? Do tell us about those."

"That's right. I actually heard one. Frances said he'd better marry her sister. She said Addy wouldn't shout at him, and was a better cook, too."

"I see," replied Bryce. "What other examples?"

"Nothing that I heard personally, you understand, but everyone knew Henry doted on Addy. It wasn't a secret, and that's why you need to get a move on."

Bryce, maintaining the warmth in his voice and a half smile on his lips, was now ready to deliver a version of Theodore Roosevelt's seminal 'speak softly and carry a big stick'.

"So, it boils down to this, Mr Ferris. You overheard one casual remark, and without any further evidence decided that Mr Ayers is guilty of murder. You've said this to Mr Cordy, to Sergeant Malan here, and now to me. I understand you also said it to Superintendent Reeves on the telephone and have put it in writing to the Chief Constable."

Ferris nodded, please that the extent of his involvement was known to the DCI, but determined not to ease up on his criticisms until the case was concluded and his contributions properly acknowledged.

"Let me put you in the picture, Mr Ferris. First, we've heard about the conversation you mention. Not just from the Ayers themselves, but from a third-party who was at the same bridge table with them and Mrs Marner. There is no doubt whatsoever that you have misread and misunderstood the exchange. It was nothing more than a joke between husband and wife – one which was shared by Mrs Marner, moreover.

"Had you bothered to think about it at the time, you should have realised that your conclusion was nonsense. Think about it now, Mr Ferris. Your suggestion could only have made some sense if Frances had been killed – not her sister. Only then would Henry Ayers be free to marry Adelaide.

"Second, Henry Ayers has a cast-iron alibi for Monday, completely covering him for the full range of possible times for the murder.

Ferris sat, open-mouthed and shaking his head.

"No use shaking your head at me, Mr Ferris; those are the facts. You keep repeating the same thing to different people …"

Ferris angrily interrupted. "Yes, I do! And I shall continue – as is my duty as a citizen and my obligation as a scholar of criminal cases."

"All well and good, if only you restricted your comments and correspondence to the police, where you are covered by qualified legal privilege – although malice may remove that privilege. But you don't restrict yourself. The damages against you could be quite significant if one of your libellous letters was actually published by the press. So far, I suspect you've been protected by the fourth estate's desire not to find themselves defending a civil suit alongside you. But you're a fool if you don't think about how many staff read your correspondence to the newspapers.

"There is also a rarely used Common Law offence of defamatory, or criminal, libel. It would be interesting to see you prosecuted for that.

Ferris stood up, not just shaking his head now, but shaking all over. "You're threatening me, Chief Inspector!" he shouted. I won't put up with it. I'll inform the Chief Constable and your Commissioner about your hostility towards me – the ultimate mark of an inferior man, if I'm not mistaken!"

Malan already shocked by Ferris' conduct, anticipated that the Chief Inspector would be fully justified in becoming angry at the insults. But Bryce continued, calmly and politely, every bit as unperturbed as before.

"I believe you are mistaken, but you're free to do what you like, Mr Ferris. I'm not threatening you; I'm merely warning you." Bryce smiled. "In the spirit of helpfulness, I'll add another warning. If you broadcast any calumnies – spoken or written – about me in any forum, or about Sergeant Malan here, I shall personally see you in court. I should tell you that I'm a barrister myself, and that I have both the contacts and the means to ensure that you are successfully sued or prosecuted. Or both!"

Malan was now inwardly roaring with laughter at this. The DCI wasn't done with Ferris.

"Finally, if you obstruct our investigation any further by effectively wasting police time, I shall arrest and charge you. You can take that as a threat, if you like."

Ferris sank into his chair and seemed to be short of breath. The two officers eyed him dispassionately. After a minute, he stood again and unsteadily walked out without saying a word.

"Blimey, sir; that's told him all right!"

"Maybe. If the threat – I'm sorry, warning – deters him from continuing, that'll be good enough for me.

"It's a bit too early for our appointment with the Ayers. I wonder if the librarian chap is at work yet. I wouldn't expect the library to be open, but the staff must come in ahead of opening time. While I get hold him, find another telephone and see what you can learn from the exchange."

Bryce placed his call giving the number provided in the librarian's message. It took a minute or two to be connected, and there was a lot of extraneous noise on the line. Eventually, he managed to speak to the person he wanted. He identified himself, and then listened, putting in a question here and there, mainly to request a repeat of something which had been lost in the buzzing.

"That's most useful, Mr Sissons; thank you very much for contacting us. It may be that I'll ask you to attend an identification parade, but that might be some time ahead."

Replacing the handset, he turned over the implications of what he had just been told. His meditations were disturbed by the return of Malan.

"No joy with the exchange, sir. They don't keep records of local calls, and there's so many of them that it would be impossible to remember, especially four days ago. I managed to speak to all three of the girls who were on duty on Monday – none could help. Sorry, sir.

"But there's another message arrived from Lynn. A Miss Featherstone saw something while walking her dog on Monday. She's not on the telephone and made her call from a public call box, but I've got an address.

"Let's start with her, then. If she's home, we should still be in time to see the Ayers by ten o'clock."

Miss Featherstone lived in Hildgate Road. Although also close to the beach and very respectable, the street was a far cry from the large and imposing properties around the Cliff

Parade area of the town. As they walked down from the police station, Bryce outlined what the librarian had said.

"Apparently Mrs Marner comes into the Lynn library every fortnight or so. She's been doing that for years, and the staff obviously know her by sight. On the last two occasions she came in, she was accompanied by a gentleman. He's not a library cardholder, and Sissons – the librarian – doesn't know his name. Sissons didn't take much notice of him. He just browsed the shelves while Mrs Marner was making her own selection and left with her after her books had been stamped. He wasn't heard to speak. Sissons hadn't thought anything of it until reading the paper this morning.

"The key point is that her companion wasn't a young man. Sissons guessed he was in his fifties or a bit older. His description is maddeningly vague. I said that we might want him to take part in an ID parade, but even if we identify this man, it doesn't follow that he is the murderer. And even if he is, his safest course would be to admit he was with her in the library. It's not a crime."

"No, but it does mean that Arthur Trevelyan and Prentice are properly ruled out because they're nowhere near old enough to be mistaken for fifty-ish. Still leaves all the other men, though," said Malan.

The two officers turned into Hildgate

Road, The houses here were semi-detached or small terraced properties. All had only a short distance between their boundary wall and the front door, but most occupiers had made some effort to plant the small gardens. Miss Featherstone was one of these, and the detectives found her kneeling with a hand fork and a bucket of weeds. A small black and tan dog was lying on the harlequin tiled path leading from the gate to the front door. He stood up and wagged his tail as the officers stopped. The lady of the house, who appeared to be about forty-five, also rose, and guessed correctly who her visitors were.

"I was expecting someone from the police," she said, after Bryce had introduced himself and Malan, "but a local constable, not senior detectives. Will you come in?"

Declining this offer with thanks, the DCI explained that they wouldn't need to disturb her for more than a few minutes and asked her to recall what she had seen on Monday evening. Miss Featherstone perched on her low wall, and the officers remained on the pavement.

"I was walking Bobby-Boy along the promenade on Monday at about quarter past seven. There were hardly any people about. I was facing Old Hunstanton, and had just passed the pier, so I suppose I was about fifty or sixty yards from the end of the prom. I saw a woman who fits the description in the Lynn News today. Going by the description of her clothes, that is, her cream jacket and black skirt – I didn't know the lady and wasn't close enough to see her face. But she was definitely coming down the steps from the green by Cliff Parade, the ones nearest to the end of the prom."

Malan, recording all of this in his notebook, started to feel excited. Finally, a good clue might emerge.

"On the prom, leaning against the concrete wall with his back to the sea, was a man. I think he must have been waiting for her, because when the woman reached the prom she walked straight over to him, and he walked a few steps towards her. They seemed to speak for a few seconds, and then the man took the woman's arm and they walked on. They went down the far steps to the beach, but I'd done my walk by then and turned around almost immediately after they dropped out of sight. I didn't think of it again until I read your notice in the paper today and saw the picture."

"We're very glad you contacted us, Miss Featherstone. Your evidence could be vital. What can you tell us about the man?"

The woman shook her head. "Nothing much. I never saw his face properly. He was sideways on when I first noticed him, and of course they moved away from me, so the gap between us never closed after they started walking and all I saw then was his back. I'm pretty sure he was wearing a suit, though."

"What about his age, Miss Featherstone – could you get any idea about that?"

"Thinking about it, I don't believe he was young. He didn't move like a young man." She frowned and compressed her lips. "But I don't think he was aged either – he wasn't at all doddery." She considered for a moment. "Fifty or sixty; that sort of age range, perhaps, but I really can't be sure because I didn't take very much notice of them. I think I only noticed them at all because of her cream jacket."

"Because the brightness of it stood out?" queried Malan.

"No, Sergeant. I have a cream jacket myself, but it's still early in the year for cream. It's a summer wardrobe colour. But the woman I saw looked perfect in hers – elegant – and of course it had been a very mild day; she'd cleverly dressed for the weather rather than the season. I think that's why I noticed her and then him."

Bryce, disappointed that the description so far provided no more than the librarian had offered, asked about the man's height.

"She didn't seem to be a tall woman, and I'd say he was only an inch or so above her. There was no great discrepancy in height, I'm absolutely sure about that."

"What about a dog, did the man have a dog with him?"

"No, definitely not. I'd have taken much more notice if he had. Bobby-Boy is a Norwich terrier, and he likes to meet other animals, but not all of them appreciate his interest. He's not very big, as you can see – his ancestors were bred for ratting in tight places. Most other dogs are far larger, so I always have to be on the lookout."

The DCI thanked Miss Featherstone, telling her she had been very helpful. "If you think of anything else, you must contact us immediately, please ."

The detectives took their leave. Cutting through to the seafront a few yards away, they walked along the promenade towards the pier. On reaching the wooden structure, Bryce stopped underneath it.

"You go on ahead, Malan, until you reach the last steps up to the green. Lean against the sea wall as Miss Featherstone described. Look at the steps, not towards me. "I'll walk along and see how much of you I can discern as I move along. Admittedly the light is different – presumably better – but it'll give me some idea."

When Malan was in position, Bryce moved forward, his eyes swivelling between the bottom of the steps and his Sergeant. On reaching Malan, he joined him in leaning against the wall, but facing the sea.

"I'm sure Miss Featherstone saw exactly what she described," he reported. "And we'll have to get her to make a statement. As for her giving evidence in court, we'll probably have to forget that."

"But it's another indicator to add to the library man's report, sir, surely?"

"Certainly is. And a far more telling one actually, because I believe what we've just heard happened shortly before the murder. It's not likely that Mrs Marner took a walk under the cliffs with the man Miss Featherstone saw, then ditched him and went on to meet another man."

Bryce looked towards the beach past the end of the promenade. "How far along was she killed?" he asked.

"Almost as far as you can see; just before the cliffs curve away around a bit of a bend."

"Hmmm. Nobody on the end of the prom here could have seen what was happening at that distance."

"Not without a good pair of binoculars; and depending on the light, maybe not even then." agreed Malan.

"I'll go down and look at the exact spot soon, but for now let's go up these steps, and cut across the green to the Ayers' house," said the DCI.

As they walked over the grassy top of the cliffs towards the houses past Lincoln square, Bryce expressed his thoughts aloud. "We're looking for someone who isn't much taller than Adelaide Marner – and Ferris isn't a tall man. I'm sure we'd both be delighted if he was our murderer," he said with a laugh. "So would Mr Cordy, no doubt. However, from what we know at the moment Ferris is just one of five possibles; Seymour Marner, Connor Proudlove being eliminated by virtue of their height. Neither of us has actually seen Webster, Pullen, Wynterflood or the senior Trevelyan. We must put all that right today. But we'll see the Ayers first.

# CHAPTER 11

The door was opened by Henry Ayers, but Frances was standing in the hallway just behind him. Malan introduced the DCI.

"Do come into the living room. Can we get you a coffee or something?" offered Mrs Ayers.

"No, thank you," replied Bryce, answering for his Sergeant as well. "We don't intend to keep you long."

The detectives took their seats and the DCI broached his question. "Did you have any more thoughts about acquaintances that your sister may have had?"

"Frances told me what you were after, and we've certainly been thinking about it," replied her husband. "However, I'm afraid we've come up with nothing. As you've already been told, I think, in some ways Addy was very shy. She took to the bridge group, and became good friends with everyone in it. But that was unusual for her. In fact we don't know of a single person outside that group with whom she had any sort or relationship other than, say, that of customer to shopkeeper, or rail traveller to ticket collector."

"That's right, confirmed Mrs Ayers. "Addy rarely needed a doctor, but when she did she went to Dr Fisher. Pippa Trevelyan acts as his *locum*, occasionally, and we and Addy have met him over supper at Pippa's house occasionally. Perhaps it's the fact that Ronald doesn't play bridge, and only seemed to be there for a meal, but Addy never treated him in the same way as she did the others. She knew him well enough, but to her he remained a sort of social outsider, you see."

"How old is Dr Fisher?" asked Malan. "Early thirties, I suppose," replied Ayers. "He qualified just on the outbreak of war, spent the next few years as a naval surgeon, and set up as a GP here soon afterwards. Why do you ask?"

"We have some reason to believe that your sister was in the company of an older man on Monday," replied Bryce. "While not completely eliminating younger males from our enquiries just yet, we're leaving them in abeyance for the time being, and concentrating our efforts on the more senior ones.

"Sergeant Malan tells me he has confirmed that on Monday you were both with friends in a cinema in King's Lynn, and that afterwards you were having dinner with the same people. So, even if you were in the age group we're looking at, Mr Ayers, your alibi is good and you're no longer under suspicion."

"Something has just occurred to me, my dear!" exclaimed Mrs Ayers. "You weren't originally going to come to the cinema." She turned to Malan, "As I told you the other day, Sergeant, we'd already seen the film together. But I wanted to go again and my friend, Pat Bingham, who hadn't seen the film, said we should go together. That's how it was fixed, just the two of us. But she cried off on the Monday morning and said she thought one of her migraine headaches was starting, so the last thing she was up for was a flickering screen in a cinema that evening. By pure coincidence, our Downham friends rang shortly afterwards and said, on the spur of the moment they were planning to go to the last showing, and did we fancy joining them and having some dinner beforehand. That was when Henry stepped in again."

"Absolutely right," said Ayers. "But if things had gone according to the original plan, Frances would have been out and I'd have been here alone that evening with no alibi whatsoever because Monday is our maid's day and evening off, Chief Inspector."

"I see," said Bryce. "I wonder if that might be even more significant than you think. Who else knew in advance that you were going to the cinema, Mrs Ayers – and even more importantly, who knew that your husband wasn't accompanying you?"

The Ayers looked at each other, quickly

realising the implication of the question.

"I'm pretty sure it was mentioned over cards at Connor's house on the Saturday evening," said Ayers. "Yes – I'm sure it was, because our table was between rubbers, and there was a chat about the merits of the film. Everyone present had seen it."

"And were those present that evening all the usual people?" asked Malan.

"Yes, we had enough for three tables, as Arthur was here," replied Mrs Ayers. "Oh, Maisie came as well, so it was thirteen. She didn't play that night – she was perfectly happy to sit and read, and she'd come round to top up drinks, or go and make coffee, and so on."

"Do you think knowledge of your maid's days off would be commonly known in the group?" enquired the DCI.

The Ayers looked at each other again. "Ye..e..s," said Frances Ayers very slowly and with a frown. "I think it must be. You see we never host bridge evenings on Mondays – nor on Fridays either – because Sybil is off. That's been the case since we started the sessions soon after the war, and I'm sure we will have mentioned it from time to time anyway."

A taut silence fell over the room as the company pieced together the significance of this new information.

"You aren't prepared to say who made the suggestion about my guilt, I suppose, Chief

Inspector?" asked Ayers at last. "Because if, as you're clearly implying, someone was banking on my not having an alibi, it would seem to be logical that it was the same person who made the accusation."

"It would indeed," replied Bryce. "Not a certainty, but a high probability. But let's look at this another way. Who, among these people, might you have annoyed lately?"

"I really don't think there's anyone. These are our friends – although perhaps one of them isn't as good a friend as I had supposed."

"I wonder," said his wife. You did say something to Guy a few weeks ago. He'd been telling us about some case he'd been working on with the police somewhere. And you implied that you had doubts about all these cases – you made a remark about the brothers Grimm, as I recall."

"I see," said the DCI. "From which the only possible inference he could make is that you thought he told fairy stories."

"Yes. I mean, Guy's not the only one who reads the crime reports in the papers. I don't suppose he ever has any more to go on that the rest of us do. Sometimes, when he's expounding his 'whodunnit' theories I've not so much poked holes in them, as driven a coach and horses through the gaps he's left. I daresay I haven't endeared myself by calling him a fantasist."

The Chief Inspector thought he had heard

enough to start forming opinions. He looked enquiringly at Malan to check if he had any questions. Receiving a shake of the head he stood up, Malan following.

"Thank you very much," said the DCI. "Please don't draw conclusions from any of this. There are lots of possibilities remaining. And it would be best if you don't talk about this with anyone. If you think of anything else which might help, you can contact us via the Hunstanton police station."

\*\*\*

"Looking better and better, sir," remarked Malan optimistically after they had crossed the road and were on the green, sitting on another public bench.

"Perhaps yes, perhaps no," replied Bryce, appreciating the view over The Wash where a small coaster was passing, no doubt on its way to the King's Lynn docks. "From what we've heard, Ferris might now be the current favourite, but not to the extent that he's odds-on. In fact, at this stage I'd still offer two to one against, although he might move ahead after we've seen the other runners. But I'd say fifty to one against a conviction if we went ahead with what we have so far."

"I'm sure I remember you telling me you're not a betting man, sir," grinned Malan, "but you seem to know the terminology!"

Bryce laughed. "*Touché*. All right, we've got some time left before lunch. Let's see if we can find one or two of these putative suspects."

Rear Admiral Wynterflood's house was nearest, and Malan rang the doorbell. It opened almost instantly, and it was clear that the occupier, accompanied by two English setters, was on the point of going out.

"Sorry to disturb you Admiral – I'm Chief Inspector Bryce from Scotland Yard, and this is Sergeant Malan. We won't take up too much of your time."

"Ah," said Wynterflood, "so the powers that be decided to call in the Yard. Good thinking, to my mind. That Inspector chappie; decent man, I thought, but seemed very timid and unsure in his approach." He stood back from the door. "Come inside, come inside."

"No, if you'll excuse us, we won't, said Bryce. "We just wanted to meet all of Mrs Marner's friends, to get a full picture, as it were. Is there anything you can think of that might help us?"

"Alas, no. I gather Seymour has provided an alibi and he was top of my list, I have to confess. As a matter of fact, his was the only name on my list. Are you sure that this wasn't done by a complete stranger?"

"We're pretty certain it wasn't, Admiral. All the evidence suggests that Mrs Marner wasn't in the habit of walking alone anywhere, let alone on that rather isolated bit of beach."

"Fair comment – I've never seen her down there. I saw your appeal in the Lynn News today – excellent notion. Any results yet, or is it a bit soon?"

"We've received two useful tips already, and are hoping for more later today. Just two further questions. Do you recall a conversation during a bridge game a few weeks ago, in which Frances Ayer made a remark to her husband to the effect that he'd better marry her sister?"

Wynterflood guffawed. "Oh yes; hilarious. And it's true that Frances can be pretty sharp with any partner who makes an error in play, whereas Adelaide was endlessly tolerant."

Wynterflood's voice cracked a little, "Such a dear girl. Anyone who suggests, on the strength of that remark, that Frances was hinting at anything untoward between her husband and her sister, is barking up the wrong tree – or just plain barking!"

The Admiral caught Bryce's expression and almost recoiled in amazement. "Someone does? Who? Who the hell thinks that? No sane person hearing the exchange could possibly draw that conclusion from it. Especially knowing the people concerned. It was a joke, nothing more."

"One last thing, Admiral. Are you aware of any, let's say discord, between any of the members of your bridge group? Between male members in particular?"

"Don't recall anything of that sort. We all get on, despite the wide age range. We have people like young Trevelyan, and Proudlove's pretty new girl. They must be all of thirty years – and then some – younger than people like Ferris and me. And I fancy Webster is older still. Perhaps it's surprising that we all meld without any difficulty."

"Thank you, Admiral – we'll let you get on. Your setters have sat very patiently while we've delayed their walk."

\*\*\*

"Did you decline the offer to go inside just because of his height, sir?" enquired Malan as they walked away.

"To be honest, yes. He must be six foot two at least. If Mrs Marner was of average female height or even less, he would be more like a foot taller than her – not a mere inch or so. Also, from what you say he told Cordy, he has an alibi.

"Let's move on. Who's next nearest?"

"The Websters, sir. Only another hundred yards."

They found Mr Webster at home alone. Within minutes, both officers decided that he wasn't the man seen by Miss Featherstone. Although he would have been a good fit as far as his height was concerned, he used a walking stick to get around, even indoors. Webster raised the subject himself, as he showed them into the living room. "Rheumatism, gentlemen, plus a dodgy knee. The penalties of age."

Everything Webster said reinforced the statements of the Ayers and Wynterflood. Yes, he had heard Frances suggest that Henry should marry Adelaide, and no, of course it wasn't serious – a ridiculous interpretation to put on the exchange. Yes, he did hear Henry's remark about the Grimm brothers, but no, he didn't see any sign that Guy had taken offence. Yes, it was true that he personally took some of Guy's reported exploits with a pinch of salt. Yes, he remembered some mention of *'Kind Hearts and Coronets'*, but he wasn't paying much attention to a conversation at the next table. "Fighting our opponents' cheeky little slam bid at that moment – needed to concentrate!"

\*\*\*

After thanking Mr Webster and leaving the house, the detectives decided to eat at the Golden Lion. Over good servings of cottage pie and peas, and seated in a corner where nobody could overhear them, they reviewed the case.

"Are we agreed Wynterflood and Webster are both out of contention – one because of his height, and the other his mobility?"

"Yes, sir. Apart from Miss Featherstone's specific mention that the man she saw wasn't 'doddery', I really can't think that Mr Webster could manage to go down the steps and pick his way over the rocks and through the sand – over a distance, too."

"Do you still feel that Miss Featherstone saw Adelaide Marner; or might she have seen someone else similarly dressed?"

Malan looked up from his plate and paused. Seeing the DCI lift an eyebrow, he explained himself. "I'm not hesitating because I'm doubtful; I'm just trying to find a way to explain my certainty! Miss Featherstone said there weren't many people about. Very unlikely there would be a second woman in a cream jacket. It's the right place; the right time; the right clothing. It must have been Mrs Marner. If so, the man must be her killer. And he's not young, and not very tall."

"I agree. Pullen doesn't get back until tomorrow – and probably quite late. He has an alibi anyway. You say Trevelyan was at work in King's Lynn until his wife met him at the hospital at about eight o'clock. If that's correct, he couldn't be the man Miss Featherstone saw. What sort of height is he?"

"Average, I suppose, sir. About five foot eight or nine."

"Better be safe than sorry. Check with the hospital after lunch – see if they can confirm he was in the hospital between five and eight. Chances are he's at work now, so we won't be able to see him this afternoon. I'd still like to see him sometime though, just for completeness. But if the alibi checks out there's no urgency.

The two men chatted about various other topics for the remainder of the meal and then returned to the police station.

# CHAPTER 12

In James Street, they were handed a little sheaf of messages, all but one forwarded from Kings Lynn as a direct result of the newspaper appeal. The exception was a note from the Coroner's Officer, informing them that the inquest would be opened formally on Monday morning at ten o'clock. The Coroner would be obliged if the senior officer would contact him at some convenient time today. Sitting in their little room, Bryce informed Malan about the inquest, and then started scanning the other messages in turn. Without comment, he passed each of these to the Sergeant.

"Not as helpful as the first two, sir," opined Malan, "apart from the one from Mrs Pollard, who works in the bank used by Mrs Marner, and knows her by sight."

"Exactly. She pinpoints the time Mrs Marner was going through the gardens towards the steps. Taken with Miss Featherstone's sighting we know for sure it was Adelaide Marner. And the two witnesses together actually confirm something else that we've almost taken for granted. Both victim and killer started along the beach from the town end – it wasn't that they started at opposite ends and met in the middle; nor did they both start from the Old Hunstanton end.

"See if you can find Mrs Pollard this afternoon, and get a written statement from her. I see she's given both her home and the bank as contact points. Get something from Miss Featherstone as well.

"But, as you say, the other eight messages don't seem to take us anywhere."

The DCI thought for a minute. "Neither you nor DI Cordy actually went to Ferris's house – is that right?"

"That's right, sir. Mr Cordy said he'd walked past it. Quite sizeable, he said, and couldn't see why the man never took a turn to entertain the other card players. Someone did say that Ferris employs a servant."

"Does he now; that's good. I want to speak to her. Or him, as I suppose it could be a valet. I wonder what would be the best way of ensuring that Ferris is out when we call."

"We could keep watch, sir, and move when we know he's taken his dog for a walk?"

"That might be hours away. Also, I suspect concealment might be a bit tricky. No, we need to be proactive. We'll invite him in here. You told him you wanted a statement about what he knew of Henry Ayer's relationship. We've shot that down already, of course, so he'll refuse to make one, but let's ask anyway. We can insist that he must turn up in person to explain. We'll get Sergeant Timmins to make the call. When I see Ferris arriving here, I'll nip straight down and hope to find the servant in the house. You can keep him occupied here for twenty minutes. Waffle as much as you want, but no suggestion he's under any suspicion of the murder, of course."

Bryce left the room and walked the short distance to the front desk. He found the Sergeant muttering over some paperwork, and took him back to the other room. Here, he explained exactly what Timmins was to do and say.

The Sergeant found Ferris's telephone number and asked the operator to connect him. It quickly emerged that the planned artifice was unnecessary, as the servant – female – reported that her master had left the house five minutes earlier, with his dog. He would not be back home for at least an hour and a half, she thought. Timmins, hand over the mouthpiece, passed on this information. "Tell her Chief Inspector Bryce will come to talk to her within ten minutes," instructed the DCI. There was a squealing noise from the telephone, and Timmins once again looked at Bryce. "She wants to come here and see you at once," he reported.

"Tell her yes – we'll expect her in about ten

minutes. Oh, and get her name, please."

Sergeant Timmins, having relayed the information that the woman was Miss Elaine Trott, was sent back to his normal duties.

"I'm not sure whether or not I like the implication of her not apparently wanting to talk to us at Ferris's residence," said Bryce. "Go and wait at the front, Malan, and bring her straight in here when she arrives. I have to call the Coroner, so I'll do that now."

The message from the Coroner's Officer had provided a telephone number. Bryce was very quickly connected by the operator and found himself talking to the Coroner within a minute. The two men had met before, during the inquests on the Railway murders a few months before.

"I heard the Yard had been called in again, Chief Inspector. At this rate you'll need a season ticket for the London to Hunstanton service!" Bryce laughed. "Let's hope this is my last visit, sir – and let's also hope that this isn't the first of three like last time."

"Amen to that," replied the lawyer. "Now, I need to open the inquest soon, but I assume you'll want an adjournment?"

"Almost certainly yes," replied the DCI; "I haven't been here twenty-four hours yet. But your officer mentioned Monday. A lot of things might happen by then."

"Very well. I'll open proceedings at ten

o'clock on Monday morning. I was intending to use the Guildhall here in Lynn, but I think it's preferable to find somewhere in Hunstanton. The Town Hall would be favourite – chances are that either the assembly hall or the council chamber will be available. If not, I'm not sure where we can go. We're barred from holding inquests in public houses nowadays, however respectable they might be. Will you liaise with PC Potter, Chief Inspector, regarding summonses and so on? He'll inform you if we can't get the Town Hall."

Bryce agreed to talk to Potter, and the call ended.

He sat still for a minute after putting down the receiver, but had no time to sort this thoughts, as Malan arrived, leading a very worried-looking woman into the room. Bryce rose and shook her hand.

"Do sit down, Miss Trott. I'm Detective Chief Inspector Bryce, and no doubt Sergeant Malan has already introduced himself. I'm sorry that we aren't in a position to offer you a cup of tea, or anything – there are no suitable facilities in this building."

"That's all right, sir – I want for nothing," she said.

Bryce was surprised to detect a trace of a London accent in the woman's voice. He saw that Miss Trott was somewhere in her mid-fifties, with short grey hair. She wore a simple navy-blue dress, with a black cardigan. She wore absolutely no ornament; no rings, brooch, necklace, bracelet, or even, as far as he could see, a watch. She wasn't wearing spectacles, but the DCI thought he detected marks on the bridge of her nose, and deduced that Miss Trott probably had spectacles, perhaps for reading and sewing.

He and Miss Trott eyed each other almost curiously for a moment. "As you must know, we are looking into the death of Mrs Adelaide Marner, who was killed on Monday evening. We want to talk to everyone who had any connection, however remote that might be, with the dead woman. We have spoken two or three times to Mr Ferris, and now we're widening our investigation."

"Yes, sir, I see. Well, I wanted to talk to someone anyway. My friend a few doors down the road, Annie Taylor – works for Mrs Crawford – she come round the kitchen door late this morning, waving a newspaper. Showed me the front page about this awful murder. Annie thought I already knew about it, see, and she wanted to show me where it asked for information. But I hadn't heard about it. And when I saw who was dead, I knew what even Annie didn't know – that the poor woman was a friend of Mr Ferris. I thought, why hasn't he mentioned it? He gets the same paper as Mrs Crawford takes, delivered every day, and I know the boy brought it this morning as usual. Yet he said nothing to me, even though I've taken and cleared his breakfast, and taken him coffee.

"After Annie left, I read the page properly again, and the extra bit inside. In my head I went back to Monday. What I want to tell you is that the Master went out of the house that evening at four or five minutes past seven. He hadn't said he was going out, but I saw him because I was standing at my window, looking out at the sea and the sky and wondering if we were going to have another glorious sunset that evening. He didn't take Xanthe, which is unusual. And he came back best part of an hour later."

Miss Trott now looked much more upset than when she arrived.

"You've done quite right to tell us all this," Bryce told her. "It may not be important, of course, but on the other hand it could be." His words, he noticed, didn't seem to have their usual effect. Most people would show visible relief after such reassurance, and pleased that they had been thanked. This was not the case for Miss Trott. He fished for the reason, "But you don't look at all happy. Is it just coming here, or is there something else?"

Elaine Trott burst into tears. Bryce provided a large man-sized handkerchief, as her own was singularly inadequate for the task of stemming the flow. Malan left the room and returned with a mug of water. After a few minutes, she recovered sufficiently to speak again.

"Sorry, sir. It's not just coming here and telling what I said. There's something else."

"Take your time, Miss Trott, and tell us everything, please."

The woman took him at his word. "It started well over thirty years ago," she began. My young man died in Salonika in 1917. It was typhoid, though he'd likely have been killed in action later anyway. I took it very, very hard, sir. They had to put me in the asylum for a bit. When I come out in March 1920, my Mother told me I needed to move right away from Dalston and all my memories. She'd been to Hunstanton as a girl and said it would be good for my health all round to be here. She fixed up with Mr and Mrs Ferris to take me on – told them everything, no secrets – and they were extremely kind to me." More tears needed to be wiped away at the memory of this kindness.

"At that time, there were three of us keeping the house for them, and it was the other girls who told me about the son, Mister Guy. The Master and Mistress never mentioned him. The girls told me he'd been sent overseas a few months before I arrived. They said nobody knew why, but the gossip was that he must've done something bad. I never thought about him again 'cos nobody mentioned him again. It was like he'd never existed. The only time I thought about him in those early years was once when

I was in the Mistress's bedroom, tidying away. I saw a photograph of a man in an officer's army uniform in a drawer. I guessed it must be the son. Very ordinary to look at, even in uniform.

"Years went by, and then one day in the middle of the last war I overheard the Master and Mistress talking about Guy. I shouldn't have listened, I know, but I was so astonished to hear his name that I think I just froze like a statue by the door. They'd heard from people they knew who had friends out in Ceylon. They were talking over what they'd been told – that the woman Mister Guy lived with had died suddenly years before, and that her family and other people suspected foul play. But there was no proof, and so the case had been closed. The Master said that there was nothing to be done and the Mistress just cried.

"I never heard no more about it. Then, about two years ago, I heard Mister Guy was coming home. That was the first time the Master and Mistress mentioned his name to me in nearly thirty years, and only the second time I'd heard them talk of him. They seemed hot and bothered about it, but…at the same time I think they were excited about it, too. It's understandable; they hadn't seen him in all that time, and they were getting very old. I think they wanted their only child back after so long away, because he never came home between the wars, and I know they never went out there to see him because they never went further afield than the Lake District, and only for a fortnight at a time."

"What about letters?" asked Bryce.

"No," Miss Trott shook her head. "If there were letters, I never saw them."

Malan was perplexed. "Did they explain to you how it was they suddenly had a son – whom they had no contact with – coming back into their lives?"

The maid nodded. "Yes, sort of. They just mentioned the parable of the prodigal son, but gave no explanations. Anyway, when Mister Guy arrived, he settled straight in. He was very eager to please and was very polite to me. I was the only live-in left by then, with help from dailies for all the heavy work and the cooking."

Miss Trott paused and appeared to be flagging in her recollections. Bryce, not wishing to interrupt her earlier on, now put an important question. "This alleged suspicious incident with his companion in Ceylon. Do you know whereabouts Guy Ferris was living at the time?" That there might have been a murder already in Ferris' past was of great interest to the DCI.

The maid replied apologetically. "He did tell me once, sir, but the name was ever so long and unpronounceable. I remember he laughed and bowed after he told it to me – like he'd done a tongue-twister for a party piece. I never saw it written down, which might have helped me remember some of the letters. When he first arrived home, he was talkative about Ceylon. He'd come into the kitchen when I was making tea and tell me about the way tea plants grow, and how you must only pick certain leaves. The way he spoke about it sounded like he'd lived in paradise. I said I wouldn't mind being a tea picker in all that sunshine and warmth, but he said the work was back breaking and the heat killing for some people."

Bryce listened. Without a location, he had little hope of a link to follow in the death of Ferris' Sri Lankan friend. He wasn't quite ready to give up, however. If he couldn't discover the location, perhaps he could find out the time.

"Can you remember roughly when it was you heard his parents talk about the death of the lady?"

"Yes. That's something I'll never forget because it was a day later we heard about the attack on Pearl Harbour, and all the papers were full of it and what it meant for us and the war."

"Good, that means the conversation was around the $5^{th}$ of December 1941, then. But from what you say, the actual death occurred years earlier, and you don't know when or where?"

"That's right, but...I do know the name of where he had his holidays on the island; a place called Kandy. He said it was on the higher part of the island where it's a lot cooler and that he always went up there every year. I remember saying the name was a lot easier than his plantation, and I asked was it spelled like American sweets. He said yes, except with a 'k' and not 'c'. The thing is, when I was eavesdropping, I heard his Father mention Kandy as well. I know he did because I thought the same thing about American sweets – it's all they ever call them in the pictures.

"Mister Guy hadn't been back a fortnight when the Master died. He was well over eighty, of course. 'Natural causes', the doctor said. Then a week later, the Mistress passed too. Of a broken heart, Mister Guy said. The doctor put it down as mycardal infection."

"Myocardial infarction, yes – that's basically a heart attack," explained Bryce. "What were their first names?"

"Samuel and Theresa, sir."

"So there was no inquest; no autopsy? And were they buried, or cremated?"

"Buried, sir. No, there wasn't an enquiry or anything. Both times the doctor just said he'd sign the certificate. When they died, though, Mister Guy wasn't broken hearted; he was happy. It made me look back over things and have a good think. As soon as his mother was buried, he never chatted to me again – only work conversations. It made me look back at how he'd been before and I wondered if he was, you know, keeping me unsuspecting of what he was really like. I know I might be completely wrong, but having heard about poor Mrs Marner, I just had to speak up now and say all that before it's too late, and I'm taken to meet my Maker as well."

Bryce looked at the woman with raised eyebrows. There was an emotion in her voice that he couldn't quite fathom. "How do you mean?" he asked.

"I'm dying, sir – they've given me perhaps six more months. I've said nothing before, 'cos if I did I'd have been thrown out, with nowhere to go, and I couldn't prove nothing, as I said.

"But now, I won't be able to work more'n another few weeks anyway, so I must speak. Don't know what I'll do now, though." She started to sob again.

Bryce conferred quietly with Malan. Then he spoke to Miss Trott again.

"Sergeant Malan will take a written statement from you now. At this stage, it will only say about seeing Mr Ferris leave the house on Monday, and his return. Nothing else for the moment. When you've done that, and signed it, go back to the house. Say nothing to Mr Ferris if he's there, and behave as if nothing has happened. I'll make some enquiries and see what can be done for you. You've been more helpful than you can realise."

The woman nodded. "Thank you, sir; I'm glad you think so. It's a weight off me, it really is."

Bryce left her talking with Malan and went to the front desk to make a telephone call there. Connected with the Scotland Yard operator, he asked for Sergeant Haig, if he was in the building. The Scots burr of his colleague came into his ear.

"Glad you're back, Sergeant, I have a couple of little jobs for you, one of which may be impossible. Sometime around 1937 there was a suspicious death of a Sinhalese woman, probably living with a Briton named Guy Ferris, on a tea plantation in Ceylon. Try the Colonial Office first. It's quite possible that there was a colonial police officer involved, and possible – although I accept unlikely – that he has retired to this country and can be contacted. If that idea fails, and of course it's a very long shot, maybe the Colonial Office can suggest some other means of finding out about it. Also improbable, I realise. But if nothing else I'd like to know the name of the woman, and the official cause of death. I'll give you the background later.

"The second job is this. Talk to Inspector Lessing, and ask him from me to see what he can find at the War Office about Guy Ferris. Probably a commissioned officer during the Great War. Unfortunately, I don't have his rank or regiment.

"Got it, sir," replied the dependable Haig. "I'll deal with it right away."

Bryce gave Haig the Hunstanton police station number, and cleared the call. He now made another, this time a local one to the Trevelyan household. Once again, he was in luck, as Philippa Trevelyan answered the telephone. Bryce explained the position regarding Miss

Trott, but without mentioning her testimony.

"Ideally, I should like her in hospital or a nursing home for a week, to keep her out of circulation. If cost is an issue, I'll cover the expense."

Dr Trevelyan didn't hesitate. "I see what you're after, Chief Inspector, and I won't waste time asking questions. I can sort this out very quickly, and get her into a nursing home. Where is she now?"

"Here in the James Street police station. But she might want to go back and collect a few things."

"Very well. I'll have an ambulance at Guy Ferris's house in thirty minutes."

Bryce thanked her and concluded the call. Returning to Malan and Miss Trott, he saw that the handwritten statement, only a couple of paragraphs in length, was just being signed.

"Good," said Bryce. "Miss Trott, I've arranged for you to spend some time in a nursing home because I think you need a bit of a rest. Go back now and pack some things for a week away. Sergeant Malan will get a uniformed officer to accompany you back to the house, in case Mr Ferris returns earlier than expected. If he does, the officer will tell Mr Ferris that you had a turn and you're being taken to hospital by ambulance."

Malan escorted Miss Trott out, and passed on the necessary instructions to Constable

Booth, and returned a few minutes later. "All done, sir. I won't ask how you fixed that! She's gone off a little happier, though. Must be a terrible thing, knowing you only have a short time left."

"Yes – as Dr Johnson said: 'Depend upon it, sir, when a man knows he is to be hanged in a fortnight, it concentrates his mind wonderfully.' I think we can assume that's why she came to us."

"Do you really think there's a chance of getting evidence to show the old Ferris couple were murdered, sir?"

"None whatsoever. The Home Office is rightly extremely reluctant to authorise exhumations, and the vague suspicions of Miss Trott wouldn't even merit consideration.

"Nor is there any chance of re-opening the case about the death in Ceylon, although I've got the Yard trying to find out about that.

"However, I think that both matters might be useful – a bit of ammunition to fire when questioning Ferris. Blank ammunition, I grant you!"

Malan grinned. "Are you going to arrest him now?"

"Soon, I think. Let's just get the two outstanding statements first. You go back to Miss Featherstone, and I'll try to find Mrs Pollard."

Bryce walked the hundred or so yards down to the bank where Mrs Pollard worked. Inside, were two tellers, one male and one female. Neither was currently occupied. He approached the woman and saw a printed sign at her till – *Mrs E Pollard*. The DCI identified himself, showing his warrant card.

"Oh, yes – I hoped my message would get through. What more can I do to help?"

"A brief chat, please, Mrs Pollard, and then I'd like you to write and sign a very short statement, if you would. Can we go somewhere away from the counter?"

"Yes; I alerted the manager that you might come in, and he said we can use his office – he'll move out for as long as it takes." She pointed to a door beside her colleague's window. "I'll open the security door and let you through."

Within half a minute, Bryce was seated in the manager's office. The occupant was in the process of leaving anyway, to visit a client. As the man passed, the DCI thanked him, with an apology.

"Anything to assist in the apprehension of this killer," replied the manager.

Mrs Pollard was a 'good' witness. She was very clear who it was that she had seen; and knew to within a few minutes the time. She was also adamant that Mrs Marner could only have been going to descend the steps to the promenade, although she admitted that she hadn't actually seen her start the descent. Mrs Pollard had not seen anyone else – male or female – in the gardens at the time. She didn't think

Mrs Marner had seen her because of their relative positions.

Bryce was content. He took a pad of paper from the briefcase he was carrying, and asked "Would you like me to write a statement for you to sign, or would you like to write your own?"

Mrs Pollard opted to scribe for herself. Bryce dictated the conventional opening. "Now just say what you've told me – about being in the gardens, the time, how you can fix that time, who was there, and what she was doing."

The witness wrote steadily for several minutes, and then handed the pad to the DCI.

"Absolutely perfect, thank you," he said. "Just sign it here, and here."

"Does my statement tie in with anything else you know, Chief Inspector?"

"Yes, it does. However, I have to say that we are still short of hard evidence at the moment. The inquest will open on Monday. It's quite possible that you'll be called to give evidence there. If we manage to charge anyone with this crime, you'll certainly be needed at the trial."

"I only knew her across the counter, of course. She always seemed a bit shy and underconfident somehow. But she was always pleasant – not all our customers are!"

Bryce returned to the police station and had hardly sat down again when Malan joined him, carrying another short statement. The two officers exchanged their papers.

The DCI barely had time to say "Excellent," when the telephone rang. He picked up the handset, and heard Sergeant Haig on the other end of the line. He listened for a couple of minutes and made some notes while doing so.

"I'm used to seeing your efficiency in action, Sergeant, but you've excelled yourself this time!" He listened again and said "I see; it's who you know, then! But very well done all the same. Keep pushing on the other search. By the way, Peter Malan is working with me here – he's been made up to sergeant and sends his best to you."

A few more remarks, and Bryce ended the call. Malan looked at him enquiringly.

"It seems that on a previous case Haig made an acquaintance at the Colonial Office. This chap put him straight on to someone in the know. In a nutshell, my hopeful hunch came good. Haig was given details of a retired chap who, until Independence, had been a senior colonial policeman in Kandy – and was able to reach him by telephone. I've got the name of the unfortunate woman, and an outline of what happened. She slipped while walking with Ferris on a hillside, and died when her head came into contact with a stone."

Malan's head jerked up sharply on hearing this intelligence. "What an extraordinary coincidence," he said, disbelievingly.

"Indeed. There was a lot of suspicion,

because it was known the couple had been having violent arguments. The woman's family also claimed she was three months pregnant, and witnesses suggested that Ferris didn't want a child by his mistress. They knew he would one day return to England and thought he never had any intention of bringing his companion back – much less a child. However, there was absolutely no proof of criminal behaviour, and the matter was dropped. Within two weeks, Ferris moved another young Sinhalese woman into his house.

"I've also asked Haig to look into Ferris's army history – I'd like to know if it was something that happened whilst he was in the service that resulted in him being 'sent away' as Miss Trott put it."

"Do we have enough to bring him in, sir?" asked Malan, eager to start the process of arrest and conviction.

"Enough to bring him in for questioning, yes – enough to charge him, no," replied the DCI. "Trouble is, beyond what Mrs Pollard and Miss Featherstone have told us, I can't see how we're going to get any more evidence. Unsurprisingly, nobody has come forward to say they saw a woman being bludgeoned to death on the beach. We'll have to see what we can make out of what we already have.

"Let's invite Ferris to come and have a little discussion. I think we might arrest him and do the interview under caution. We'll take him straight to King's Lynn.

"Ah – I've just remembered the dog. I wonder if one of the bridge players would take him in for a while. Any suggestions?"

"Wynterflood has some of his own, sir, and they might not get on. What about Prentice? He works from home, has a big house and no apparent commitments. Or perhaps Proudlove. Ayers told me he took in a stray cat once."

"Yes – okay, try Proudlove first. If he's agreeable, get one of the local officers to come with us. He can walk the animal round to Cliff Parade."

Within two minutes, this arrangement was agreed. Proudlove, who had taken the call himself, expressed the same attitude as Dr Trevelyan had earlier. "I shan't badger you for an explanation," he said. "No doubt you'll explain in due course."

Ready to leave, Bryce suddenly remembered he had promised to speak to the Coroner's Officer. He made the call to the number the Coroner had provided, and had a brief conversation, giving the man a short list of names. These were suggestions of people whom the Coroner would probably need to call to give evidence at the inquest.

# CHAPTER 13

Accompanied by Constable Wren, the two detectives drove to Ferris's house. Ferris came to the door himself. "You lot again!" he exclaimed angrily. "And three of you this time – what a waste of my taxes. What do you want now?"

"We'd like you to come with us and discuss a few things," replied Bryce, his voice and manner as pleasant as in the previous encounter.

"You're harassing me because I criticised you and your predecessor," shouted Ferris. "I'm not coming. And don't you doubt that I shall break you too!"

"You have no choice about coming with us, Mr Ferris. I'm arresting you on suspicion of murder. You do not have to say anything, but anything you do say may be taken down and used in evidence.

"Handcuff him, Sergeant, and put him in the car."

For a moment it looked as though Ferris was going to resist, but he suddenly drooped, and made no trouble.

"Mr Proudlove is going to look after your dog for the time being, so that'll be one less worry for you."

"Ridiculous! Whatever for? Elaine, my maid, can feed Xanthe."

"No, she can't. Miss Trott is seriously ill and has been taken to hospital."

Bryce turned his back on Ferris and instructed Malan. "There's a mortice lock on this door as well as the usual. Find the keys – I'm sure Mr Ferris realises it would be sensible to hand them over without any fuss – then put him in the car."

Ferris removed a bunch of keys from his pocket and sullenly passed them to Malan, unnecessarily pushing the keys end-on into the Sergeant's waiting hand, rather than laying them lengthways into his palm.

Bryce, addressing Wren, missed this spiteful display of petulance.

"When you've located and befriended the dog, Constable, you can take her round to Mr Proudlove – you know the address?"

Wren nodded, "Sir!"

Malan passed the keys to his uniformed colleague and took Ferris down the steps to the waiting car.

"Make sure the house is properly secure throughout before you leave," continued Bryce, "then give the keys to Sergeant Timmins for safe keeping."

Bryce returned to the car and took the driver's seat, firing up the engine of the big car. Malan sat in the back with Ferris.

"We're going to King's Lynn, Mr Ferris," said the DCI. "Conversation can wait until we get you settled in at the police station, but in the meantime, you might care to be thinking about which solicitor you'd like to contact, if you think you need a representative."

Ferris, having been told to remain silent, immediately found his voice. "I demand that you explain this audacious outrage!"

The detectives pointedly ignored him. A few minutes later he tried again, with the same result. For the remainder of the journey, he sat glowering at the back of the DCI's head.

At Lynn police station, Ferris was taken to the front desk. The Custody Sergeant recognised the DCI from his previous visit and snapped to attention. Malan handled the booking-in of their prisoner who, although looking as though he might explode, said nothing.

"Put him in a cell for the time being, Sergeant," Bryce instructed the Custody officer. "If he asks for a lawyer, please arrange it. We'll come and talk to him later."

Malan, taking the hint that the DCI intended to let Ferris sweat for a time, took his boss to his own deserted office. He indicated that Bryce should sit at Cordy's desk.

"I'm undecided, Sergeant. Do we leave

Ferris in the cell overnight, and not talk to him at all until the morning? Or shall we have a bite to eat in Lynn, and tackle him later in the evening?"

"I dunno, sir. Maybe if we leave him all night he'd have more time to think and realise he'd better ask for a mouthpiece – who'd probably tell him not to talk. Whereas later tonight he might be getting a bit tired and not so quick-witted."

"Well reasoned, Sergeant!" said Bryce warmly. "We'll eat and then come and talk to him. He may choose to maintain his silence, of course, in which case we have a problem – to charge him or release him. Go to the desk and see if they can arrange a shorthand writer to come in at about half past eight. A civilian, if they can't rustle up a uniformed one. I'll join you out front when I've rung my wife."

As Malan left the room Bryce picked up the telephone and asked for his home number. After five minutes of conversation, he put the receiver back into its cradle.

"I admired the Duke's Head from the outside when I was here before," said Bryce as the detectives left the police station . "No doubt they cater for non-residents, so let's see what they can offer us for dinner."

Malan wondered what County Hall would say about a bill for policemen eating at the town's best hotel. Remembering that the DCI had told Ferris he had private means, he realised that it was unlikely a claim would be submitted for this particular meal.

Although Malan, like most detectives, was wearing a suit, he still felt underdressed in the up-market dining room of the old building. His superior, on the other hand, always managed to look smart regardless of how tired he was, or how many days he'd been away from home.

As before, the DCI made the Sergeant feel comfortable, reverting to the informal 'Peter' and 'Guv' format as soon as they entered the front door of the establishment. The two men enjoyed an excellent meal, and afterwards took coffee in the lounge. At half past eight, Bryce checked his watch.

"The time has come to make a start on Ferris. Let's go."

Five minutes later the two men were back in the police station and the Custody Officer instructed to bring Ferris to an interview room. "Has he said anything?" asked Bryce.

"He shouted quite a bit at first. Regular little potty mouth. He doesn't seem to like you at all, sir. If he'd been in the street, he'd have been arrested under Section 5."

Bryce grinned. "I won't ask for all the graphic detail. I'll take it as sticks and stones instead."

"He calmed down after half an hour or so. I think he'd worn himself out – either that or he'd run through his repertoire," said the officer, returning Bryce's grin.

A hefty constable standing nearby was given instructions to fetch Ferris and take him to room two.

The Custody Officer turned back to Bryce. "Oh, and he turned down the suggestion of a lawyer."

Malan led the DCI to an interview room, where a female shorthand writer was waiting for them. Bryce introduced Malan and himself, and briefly explained what she was to do. He learned her name was Betty Gould. A few moments later Ferris arrived, escorted by the large officer.

"You can leave him with us, Constable," said Bryce.

"Shall I put cuffs on him first, sir?" enquired the officer, whose demeanour gave the impression that he thought a ball and chain would be advisable in addition to the handcuffs. Bryce declined the offer.

Ferris sat glaring angrily at Bryce, extreme tension evident in his rigid posture. "You've exceeded your authority this time," he snarled, "I have friends in high places in police circles – including at Scotland Yard. And I have the ear of the Press. I'll break you for this."

"You're really frightening me, Mr Ferris," remarked the DCI mildly. "Would these be the same 'friends' who wrote caustic comments on your letters to the Yard?

"Perhaps you mean the senior officers in

Sussex and Yorkshire, who, among others, found that your suggestions were worse than useless?

"Possibly you're referring instead to the provincial and national newspaper editors who never print your letters because they know your offerings are libellous?"

Ferris fulminated but said nothing.

"I must remind you that you're still under caution. Let's move away from your imaginary friends and consider something real. Murder, Mr Ferris."

"Don't even try and pin that on me! Adelaide was my friend."

"Who mentioned Adelaide Marner, Mr Ferris? It's another matter I want to talk about first. I understand you lived for many years in Ceylon?

Ferris looked surprised. "I did; what of it?"

"There was an interesting case there, in December 1937. A Sinhalese woman, Ravima Fernando, was found dead. I believe you knew her?"

Ferris seemed to have lost the bravado he'd been demonstrating only seconds before. He replied very warily. "She was a worker on the tea plantation I managed."

"No doubt she had been. But later she became your mistress." The DCI spoke slowly and deliberately, every one of his words delivering a sharp dig at Ferris. "Her family says she didn't pick much tea after that. The also say she was carrying your child when she died."

Ferris' face was florid, and his eyes were on stalks. He had held his breath as the implications of his companion's death were set before him and his response now burst out of him. "What right do you have to pry into my private life overseas? I warn you, Bryce, I won't discuss it!"

"Perhaps you don't *want* to discuss it, Mr Ferris. But when the newly-formed Dominion of Ceylon makes a formal request for your extradition to face trial for murder, what response do you think His Majesty's Government should make? I assume you'd like some discussion to take place then, rather than rubber stamp compliance?"

Ferris was now looking wildly at Bryce. "It would be a witch-hunt, nothing more, and the Government should rebuff any such request out of hand! Anyway, she died as a result of a fall."

"Yes, I gather that's what you maintained at the time, Mr Ferris. Certainly, we can agree she died as a result of an impact between her head and a large stone. The only question really is this: which of the two was moving at the moment of impact – her head which struck the stationary rock; or the rock which someone used to strike her head?

"Of course, with your knowledge of detective work you will know that forensic techniques have improved in the last eight years or so. Anyway, we'll have to await the request for your extradition."

The florid complexion had given way to a pasty pallor during this. "You can't allow it," Ferris muttered. "It would be the most monumental miscarriage of justice."

"Oh, not my decision," replied Bryce. "Ultimately, it's down to the Home Secretary. Perhaps he is another one of your friends in high places?"

Ferris said nothing.

"Just now you seemed to want talk about the late Adelaide Marner. So let's come forward in time. You said she was your friend. How well did you know her?"

"We were members of the same bridge circle; had been since I came back to England. We met once a fortnight, at least. A lovely woman who held me in high regard. Her husband was vile."

"Ah yes; if you hadn't been so certain that Henry Ayers was the murderer, I'm sure Seymour Marner would have been your second choice. So inconvenient for you that neither of them could have done it."

Ferris flushed in annoyance, but didn't react.

"So you met for card evenings fairly frequently. Did you see her at any other times?"

"No. I give Xanthe a good walk at least once a day, and I have never seen Adelaide outside. She didn't have a dog, of course, but Hunstanton isn't a big town, and one might have expected to meet her out and about occasionally."

"We understand her husband was away on business quite a lot. Did you ever escort her anywhere – take her out for a meal, for example?"

"Certainly not. I know there were rumours that Seymour had interests other than business which took him away so often, but Adelaide was a loyal wife, Chief Inspector."

"I'm quite sure she was, Mr Ferris. I think it's quite possible that was why she was killed.

"But we'll go back again a couple of years. Your parents, Walter and Theresa, died in very quick succession soon after your return, did they not?"

Both Bryce and Malan thought they detected a flash of fear pass over Ferris's face, although neither could have sworn to it.

"I don't know why you raise that sad business. They were both old. Father died from heart failure, the doctor said so. Poor Mother too, although Ebbs said hers was probably brought on by grief."

"When all is said and done, Mr Ferris, everyone dies from heart failure. When your parents' bodies are exhumed, I wonder whether a more specific cause of death will be found. We'll have to wait and see."

Ferris looked completely floored. He sat looking down at the table in front of him. "I'm sure you can't do that," he said, feebly.

"We'll have to see," repeated the DCI. "Let's look at your relationship with Mrs Marner. I enjoy a game of bridge myself, although I have little time these days. But apart from your bridge sessions, you say didn't see Mrs Marner?"

"No."

"So if people said they had seen you more than once in the King's Lynn library, coming in with Mrs Marner and leaving with her, but not taking out any books yourself, those people would be lying?"

Ferris looked flustered. "You're trying to trap me. I might have gone to the library with her once or twice. I said I didn't take her out for a meal."

"No, Mr Ferris. I put the same question three different ways."

Bryce turned to Mrs Gould. "I'm going to summarise for Mr Ferris. Would you find the relevant places in your notes, please, and when I've finished either confirm, or correct, what I'm about to say."

The shorthand typist gave an alert, "Of course, Chief Inspector."

"To my question about whether you saw Adelaide Marner apart from the bridge sessions, you replied 'no', Mr Ferris. I asked if you had ever escorted her anywhere; you clearly replied 'certainly not'. I asked if you saw her at any times other than at the card table, and again you said 'no'. The questions were not ambiguous, and neither were your responses."

Bryce looked at Mrs Gould. The secretary nodded, "Yes, exactly what I've recorded."

"You didn't want us to know that you saw Mrs Marner more often than just having a game of cards with her, did you?"

Ferris said nothing, but he looked as though he sensed worse was to come.

"Let's turn to your accusation against Henry Ayers. You had reason to fear his tongue, and although I doubt you knew this at the time, he has a close relative in Sussex who works with the police. You realised that, somehow or other, Mr Ayers had learned that your boast of solving the Sussex murder case was totally unfounded. In fact he didn't, as he might have done, totally humiliate you in public, but he did make a passing reference to Grimms' Fairy Tales. At the time, few people seemed to realise that the remark was more than a joke. But you knew your reputation was seriously at risk if Ayers expanded on it.

"I don't know if you initially intended to kill Ayers, but I do know that at some point you decided to kill Mrs Marner. We will get to the reason for that; but arising out of that decision, you quickly realised that you had a golden opportunity to get Ayers hanged for the crime.

"You knew, as did your fellow players, that Henry Ayers was going to be at home, quite alone and without any witnesses, on the Monday evening. His wife would be in Kings Lynn, and his maid had the evening off. In your attempt to push Ayers to the forefront as a suspect, you had to rely on an exchange over the bridge table. As I pointed out to you yesterday, your suggestion of a motive for Ayers was ludicrous. Had he been in love with Adelaide, as you claimed, his victim would have been Frances – not the object of his affection."

"Am I making any mistakes so far, Mr Ferris?"

Astonishingly, Ferris came back strongly to this. "Too many to count! And none of it amounts to any sort of evidence."

"Well, it's circumstantial, I grant you – but then most murder cases hinge on that sort of evidence to a degree.

"To continue. Did you go for a walk on Monday evening, and did you see Mrs Marner?"

"No, I didn't go out, so I couldn't have seen Adelaide."

Bryce looked at Malan. The Sergeant gave a wordless shake of his head and an expression that conveyed what he was thinking.

"You're lying again, Mr Ferris. You did go out. You left your house on Monday evening a few minutes after seven. You didn't take Xanthe, although that was unusual when you took an evening walk. You returned about an hour later."

Ferris was quick to identify the source of this information. "I suppose Elaine saw me. Well, she's never been right in the head. You can't rely on anything she says."

"As far as relying on her evidence is concerned, I'll tell you something. Miss Trott is terminally ill, and almost certainly won't live until your trial. What she will do is this. She'll make what's called a 'dying deposition', witnessed by a magistrate. Your legal representative, if you have one, can be present and may question her. That deposition will be admissible at your trial. For hundreds of years it has been the assumption that a dying person doesn't want to meet their Maker with a lie on their lips, and so the deposition will carry particular weight with the jury. However, her testimony won't actually be necessary."

Bryce stopped speaking. Betty Gould looked up, pencil poised. "Read that last exchange back to us all, would you please," Bryce asked.

Mrs Gould obliged.

"You said: 'I suppose Elaine saw me'. Not 'I suppose Elaine *said* she saw me.' That's a crystal-clear admission that you did go out. Mrs Gould, Sergeant Malan, and I all heard you; and you have just heard Mrs Gould read back your exact words to you.

"We'll go on. When you left your house, you went down onto the promenade. There, a witness was present, although you probably didn't see her. You leaned up against the sea wall with your back to the sea. Very shortly after that, Adelaide Marner walked down the steps from the gardens and joined you. You took her arm, and walked her down onto the beach, in the direction of Old Hunstanton. A few hundred yards further along, you slammed a lump of stone onto her head, and she died.

"Guy Ferris, I charge you with the murder of Adelaide Marner in Hunstanton, on or about Monday April the 26th, contrary to Common Law. It's you, not Henry Ayers, who will hang, Mr Ferris."

Ferris didn't rise from the table; instead he began to scream and howl in anger. The large Constable waiting outside, burst in. Malan told him to return Ferris to his cell.

"Sorry about all that, Mrs Gould," said Bryce. "Not a pleasant incident, but murder isn't a pleasant business. Please transcribe your shorthand and let DS Malan have the transcript in the CID office here tomorrow. And thank you very much.; I appreciate this has all been well outside of office hours."

Mrs Gould picked up her handbag and departed. The two officers were alone in the room. "Do you reckon he's mad, sir?" asked Malan.

"God knows," replied Bryce, suddenly feeling quite drained after the concentration required in the interview. He stood up, and led the way back to the front desk. Ferris could still be heard screaming. "I suggest you get Doctor Bartlett to come and take a look at him, Sergeant. And better pick a likely solicitor and offer him the chance to talk to things over, either tonight or first thing in the morning. Ferris will have to appear before a magistrate tomorrow if you have a Saturday court."

"There's nobody else in the cells so far tonight, sir, but we'll find a JP anyway. Out of hours, what we usually do is use the Superintendent's room as a remand court. Is ten o'clock suitable?"

"Yes; that should give enough time for Ferris to speak to a solicitor, if he chooses to co-operate. You'd better arrange for a prosecutor too. Ferris already thinks I'm harassing him – so I really don't want to have to fulfil that role!"

***

"It's getting late, so I'll drop you at your car, and you can get off home," said Bryce on the journey back to Hunstanton. You'd better come to the remand hearing tomorrow, and after that, if you aren't doing anything else, I want to search Ferris's house thoroughly. Strictly speaking we don't need a warrant to do that, but I think I'll ask the magistrate tomorrow to issue one. When we've been over the house, I think I'll go home for twenty-four hours."

"I'm free tomorrow, sir. Even if I'd had something else on I'd have cancelled it!"

"Good. Another thing I want to do before I join you in Lynn tomorrow morning, is inform the various interested parties what's happening, before they go to the inquest on Monday. Particularly Mrs Ayers and Mr Marner, of course.

"I'll drop into the Hunstanton police station as well, just in case there are any more messages.

"Incidentally, I don't think I told you this, but I was trying to arrange for a copy of Proudlove's painting of Mrs Marner to appear in the national press tomorrow – to see if a more striking picture might prompt a better response. If the paper did manage to get a copy, it looks as if publishing it will be a waste of time. More publicity for Proudlove, though, not that he probably needs it nowadays."

After dropping Malan at his car, Bryce went into the police station – only just in time, as Constable Wren was locking up for the night. "Letter for you on the desk, sir" announced the officer.

With an apology for delaying the man, Bryce found the envelope, picked it up and slipped it into his pocket.

"Took the dog round to Mr Proudlove, sir. He and his young lady seemed very pleased to have her. And the dog took to the two of them."

"That's good, because she may have to be there a long time. Ferris won't be coming back for the time being – probably never. Right, Wren, you can carry on with shutting up the shop."

Bryce left his car beside the station and walked to his hotel. In his room, he tore open the envelope. The note inside was a transcript of a call made by DS Haig. In essence, it reported that Second Lieutenant Guy Ferris had been cashiered in June 1918, as a result of an assault on a senior officer.

Bryce nodded to himself, filed the note in his briefcase, and turned in for the night.

# CHAPTER 14

Bryce rose early on Saturday morning and went for a brisk walk along the promenade. Returning to the hotel, he enjoyed a full breakfast. He found the manager and informed him that he would be away for the night, but would be back for Sunday night. "I'll leave my things, and pay for tonight, of course."

He walked to the police station, and greeted Sergeant Timmins who was also just arriving. He explained what had happened during the interview at Lynn.

In the little office, he picked up the telephone, and made a number of telephone calls. The first was to the Coroner's Officer. This contact took some time to make, but eventually Bryce found the man at home. Next, he telephoned in turn all the other people with an interest in the case. To each person he reported the arrest and charge of Guy Ferris but emphasised that a charge was far from equalling a conviction. The information he imparted was received in various ways.

Marner, to the DCI's surprise, thanked him for finding the culprit so soon. "I suppose I'm being selfish, Chief Inspector, but people have already been looking at me and thinking I must have done it."

Mrs Ayers congratulated him heartily, and while still on the telephone called to her husband to pass on the news. "I always thought Guy was a liar, but I never had him marked down as a murderer," Bryce heard Ayers say.

Proudlove's phone was answered by Maisie Lawrence. "Oooh how wonderful," she trilled. "Perhaps we can keep Xanthe now." Bryce almost queried how long she thought her own tenure might last at the artist's residence, but decided the question was better unasked.

Dr Trevelyan also answered her own telephone. The incident with Elaine Trott had of course been something of advance notice, but she too was congratulatory. "I'll inform John and Arthur, Chief Inspector. Arthur in particular will be glad the police aren't still suspecting him! Is it all right if I pop into the nursing home and inform Miss Trott?"

Bryce confirmed that he had hoped the doctor would do just that. The Websters had already gone out, so he left a brief message with the maid who answered the telephone.

Rear Admiral Wynterflood made a lot of spluttering noises, and then said "Ferris? Ferris? Guy Ferris? Are you certain?"

"I am, Admiral, but the jury will be the final arbiters."

David Prentice simply said, "Well done, Chief Inspector. I'm not totally surprised. Everything pointed to one of us bridge players being responsible. Once you told us that Seymour was eliminated from the list of suspects, I mentally trawled through everyone else. Without knowing the details of anyone's alibi, of course, I just went through all the names, and rejected them one by one. Guy's was the only name I couldn't quite bring myself to reject."

Returning to the front desk, Bryce asked Timmins to do him a favour. "Get Wren or someone to go and see these two ladies, would you, and tell them that we've charged a man with the murder of Adelaide Marner."

The DCI passed over a note with the names and addresses of Miss Featherstone and Mrs Pollard. "I'm off to the remand hearing now," he said, but Malan and I will be back later to search the house. Presumably Wren gave you the keys. I may as well take them while I'm here."

\*\*\*

On arrival at the Lynn police station, Bryce found Malan talking to a different Custody Sergeant. With them stood a very tall, uniformed Inspector. Horn-rimmed spectacles and a moustache added to the dignified bearing of the man. Introductions were quickly performed and Bryce learned that Inspector Rose would be prosecuting.

"How is Ferris this morning, Sergeant?" enquired the DCI of the Custody officer.

"I think the word is 'morose', sir. I hear he did a lot of shouting and screaming yesterday evening, but this morning he's been quiet. Doc Bartlett saw him last night – maybe he gave him something. Anyway, Jack Courtenay is with him at the moment; he's one of our local solicitors."

"Good luck to him," muttered Malan. "Ferris might be more high-profile than his usual clients, but I doubt if he's ever had a more difficult one." The other two local officers nodded sympathetically.

"Mrs Gould handed this in half an hour ago, sir" the Custody Sergeant held out an envelope. "She said there's a carbon copy as well."

Bryce quickly opened the envelope and leafed through the fair copy. "Good," he replied. Take the carbon to the solicitor, please, Sergeant." Turning to Rose he asked, "Are you ready for the prosecution this morning, Inspector?"

"I am sir. Never handled a murder before, but I'm planning to request an adjournment to a committal date, and then ask for a remand in custody. The JP is Mr Halliday – don't suppose he's ever seen a murder case before either, but he's very competent. And the Clerk to the Justices will know what to do if the rest of us get stuck!"

Bryce retired to the CID office as Malan

disappeared to find some refreshment. On his return with two mugs of coffee, the DCI passed him the interview transcript. After reading it, Malan looked up to find the DCI looking pensive. "Problems, sir?" he enquired.

"Oh no; I'm just trying to decide whether to drive back to London this evening, or take a train. It'll take me nearly four hours to get back, either way. I could leave here at six and reach home by ten. Then tomorrow I'd have to start back again by six o'clock, so not even twenty-four hours at home. I did think about returning here on Monday morning, but that'd mean a very early start to be sure of being able to attend the inquest at ten o'clock."

"Don't suppose you'll like this suggestion, sir, but can't the search wait until after the inquest? That way, you could leave here within the hour."

"I like that idea very much, Sergeant, but I have an even better one. I shall leave after the remand hearing – and you go and search the house. I have no more clue of what to look for than you do, and I'm not sure we should expect to find anything incriminating anyway. It's just one of those jobs that must be done. So, you take Ferris' keys and spend a couple of hours looking through the house."

DS Malan was delighted to be entrusted with this task and said so.

"I trust you completely, Sergeant, and

you'll soon have to do these things for yourself anyway. One day, you'll be a DI."

Malan's telephone started to ring before he could say anything in response. Replacing the receiver after only a few seconds, he announced that the Police Surgeon would like a word and was on his way up. There was a tap on the door, and Dr Bartlett came into the room. He had met Bryce during the inquests in the railway case a few months earlier and greeted him warmly, smiling at Malan as he took the seat the Sergeant pulled out for him.

"Can't stay long," he said; "got to get back to my bread-and-butter job, even on a Saturday. I just wanted to report what I found with your man Ferris. I had half an hour with him last night. Most entertaining. Started off screaming, then calmed right down, then began the screams again. Several cycles of that. Perfectly coherent during his quiet periods, though.

"What I tell you now isn't official – you'll need to get the prison medic to spend a lot longer with him than I have. And at some time I don't doubt the Crown will need the opinion of a professional alienist. But at this stage, in my opinion, I'd say the man is faking insanity. That's all; I'll see you at the inquest, no doubt."

Bartlett stood up and was gone before Bryce could say more than "Thanks, Doc".

The medic was scarcely out of the room when the telephone rang again. As before, the call was very short.

"Mr Courtenay would like a word before the hearing starts, sir, reported Malan as he replaced the receiver again." The two men trotted downstairs, where the custody sergeant told them that Ferris was back in his cell, and Courtenay was in the interview room.

The solicitor was a burly man of forty, with dark wavy hair of the sort that many women paid good money to achieve with their own locks. He was reading a document as they entered, through a pair of too small *pince nez* glasses, which he removed and left hanging from a lanyard as he rose to greet the officers. Malan, who knew Courtenay, performed the introductions.

The three men sat down. Courtenay was hesitant. "Frankly, and I haven't experienced it often in my career, I'm not sure quite what to do," he announced. "I've scanned through your interview record. As yet, of course, I've seen nothing in the way of statements and so on. I see that there are suggestions about other serious matters, both in this country and in Ceylon, but as you've only charged him with one offence, I assume this morning's remand hearing will be restricted to that?"

Bryce nodded.

"Well, my problem is that I can't communicate with him. He smiled at me and shook hands when we met, and he looks at me in a perfectly normal manner. But he says absolutely nothing in response to my questions. I'm not sure how much he understands – so I'm not even sure that he realises his position, and that I'm trying to represent him. Obviously, I have no instructions, and so am in no position to object to your inevitable request for a remand.

"Incidentally, I heard from Clarissa Mayhew, after her husband's murder, that you are a member of the legal profession yourself, Chief Inspector. Are you prosecuting this morning?"

"No; Inspector Rose will handle it. I see your difficulty with Ferris, but I can't advise you. I think you're lumbered with him unless a court relieves you of the responsibility and gives it to someone else. Soon, of course, you'll have to look for counsel.

"But if it helps you, I think that without breaching any professional ethics I can say that Dr Bartlett' provisional opinion is that your client is faking insanity and is perfectly *compos mentis*."

"Well, I can't comment on that, Chief Inspector, of course. No doubt if this gets to trial – or even before – there will be various medical opinions tendered from both sides." The solicitor looked gloomy.

A constable put his head into the room. "Mr Halliday is here, gentlemen." He led the way upstairs to Superintendent Reeve's office, where

Inspector Rose was talking to a diminutive bald-headed man wearing a pinstripe suit. About seventy years of age, he wore a wing collar which appeared even more incongruous than Courtenay's *pince nez*. Before he was introduced, Bryce assumed that this was the local Clerk to the Justices, but discovered he was a last-minute stand-in, the regular Clerk being indisposed.

Rose and Courtenay conferred for a minute, and then announced that they were ready. Rose told the waiting constable to bring the defendant up, and the Clerk went to the next room to fetch the Magistrate.

The proceedings took very little time. The defendant agreed that he was Guy Franklyn Alwyn Ferris, and spoke to give his address. Inspector Rose outlined the charge, and asked for a remand in custody to a date when committal proceedings could take place.

Courtenay stood up, and explained his difficulty. "I'm not in a position to object to the prosecution's request, sir. However, I would ask that the defendant be remanded to the prison hospital, for proper observation and assessment."

The Magistrate replied that he had no power to order that, saying it was a matter for the prison governor. He agreed that a note could be attached to the warrant to draw the governor's attention to the defence request. No doubt the view of the prison medical officer would be sought. He adjourned the matter for six days, and remanded Ferris in custody.

Ferris, who had been silent after giving his details, began to scream again as the officer was taking him back downstairs.

Before the Magistrate retired, Bryce approached him to seek a search warrant for Ferris's house. The DCI had written out an 'information' earlier, and he now took the oath to confirm the contents were 'true to the best of my knowledge and belief'. The JP remarked that strictly speaking a Hunstanton magistrate should deal with the matter, but accepted that he had jurisdiction across the county. He asked a couple of questions, and then agreed to issue the warrant. The paperwork completed, he left the room.

Bryce turned back to Courtenay. "I don't know if anyone has advised you of this, but the inquest is being opened on Monday, in the Hunstanton Town Hall. Will you attend?"

"I suppose I should keep a sort of watching brief. Almost inevitably my client will be named as guilty. Ridiculous state of affairs, that a coroner's jury can make that statement without hearing anything in the person's defence. It's not even as if the court has to observe the normal laws of evidence."

"I tend to agree, although in effect the jury is only indicting him," said Bryce.

"In effect, yes. But the Coroners' Act says

something like *'the persons if any whom the jury find to have been guilty of murder'*. As far as the public is concerned my client will be guilty," grumbled Courtenay. "There was that notorious case in 1914 when a coroner's jury returned a verdict of murder, but neither the examining magistrates nor the grand jury found the defendant even had a case to answer."

"Yes, I'm familiar with the case," said Bryce. "But the authority to identify a murderer at a Coroner's Court is long enshrined in the law," said Bryce. "Maybe it'll be abolished one day. At least coroners no longer summon juries of twenty-three, with only a simple majority requirement for the verdict!

"Anyway, I feel you don't need to worry at this stage, Courtenay. As soon as I say that Ferris has been charged with murder, under an amendment Act of 1926 the Coroner is automatically required to adjourn – unless there are reasons to the contrary. There being no reasons that I know of, this jury won't have a chance to name your client – not until after his trial, anyway, by which time his name will already be public."

"Dear me; that bit of legislation has passed me by," said the solicitor. "My excuse is that this is the first capital case – or murder inquest – that I've ever been involved with!"

The elderly Clerk, who hadn't joined in this exchange, smiled at Bryce as Courtenay left the room.

"I saw you at the committal proceedings last year, Chief Inspector, although I wasn't clerking the court that day. I gathered then that you are a barrister. Young Courtenay is a nice chap, but inclined to be bumptious at times. Do him good to have someone younger than he is correct him on a point of law!" He gathered up his paper and left.

Bryce and Malan walked back towards the CID office. At the front desk, the DCI paused to ask for a copy of Bradshaw's Guide. After consulting this, he said, "I hope nobody will object, but I've decided to leave my car here and go home by train. I'll see you on Monday morning, Sergeant."

Malan offered to give him a lift to the station, but Bryce declined with thanks, saying it was only a five-minute walk, and he had over thirty minutes before the London train left.

\*\*\*

It took almost four hours for Bryce to reach home, where his wife was very surprised but delighted to see him. She wasn't quite so happy to learn that he would have to return to Norfolk twenty-four hours later. "Still, it's lovely to have you back, even if it's only for a day. But if you'd only told me you were on the way I'd have picked you up at Liverpool Street. I shall drive you there tomorrow and save you that awful journey on the tube."

"I won't say no, my love. Well before the seventeenth stop I start to think that we should have moved somewhere more convenient! I'll take the 'Fenman' back – it leaves at twenty to five."

Bryce had suggested going out to eat, as he was effectively an unexpected guest, but Veronica vetoed his on the grounds that he travelled enough for the day. While she was organising dinner, Bryce took an armchair by the French doors. Picking up the newspaper from the nearby table, the first thing he saw was Proudfoot's portrait of Adelaide Marner on the front page. The newsprint quality was poor and it was in black-and-white, of course, but nevertheless the picture was exactly as he remembered it from the Academy over ten years before. The accompanying article included an appeal for information.

Veronica, coming back into the living room, saw what he was reading. "I looked at that piece this morning," she said. "I hope it brings some useful leads for you. It's obviously another horrible case."

Later, as they relaxed in the living room, each with a glass of cognac, he explained what had been happening in Hunstanton. Veronica, as usual, asked pertinent questions.

"It's all circumstantial evidence then, Philip?"

"Yes, but that isn't unusual in a murder case."

"True, but usually you have a murder weapon – and usually a motive, both of which seem to be lacking here. Surely you won't be able to use the Ceylon case, nor the deaths of the parents?"

Bryce laughed. "Not a hope! There's no evidence that we know of in any of those cases. And even if the Ceylon authorities found some all these years later, I doubt if we have an extradition treaty.

"No; I just tried to lob different darts at him in an attempt to throw him off balance. He was caught out in two separate lies, and I decided to charge him. But you're right about the missing elements. In fact, between you and me, it's even possible that the examining magistrates won't find that he has a case to answer."

Veronica nodded. "That's marginally better than an acquittal at the Assizes, though, isn't it? You could still have another go if more evidence emerges."

"That's right. Trouble is, I can't see where additional evidence might come from. The weapon was no doubt washed out to sea within minutes of the murder. And I should have thought a motive would have emerged by now.

"However, Ferris is, in my non-medical opinion, feigning madness. If he sticks to that, the magistrates will certainly commit him to the

Assizes. The trial court will then have to make a number of decisions, the first one probably being 'is he fit to plead?' followed by questions like 'did he know what he was doing?' and 'did he know that it was wrong'.

"I do wonder, though, if his counsel will advise him against that line. If you stand a reasonable chance of acquittal, why risk being committed to Broadmoor for the rest of your life?"

Veronica changed the subject slightly. "Tell me how you're managing without Alex Haig to hold your hand." she asked archly.

Her husband laughed and threw a cushion at her. "Very well, actually. I've got Peter Malan again – I told you about him in the last Norfolk case. He's just been made up to Detective Sergeant, and one day he'll make a decent DI."

The following morning the Bryces, not being churchgoers, went for a walk in Pitshanger Park. Alongside the River Brent, they enjoyed the water view. They also watched the golfers on the course across the river. Some of the players were much less competent than their companions, but far more entertaining.

After lunch, Bryce actually fell asleep in his armchair – something he rarely did. Veronica, observing this, decided it was high time they took a holiday. She determined to visit a travel agent on Monday.

Just before three o'clock she made a pot of

tea, and set a cup down beside her husband. He woke, and slowly focused his eyes on the cup. "Many thanks, my darling. Have I been asleep long?"

"Over an hour, Philip. You needed the rest. When you've finished the tea, I'll take you into the city in the car. Will you eat on the train?"

"I don't think I'll be ready; I should be back in time to have dinner in my hotel."

The traffic on a Sunday was very light. Veronica was a good driver and enjoyed handling the burgundy Triumph Roadster. Knowing Philip had at least half his mind on the current murder case, she refrained from general chat, but after ten minutes, she spoke:

"You said the two maids at the Marners' house were both out when Mrs Marner left that evening. But I wonder if they could say whether the Ferris man ever called at the house when it wasn't a bridge evening."

"Good point, Vee. Actually, it was Cordy and Malan who questioned the maids. I did see them later, but at that stage I was only there to talk to the cook. Malan told me that the girls originally said there were two types of visitor – business colleagues of Seymour Marner, and people who came to play bridge with Adelaide. But you're right; they wouldn't have been asked about Ferris specifically, because he wasn't especially suspected at that time. I'll see them again tomorrow."

"What about the man who has been away on holiday; Pullen, is it? Will you talk to him?"

Bryce looked sideways at his wife, who maintained her gaze on the road ahead, with frequent glances in her rear-view mirror.

"Pullen, yes; a retired senior army officer. I confess I didn't intend to interview him because it's been confirmed that he was in Biarritz at the relevant time. But you're right again – as usual. It's just possible that he might have observed something earlier between Ferris and the victim. He was due back yesterday. I'll try to see him tomorrow as well."

"If Ferris had some sort or relationship with Mrs Marner – and I don't suggest it was anything untoward – have you thought that he might have written to her?"

Bryce again recognised the sense in this suggestion. "You could be right, my dear. But if there was anything, and if Mrs M retained it, I'm not sure if Marner will be very keen for it to see the light of day. And there are no grounds for applying for a search warrant at the Marner residence. I'll ask him though."

Veronica made good time and dropped her husband at Liverpool Street with twenty minutes to spare. Bryce retrieved his brief case from the dickey seat and climbed out of the car. He hadn't bothered with another overnight case because the bag he'd left in Hunstanton still had sufficient clean linen. He leaned through the driver's window to kiss his wife. "Bless you for the lift, darling – and thanks too for your suggestions. I'll call you tomorrow night."

The 'Fenman' actually ran all the way to Hunstanton, and Bryce, who had bought a return ticket from King's Lynn, considered paying an extra fare so he could stay on the train. Malan could easily give him a lift back to Lynn after the inquest. Then, he remembered that although it ran non-stop to Cambridge, between Ely and Hunstanton it stopped at almost every station. Allowing for the necessary locomotive change at Lynn so the train could reverse out onto the Hunstanton branch, plus the fact the train would then stop several more times before reaching the terminus, he reckoned that he would actually arrive before the 'Fenman' – even though he had to walk to the police station to collect his car.

On arrival at the Glebe Hotel, he found a handwritten message from Malan

*Dear Mr Bryce. Some useful material from the house. Also, more responses to the newspaper articles. I think one of these may be of help. Unless I hear to the contrary, I'll be at the Hunstanton police station at half past eight on Monday. Peter Malan, Detective Sergeant.*

The DCI was very satisfied with this. Perhaps they might yet acquire enough evidence.

# CHAPTER 15

Leaving the car at the hotel, Bryce walked down to the little police station straight after breakfast the following morning. He was greeted by Sergeant Timmins, who passed him another note. The DCI was still talking with Timmins when Malan arrived, looking very chipper. The three officers conversed by the desk for a few minutes before the detectives went to their little room.

Bryce read the note he had just been given, and passed it to his colleague. "Useless, I think," he remarked. "Have you got anything better?"

"There were five more responses on Saturday as a result of the appeal in the local papers, but like the one you've just received, no good." He pushed a little sheaf of notes across to the DCI to quickly flick through.

"But there was one response to the national newspaper, sir. This man, Edward Fairchild, doesn't take a local newspaper. So he hadn't heard about the murder until he saw Adelaide Marner's picture on Saturday. He realised he might have some information. His message said that he heard a cry from the beach at about half past seven.

"I went to see him on Saturday evening. He told me he was walking on the cliff top from the lighthouse, going towards Old Hunstanton; reckons he was about level with Queen's Drive."

"Above where Mrs Marner was found, then?"

Malan nodded. "He said he didn't think anything of it; thought it might be kids pole vaulting between the rocks – that's a bit of a sport here, dangerous though it is.

"Much more important, though, he mentioned that ten or twelve minutes after he heard the cry, he saw Ferris coming up from the beach. He knows him very slightly as a fellow dog walker and he was sure it was him. Fairchild doesn't think that Ferris saw him – they weren't within speaking range. He remembers wondering why he didn't have his dog with him and he said if they'd been closer he'd have asked after the dog – thought perhaps she was sick. He said it was rapidly getting dark at that point and there was nobody else about."

Bryce thought aloud. "From the end of the promenade to that access pathway, it's maybe twelve hundred yards, with the murder site roughly halfway along. The cliffs prevent you getting on or off the beach over that whole distance. Yes?"

"Yes. If Miss Featherstone saw a man that could have been Ferris walking onto the beach from the prom at seven-fifteen, and twenty-five minutes later Fairchild says he definitely saw Ferris north of the lighthouse coming the other way, then he must have been in the vicinity of the murder scene. I don't see how he could argue otherwise."

"I'm afraid I do see how he could argue otherwise," said Bryce, "because the new information is still circumstantial. But I'd like to think that Ferris would find it difficult to explain away this positive convincingly. Did you take a formal statement from Fairchild?"

Malan passed a paper to the DCI, who read it carefully.

"Excellent; that's exactly what we need. Now, what else do you have?"

"Ferris's house, sir. Three things, in what I think is ascending order of importance. First, he's kept scrap books for decades, with snaps of the plantation over the years and some cuttings from Ceylon newspapers here and there. There's one cutting in English referring to the death of Miss Fernando – with two exclamation marks beside where the report concludes: 'This case is now closed'.

"Second, is a half-written letter to Mrs Marner. I wouldn't say it's a love-letter, but it isn't what I'd call appropriate for an older man writing to a younger married woman. I've kept it clean for fingerprints, although I don't think there can be any doubt about who wrote it. He refers to a previously written letter, and her lack of response to that. I've made a transcript, sir, to avoid handling it any more than necessary." He passed the DCI another sheet of paper.

"Oh, first class!" exclaimed Bryce after reading the transcript. "Quite right to save it for prints, although as you say there can't be any doubt. Lynn station will have taken his prints, so when we've finished here you can do the comparisons. What's your last item?"

"His own copies of three textbooks, all bought from Foyles in the Charing Cross Road. Not sure exactly when, but it must have been recently. As far as I can find out, two of these are the latest editions, both published last year. The third has only had one edition anyway, published a few months ago. They're locked up in the station at Lynn, but I can tell you what they're about; one's a medical text book about psychiatry, one's a law book, and the third is a 'medical-legal' book. Passages have been circled or underlined; notes have been handwritten in the margins. All of the annotations concern insanity – symptoms, defences, legal implications, and so on. And the writing matches the letter."

Bryce was delighted. "Sergeant, that's marvellous! I'll look at the books later, after they've been dusted for prints. For now, let me tell you how this morning will pan out. The Coroner's Officer knows that Ferris had been arrested, so the session this morning shouldn't take very long. I imagine that most of the potential witnesses have been 'de-warned'. As soon as the inquest is adjourned, we're going to follow my wife's suggestions, and interview some more people."

The DCI smiled at the expression on Malan's face. "Oh yes," he laughed. "Veronica was instrumental in helping me solve one tricky case – I could almost say that she solved it for me. And she's helped in later cases too, including one on our honeymoon. I'm always open to any suggestion she might make, or any idea she might have. We'll talk about this later; let's get along to the Town Hall now."

\*\*\*

Constable Wren was already waiting outside the Town Hall, talking to another uniformed policeman. This was Constable Potter, the Coroner's Officer. Three more men, easily identified as reporters, were talking together a few feet away. Seeing Bryce, they moved quickly to surround him.

"I'm not saying anything today, gentlemen," announced the DCI. You'll hear my statement in the witness box in a few minutes; that's all you're getting. And please don't harass the relatives this morning!"

Grumbling, but seeing the implacable expression on Bryce's face, the reporters backed off.

"We're in the assembly hall to day, sir," reported Potter. "Mr Ellerby's not here as yet. But after you spoke to me on Saturday, I rang him at home to report. He told me to tell some of the witnesses they needn't come today after all, although they'd likely be wanted another time."

"That's sensible," agreed Bryce, "but I imagine some of them will still turn up this morning anyway, to observe."

Leaving the two constables outside, the detectives went to find the assembly hall. The room was laid out theatre-style, with seats facing a stage on which were two tables, each with a chair. At the back of the stage were more chairs, facing the audience.

The only person present was Seymour Marner, who had taken a corner seat near the back of the room. Clearly, he didn't expect to play a prominent role in the proceedings. Bryce told Malan to sit in the front row, and went to converse with the widower. Their discussion lasted only a few minutes, and the DCI rejoined Malan. Before he could sit down, the solicitor, Courtenay, arrived and approached him.

"Any further news, Chief Inspector?" he enquired.

"The investigation is continuing, of course," replied Bryce. "I expect to have it all sewn up before the committal proceedings. What about you – been hunting around various chambers for counsel, no doubt?"

The solicitor grimaced. "Unsurprisingly, it's not easy to contact barristers' clerks over the weekend. I've made a couple of calls this morning. Ferris has money, which is probably unusual among people charged with murder. I expect a reputable man – a KC in fact – will have accepted the brief by lunchtime today. No doubt he'll know more about handling questions of insanity than I do."

Based on what Malan had told him about the books Ferris had been reading, Bryce thought that Courtenay's client might actually know more than either of his lawyers. But he said nothing – it wasn't yet time to disclose the new information.

Courtenay took another seat in the front row, and as he was doing so several more people entered the hall. Mr and Mrs Ayers came and exchanged a few words with Bryce, before taking seats beside him. The Trevelyan family was represented by Doctor Trevelyan. She took a seat in the second row, where Proudlove, dressed very soberly for an artist, Bryce thought, joined her. Maisie Lawrence wasn't to be seen. David Prentice came in with Rear Admiral Wynterflood, and they also took seats in the second row. Doctor Bartlett came in looking harassed, and muttered a greeting to the DCI as he went to sit next to Malan.

Two men, whom Bryce didn't recognise, arrived separately. One, elderly and dressed in a poorly fitting suit, almost reluctantly, Bryce thought, came and sat in the front row. He was freshly shaved, but appeared to have snicked himself in the process and an angry red weal was visible on one side of his face. The second man was well-dressed and extremely upright – an archetypal soldier's bearing. The DCI provisionally identified him as Brigadier Pullen, and turned to whisper a question to Frances Ayers. Glancing behind, she confirmed his supposition. "I'd be grateful if you would introduce me, afterwards," said Bryce.

Constable Potter came in, followed by a group of six men. These he led up onto the stage, and watched as they sat down on the chairs at the back. A typical small-town jury, thought Bryce, although nowadays it was more likely than not that there would be some female representation.

Desultory conversations among the little groups died away as the hands of the big clock on the hall wall neared ten o'clock. Almost to the second, the front door banged, and a smartly dressed little man trotted down the aisle. As he ascended the steps onto the stage, the assembled people rose to their feet.

"Do sit down, ladies and gentlemen. I'm sure you all know why we're here, but I have to address the jury about their responsibilities."

The Coroner proceeded to do this speedily and clearly. It was evident that he had made the same speech many times before. The core message was that it was for the jury to decide, after hearing all the evidence, who the deceased was, and how and where she had died. He included the passage about identifying the person or persons responsible for her death.

Henry Wilkins was first to be called, and the man in the ill-fitting suit climbed onto the stage. He stood by the second table and took the oath. It took only a couple of minutes for him to describe where he had been on the previous Tuesday morning, and what he had seen and done.

He was reluctantly followed onto the stage by Frances Ayers. She confirmed that she had seen the body, and could identify it as her sister, Adelaide Ariadne Marner. Her testimony lasted an even shorter time than that of Wilkins.

Doctor Bartlett testified that he had viewed the body beneath the cliffs, and had subsequently carried out a *post mortem* examination. He described in very simple terms how the death had occurred. He explained that the injury could not, in his opinion, be accidental; nor could it be a matter of suicide. Neither the Coroner nor the jury asked any questions.

"Would Detective Chief Inspector Bryce

come forward."

Bryce ran up the steps and stood by the table. He picked up the Testament and, like Bartlett, took the oath without prompting.

He identified himself as the officer in the case. Without the Coroner needing to ask questions, the DCI explained the current position.

"The local Constabulary requested the help of Scotland Yard in this matter. I have been here since Thursday afternoon, and a local detective and I have been investigating this murder. On Friday evening, I arrested Guy Ferris on suspicion of murder. Later that night, I charged him with the murder of Adelaide Ariadne Marner. He appeared before a magistrate on Saturday and has been remanded in custody."

"Thank you, Chief Inspector," said the Coroner. "Under those circumstances, I am required to adjourn this inquest until any criminal proceedings are concluded. I shall adjourn *sine die*. That means, gentlemen of the jury, that I am putting this hearing off, but that I can't set a date for when we can resume. I'm afraid that means that you must hold yourselves in readiness to come back here – but that may not be for some months. In the meantime, you should not discuss the matter with anyone. I can advise Mr Wilkins, Mrs Ayers, and Doctor Bartlett that their attendance will almost certainly not be required at the resumed hearing."

Mr Ellerby stood, and everyone rose too as he trotted out the way he had come in.

# CHAPTER 16

Outside the hall, Bryce and Malan stood waiting. Mrs Ayers approached with the military-looking man in tow. After performing the introductions, she rejoined her husband and the two walked away. Marner, passing at that moment, nodded perfunctorily and said, "I'll expect you shortly, Chief Inspector." The other attendees went off in various directions.

"This has all come as a shock, Chief Inspector," remarked Pullen when everyone else had dispersed. I come back from holiday to find a dear friend has been killed, and not long after that I hear that another friend has been arrested and charged with her murder. You want to talk to me, although I can't think what help I can be. If it's going to take some time, I suggest you come along to my house. I gather you're going to visit Seymour now, but perhaps at about noon?"

"I don't anticipate our chat will take long, Brigadier, but it would be more comfortable to have it elsewhere. So yes, thank you; we'll come along around noon."

Bryce turned to Malan after the soldier had marched away. "Let's get along to Marner's house. I've told him what we want to look for. He was naturally not very keen. As he said, if there was any incriminating correspondence between Ferris and his wife, it was only going to sully her good name. I pointed out that on the credit side, from his own point of view, anything found could help to convict Ferris and so definitely clear his own name. That swung it, I think. He could of course be back home now trawling through her things and destroying anything he found. But I think that's unlikely.

"We'll look for any letters first, and then go downstairs and talk again to the maids".

At the house, Marner was looking out of one of the upper-ground floor front windows and spotted the detectives arriving. He was opening the door before they had reached the top of the steps.

"Come in," he instructed. With the front door closed again, he explained the layout of the house. "The two front rooms on this floor are my office and Adelaide's study – I have the one on the town side, and Adelaide had this one on the Old Hunstanton side." He opened the first door on the left of the hallway. "Search as much as you want," he said. "You can also go into Adelaide's bedroom on the second floor and look there, but there's no writing desk or any storage there, other than for clothing and so on. Go up the stairs when you're ready – it's the room directly above this one, but two floors up.

"I gather you also want to talk to the staff. You might as well do that in here. Just ring the bell when you're ready, and one of the maids will come."

After he had left the room, Malan looked at Bryce. "He's being very co-operative this morning, sir. Your hint about this helping him must have really hit the target."

Bryce grinned. "Probably. Right – there's only the desk in here, plus those drawers in the corner. Before he changes his mind, nip upstairs and look through Mrs Marner's bedroom. I've heard that females only secrete letters in their underclothing drawer if they are in love with the sender. That seems highly improbable in this case, but look carefully anyway. I'll start in here with the desk."

Malan left the room, and Bryce looked at the desk before sitting down. It was a beautiful secretaire cabinet, in walnut. The base section was a table, with two drawers. On this sat a unit with six stationery drawers, three either side of a recessed mirror. Above this sat a small bookcase on one side, and a small cupboard on the other. The whole thing fitted together apparently seamlessly. 'Almost certainly by Gillows; late nineteenth century probably,' he thought admiringly. He sat down on a chair and pulled each drawer out a short way, ready to methodically check the contents in each. In the first he found some accounts from local tradesmen. He removed nothing and shut the drawer very quickly. This process was repeated for the next three drawers until only two drawers remained pulled out. In the fifth he found what he wanted – two letters, pinned together. They were tucked into a desk diary, but the edges stuck out and there had been no attempt to conceal them. Bryce thought that Adelaide Marner could probably rely on her husband never looking through her desk. Or perhaps she really didn't care if he did?

He swivelled a quarter-turn away from the desk and glanced at the view of the sea before reading the letters. They were similar in style and length. Both letters expressed undying admiration and affection for the recipient, and deplored the state of her marriage. The second letter complained that she had not replied in writing to the first, nor given the sender a private opportunity to tell her *'...all you need to know of my plans for our future life together.'*

Each letter was signed *'Your truly and everlastingly devoted admirer, Guy'*. Bryce noted the dates. Both were written within the last three weeks.

When Malan returned downstairs empty-handed, he found his boss still staring out over The Wash, the letters lying open on the desk Without a word, the DCI handed over what he had found. Malan sat on a huge settee and read. "This is it sir, isn't it? All we need?" he asked.

"It will definitely help," said Bryce. "I'll call for one of the maids." He rang the electric bell. Faith arrived, evidently surprised to be summoned to her late mistress's room. She looked relieved to find the policemen there.

"Sit down next to Sergeant Malan, Faith. We just need to go over a few of the things you told the Sergeant and Inspector Cordy a few days ago. You said that there were two types of visitor to this house – is that right?"

"Yes, sir. The card players and the business people coming to see the master."

"I assume that you've heard that Mr Ferris, one of the bridge players, has been charged with the murder of your mistress?"

The girl nodded. "We heard on Saturday. Cook's friend …" The DCI interrupted her. "No, it doesn't matter how you heard. But now you know, is there anything else you can think of, regarding Mr Ferris specially? Did he ever visit here on a day when it wasn't a bridge day, for example?"

"Ooh," she said. "I never thought." The girl appeared to be sorting out how to say what she wanted to say. "Mr Ferris did call maybe a couple of times; only in the last week or two – not before that I know of. But the Mistress give us instructions that she was to be 'out' if he came to the house. She never did see him those times."

"What about telephone calls, Faith?" asked Malan. "Do you sometimes answer the telephone?"

"Only if the Master's out, sir," replied the girl. "He always answers if he's in. I don't remember ever hearing Mr Ferris on the telephone, anyhow."

"Good; thank you. Fetch Elsie for me now, please, and come back with her."

Elsie corroborated Faith's report.

"Thank you very much," said Bryce. "You've both been very helpful. We'll take a statement from each of you – won't take more than a few minutes. One at a time, tell me your full names, please."

The Chief Inspector produced a short draft for each girl. "There you are, young ladies," he said. "Just read these and tell me if anything is wrong and needs to be taken out, or if you want to add something."

The two maids did as he said. One after the other they nodded agreement and signed as indicated. Bryce tucked the statements and the two letters away in his briefcase.

"Thank you very much. It may be that you'll be called to give evidence in the future, but I rather doubt it. In any case, it's nothing to be worried about. Now, you get back to work, but one of you please find Mr Marner first, and tell him we'd like a quick word before we go."

Marner came in almost at once. "Find

anything useful?" he enquired.

"Yes," replied the DCI. "Two things, neither of which is in any way critical of your late wife, but both of which may help convict Ferris of her murder." He explained the letters, and Mrs Marner's refusal to see Ferris if he called. "I can also tell you, in confidence, that Ferris had started to write a letter to your wife, and in it he complains that she hasn't replied to his letters. So, all in all, it's clear that she did nothing to encourage the man."

"I'm baffled," said Marner. "She was refusing to see him or answer his letters, but she must have agreed to meet him on Monday evening."

"True, and unless we hear from Ferris himself as to why she met him, we can only surmise her reasoning. However, from the other evidence it's not improbable that she only went to tell him to his face that he was wasting his time and to stop pestering her. That's supported by the fact that he then killed her."

There was another silence. Just as Bryce was about to say they were leaving, Marner spoke again.

"I wasn't a good husband to Adelaide. I have to accept that, and if there is such a thing as the hereafter, no doubt I'll pay my penance there. If only I'd treated her differently, she would have come to me with the problem of Ferris."

Both Bryce and Malan thought that if he'd

only treated his wife properly, the opportunity for Ferris to make up to her would never have arisen in the first place. They said nothing, however, and instead took their leave.

\*\*\*

Outside, Malan gave vent to his feelings about Marner's admission that he hadn't treated his wife well. He spoke for some time as they walked along to Pullen's house. "Sorry, sir," he said eventually.

Bryce laughed. "Oh, don't apologise, Sergeant. If you hadn't said all that, I'd have had to say it myself!"

Pullen answered his own door bell and led the officers upstairs. Malan's earlier supposition was confirmed – the main living room was upstairs, with a sea view. It didn't require any detective skills to realise that this was a man's room. There was nothing about it, in decoration, furniture or ornament, to suggest the presence of a woman.

His offer of a cup of coffee being declined, Pullen leaned forward in his chair and declared himself ready for questions.

"Only one really, Brigadier," began the DCI. "We're trying to build up a picture about any interaction between Guy Ferris and Mrs Marner, especially over the last two or three weeks. Did you observe anything which, with hindsight, might have suggested something other than just two bridge-playing friends conversing? I don't necessarily just mean a friendly exchange – looking back, was there anything which might suggest any frostiness between them?"

Pullen gazed out of the window. It occurred to Bryce that a sea view provided an ideal medium for thought; he realised that he had used the same feature only a short time before. Akin to staring into a blazing fire, really.

Pullen turned to face the DCI.

"With hindsight, you said. Yes. Well, the last bridge session I attended was the Thursday before Adelaide was killed. John and Pippa Trevelyan were hosting. We always split into two or three tables, and then each table cuts for partners. The arrangement is always that the tables then remain constant for the evening. The initial splitting into tables is generally quite informally done by the host or hostess. Our group is more-or-less unchanged from week to week, so I suppose each host remembers who played together recently, and who hasn't sat with someone else for some time – that sort of thing.

"On that occasion, I remember Pippa proposed the seating, and Adelaide suggested a slight alteration. I don't suppose anyone else noticed – most probably didn't even hear at that point, as she was really only talking to Pippa. But the point is that Addy's revised suggestion meant that she didn't sit at Guy's table – where of course she would have had him facing her as her partner, or sitting beside her."

"What reason did she give for her suggestion?" asked Bryce.

"Well, that's it, really. She said 'Guy and I are a bit fed up with each other's play lately', or something like that. Anyway, Pippa switched her plan around, and Addy and Guy were placed at different tables that evening. I can't think of anything else.

"Is that of any use to you, Chief Inspector?"

"Every last crumb is useful, Brigadier. I can't go into detail, but at the trial you'll hear about a number of little examples like yours – and together they should help to convict Mrs Marner's murderer."

"Do you want me to make a statement now?"

"Not at this stage, sir. If we use this information, and we probably will, I'll get the Trevelyans to make statements, as Mrs Marner was actually speaking to them. I don't think it'll be necessary even to call you as a witness to what you overheard. But we're very grateful to you for pointing us in the right direction, as this is the first we've heard of this incident."

The police officers took their leave.

Walking back towards James Street Bryce said, "I want Ferris' books dusted for prints first. Then I'm off back to London. Two jobs for you, Malan. Go and see the Trevelyans; if they confirm what Pullen said, get a simple statement from each of them. It has little or no evidential value at trial, but we'll put it in anyway.

"Then, get your own statement prepared. Make sure everything in it is admissible. Third, liaise with your county prosecutor, and find out when the committal proceedings are to be held. I wouldn't expect it to be before next week but inform me as soon as you know. I'll be back for that hearing, of course – earlier if necessary. Finally, let me know if you hear which barrister is appointed for the defence – and for the Crown."

\*\*\*

Returning home, Bryce described to Veronica how her suggestions had in fact produced additional snippets of evidence and thanked her again. Settling into the chairs by the living room French doors, Veronica told him that she had made provisional bookings for a short holiday in France. They would fly from Lympne to Le Touquet, taking their own car on the Silver City 'air ferry'. As she had gambled, her husband was sufficiently attracted by this novel prospect and the thought of a break with Veronica to forget that he hadn't been very keen on flying on the two previous occasions when he had tried it.

\*\*\*

Ten days later, Bryce returned to King's Lynn. The committal proceedings were something of an anti-climax. Ferris said nothing except to acknowledge his name. As soon as that formality had been completed, Mr Courtenay stood up and told the examining magistrates that his client would plead not guilty, and reserve his defence. He invited the court to commit his client to the Assizes for trial, based on the depositions they would hear shortly from the Crown.

Malcolm Leeming, a young barrister from chambers in Cambridge, prosecuting for the Crown, was visibly surprised by this statement, but rapidly recovered his composure and called seven witnesses including DCI Bryce. Despite the early indication from Courtenay, it took several hours for the witnesses to have their depositions taken down, typed, and signed. Miss Trott had made her dying deposition with Courtenay present when it was made; he had raised no questions.

The clerical work concluded, the Chairman formally committed Ferris for trial at the next Assizes in Norwich.

With the hearing finished, Bryce went over to speak to Leeming. The two men knew each other by name, but had never met. The prosecutor had just mentioned that he'd never before come across a committal where the defence announced their position before any witnesses were called, when Courtenay joined them.

"Before you ask," he said, "we have Sir

William Beckett KC for the defence, leading Owen Perry. A heavyweight defence team, I'm sure you'll all agree. Just now, as you must guess, I was following Beckett's strict instructions. He's seen our client. And no, I have no more idea than you as to what line of defence he will take – not that I'd tell you if I did!"

"Well, we have Quentin Hanbury-Lee KC," remarked Leeming. "Not being pejorative, but as far as weight is concerned I'd say he more than equals Beckett and Perry put together, even without my own modest contribution."

This remark caused much laughter – Lee was by any standards a huge man, both in height and in girth.

# CHAPTER 17

Bryce had little to do with the case over the next three months. Either side of a pleasant ten days spent touring some of the battlefields of the Great War he was kept very busy on other matters. Eventually, the time came for him to travel up to Norfolk again – this time to the county town.

It was his first visit to Norwich, once the second city in Britain, and he travelled by train. He had originally intended to stay at the Maid's Head, which claimed to be the oldest hotel in Britain, but a telephone call a week before his trip revealed it was fully booked. His secretary reserved him a room in the equally prestigious Royal Hotel instead – even more convenient as it was only a minute's walk away from the Shirehall, where the trial would be held.

Over dinner on the Sunday evening, and with nobody to converse with, Bryce passed the time by reading a little booklet about the city, which had been handed to him at reception. He picked up several interesting snippets, learning that Norwich was the only English town to have been excommunicated – *in toto* – by a Pope, in 1274. Further information was not revealed, but Bryce assumed that the edict must have been lifted at some point over the following six and a half centuries.

He also learned that in the early eighteenth century Norwich was reckoned to be the wealthiest city in the country, with the best system of Poor Relief. He was much amused to read an extract from George Borrow's translation of Faust:

*'They found the people of the place modelled after so unsightly a pattern, with such ugly figures and flat features that the devil owned he had never seen them equalled, except by the inhabitants of an English town, called Norwich...'*

At nine o'clock on the Monday morning, the DCI walked across to the Shirehall, where he was due to meet with the County Prosecuting Solicitor, Peter Swindley. The two men had met briefly some months before, when the Railway case had come to trial.

"I don't know what's going on," reported Swindley. "My spies tell me that Perry arrived on Saturday, and was closeted with Courtenay for a couple of hours. The pair of them visited Ferris in prison and they talked together at length afterwards. Yesterday, Beckett arrived in the city, and the three of them held a meeting in his hotel. He didn't visit his client, though.

"The three of them have been in conference since eight o'clock this morning. I'm told that such an early start is unprecedented for Sir William. Also, as prisoners aren't brought here before nine, none of the team can have seen Ferris today, unless they've just gone to the cells now."

"Very curious. We'll see soon enough what they have up their sleeves."

The two men were joined by the prosecuting barristers. Bryce had been in the same chambers as Hanbury-Lee for a couple of years after his call to the bar, before opting to change career and join the police.

"You've done well, young Bryce," smiled the KC – "but if you'd stayed at the bar…"

"I might still be doing dock briefs at the Marylebone Magistrates' Court!" Bryce finished his old colleague's sentence for him. "Or perhaps promoted to making applications to the licensing justices!"

"Well, gentlemen, what do we know?" asked Hanbury-Lee, when everyone had finished laughing.

Swindley reported what he had heard. The four men tried to work out what this flurry of meetings might portend.

"My guess is it'll be something to do with whether or not he is fit to plead," said the DCI. "As you all know, he tried a few screaming fits when he was first charged."

"Yes, the fitness angle seems a likely strategy," agreed Leeming. "Not a straightforward procedure, though."

The four men, all lawyers (albeit Bryce was rusty), took a few minutes to talk about the law on fitness to plead. With a glance at his watch, the KC stood up. "Let's take our places in court," he suggested. "I like to spread my things out and get comfortable in a new court and I've never been in this building before."

As the men moved in the direction of the principal courtroom, Bryce saw Sergeant Malan across the foyer, talking to Mrs Ayers and her husband. He didn't join the witnesses, but raised a hand in a half-salute, which Malan acknowledged.

This part of the Shirehall dated from the early 1820s, and the principal courtroom had changed little in that time. The council chamber was actually rather more attractive, panelled in oak, but the wood in the courtroom was painted a stark white, leavened only by red upholstery and red leather inlays in the tables.

There was little room for the legal representatives. In most courts, the instructing solicitors would sit behind counsel, but there was only a small bench to do this on one side. Bryce viewed the cramped facilities unhappily.

There was no sign of the defence team, but the five tiers of public seats, facing the judge and stretching the full width of the room, were already almost full. A high-level gallery ran along one side wall, but Bryce saw this was not open to the public. The Clerk of Assize was sitting below the Judge's bench, a shorthand writer sat nearby, and a gowned usher stood overseeing the public gallery.

Within seconds, and before the prosecuting team could sit down, Owen Perry entered the court and immediately went to speak to the Clerk in a low voice. The Clerk appeared to demur, but Perry shook his head firmly, and gestured towards one of the doors behind the bench.

The Clerk shrugged his shoulders, called to the usher and gave him instructions, before leaving the courtroom himself via the rear door.

"Curiouser and curiouser," observed Hanbury-Lee.

Perry came over and spoke to the interested observers. "Sorry for all the mystery," he said, "but I think it's best if Beckett explains our position to you and the Judge at the same time."

As he spoke, the two other defence lawyers came into court. With a nod towards the prosecution team, they took their seats opposite. Nobody spoke, and Bryce thought that neither the KC nor his junior looked happy.

Within a minute, the usher could be heard outside reciting the traditional and ancient call to justice. The rear door opened, and the usher reappeared. He signalled to the four barristers to follow him. In the judge's chambers, Mr Justice Salmon was robed but not wearing his wig. He invited the four to remove their own wigs and sit.

"I understand that you have something to say, Beckett," said the judge. "I assume you have some sort of application, but I confess I don't see why it is being made in chambers. Are you aware of what is happening, Lee?"

"I have not been admitted into the confidence of the defence, Judge, so if it is an application I am unable to say whether or not the Crown will have any objections."

"I see. Very well, carry on Beckett."

"Thank you, Judge. I do most earnestly apologise to my friends opposite. It is not a matter of deliberately keeping them in the dark. Rather it is that we have been faced with a ..." he hesitated, "...a difficulty. That difficulty has not in fact yet been resolved. I confess that, even with the assistance of Perry here, and my instructing solicitor, I am not sure what to do for the best. I should like to explain, if I may.

"The Crown is well aware that from an early stage the mental state of my client caused some concern, shall we say. Frankly, until yesterday, it was my intention to ask the court to rule that he was unfit to plead to the indictment. You will all be familiar with the leading case, that of R v Pritchard in 1836, and the learned judge's decision in that matter.

"Somewhat unexpectedly, I now find myself unable to argue this point. My client is not '*mute of malice*'. Nor can it be said that he cannot comprehend the evidence or understand the processes of the court. He is able, at least in a sense, to plead to the indictment. But more recent cases have suggested that a further limb is required, and that hinges on the ability of a client to give proper instructions to his representative. This is not the forum to argue the meaning of 'proper' in this context, but I cannot dispute that the defendant has, yesterday, given me instructions – very clear written ones.

"The arrival of those instructions – out of the blue, I might say – and the last-minute indication of a plea, mean that I find myself unable to contend that the defendant is unfit to plead.

"My instructions are to enter a plea of guilty but insane, under the Trial of Lunatics Act of 1883. I should say that my client seems to be remarkably familiar with some of these cases and statutes. However, my limited experience of that Act leads me to suppose that, ordinarily, a defendant has pleaded not guilty, and only after trial does the jury finds him guilty but insane. I do not know if there is any precedent for my client's route, but I don't see any insuperable objection to it. Guilty pleas in capital cases are of course extremely rare anyway."

Mr Justice Salmon was about to thank Beckett when the barrister held up a hand.

"I beg your pardon, Judge, but there is more. I am specifically instructed to read, in full, a statement which my client has provided. He insists that this is read to the court immediately following his plea.

"In the statement, my client claims to have murdered three other persons – a woman in Ceylon in 1938, and both his own parents in 1947. I gather that the police are aware of all three matters, but of course there is only the one charge on the indictment. He also refers to deliberately interfering with police investigations into various other murders, including the one he is charged with, while posing as an amateur detective.

"So, I don't have an application as such – but I thought it only right to explain the situation to you all. I assume you will allow the plea, leaving the jury to decide only on the insanity question. The question of whether the statement should be given to the jury at all, and if so when that should be, is of course also a matter for you, Judge. I merely pass on my client's wishes. Frankly, Perry and I are undecided ourselves."

The judge was quick with his assessment of what he had just heard. "What your client believes, it would seem, is that this statement will support the contention that he is in some way insane. Reminiscent of the recent case of Haigh, perhaps, he appears to be attempting 'the more the merrier'. What does the Crown say to all this?"

After a glance at his junior, who gave a small and non-committal gesture, Hanbury-Lee replied. "We see no difficulty with accepting the guilty plea, and leaving it to the jury to decide the matter of insanity. We're also content to leave the matter of the statement to you, Judge. All I would add is that the defendant apparently did quite a bit of screaming both in interview and during his first remand hearing. If the jury is to have the statement at all, then to spare the court a further outburst perhaps it would be better to accede to his request and get it out of the way early."

"I'll decide when we get to that point," said the Judge. "For now, I think we'd better make a start."

The four barristers returned to court, where Leeming quickly whispered to Swindley and Bryce what had happened.

A few minutes later, to a call of 'all rise', the Judge entered. Placing his nosegay on the desk in front of his place, he gave a small bow and sat down. Mr Justice Salmon was not a large man. In his red robes he seemed almost to disappear as he sat in his huge red leather chair.

The defendant was brought in from the cells, and placed in the dock, with two prison officers beside and slightly behind him. Beckett immediately went and spoke to him, Ferris smiling as he leaned forward to listen. The KC returned to his place. The next half hour was taken up with empanelling a jury and getting them sworn, after which the main proceedings started. The Clerk told the defendant to stand, and had no trouble in getting him to identify himself. When the Clerk finished reading the indictment, and asked whether the defendant was guilty or not guilty, Ferris said very clearly "Guilty but insane", and a gasp ran through the public gallery.

The Clerk told him to sit down again. Hanbury-Lee rose to explain to the jury that he and Mr Malcolm Leeming prosecuted on behalf of the Crown, and that Sir William Beckett KC and Mr Owen Perry represented the defendant.

The prosecution in this courtroom was slightly inconvenienced. The jury box, raised by several feet above the floor of the court, and requiring a climb up four steps to reach it, was situated immediately behind the prosecution. The front row of the box had an angled shelf to support papers and books, and this projected in front of the box itself. The effect of this was that those sitting behind the counsel at the table could never see the jury at all, even if they were to turn around. Even standing at the table, a short prosecuting counsel would find hard to see the face of a similar sized juror in the back row of the jury box. Another defect in the layout was that whichever side was examining a witness, the barrister could only do so with his back to the jury.

Instead of continuing his opening address, the KC paused, to see what the Judge would say. After a few seconds, his lordship appeared to come to a decision, and motioned the KC to sit down again.

"Ladies and Gentlemen of the jury, this is a most unusual case. As you have heard, the defendant admits to the killing of Mrs Adelaide Marner, but says he was not responsible by reason of insanity. So, you do not have the typically onerous task of deciding guilt or innocence. However, you do have an alternative task, which may well have much the same degree of difficulty. You will have to decide, after hearing all the evidence, about the defendant's state of mind at the time of the murder.

"In this country, when a guilty plea is presented in a capital case, the prosecution is still required to bring at least a shortened form of the evidence by which the Crown intended to prove the case. That will be presented to you in a few minutes. But the defendant has made a special request – for his counsel to read a prepared statement now, rather than later on, as would be more usual. The Crown has raised no objection, and I have agreed to it." He turned to Ferris' KC. "Yes, Sir William."

"Thank you, My Lord. Ladies and gentlemen, my client's statement is very short, and I shall read it exactly as he wrote it.

"'I killed Adelaide Marner, on the beach at Hunstanton. I have no idea why. Some years ago, when I lived and worked in Ceylon, I killed the woman with whom I lived. Again, I don't know why. I came back to this country after the last war. On arrival, I killed my mother and father, within a month of each other. Nobody noticed. I became obsessed with crime – murder cases – both real and fictional. I became something of an amateur detective, and involved myself in a number of real-life cases. Ostensibly I was helping the police, but actually I was trying to mislead them – as indeed I did with the police in Adelaide's case.

'I was very fond of all the people I killed. I loved them all in different ways. I was not rational and had no idea of what I was doing. Indeed, it is only occasionally, such as now while I am writing this statement, that I can accept that I did these things at all. But as I write this I have to accept that I did them. At other times, I don't seem to recognise myself in any of this.

'I served as a soldier in the Great War, and saw many horrors. It was a conflict of exceptional and shocking violence. I do not know if those experiences turned my mind, but I can think of no other cause.

'I have pleaded guilty to the charge of

killing Adelaide Marner, because I understand that I must have done so. But I can assure you all, ladies and gentlemen of the jury, that I certainly did not do it consciously, or with malice, and I have no memory of it. Thank you for hearing me.'

"That is the statement, my lord." Beckett resumed his seat.

In the jury box, and in the packed gallery, there had been absolute silence as the confessions were read out. Now that Beckett had finished, there was a collective release of breath. Perhaps surprisingly, not a single person spoke.

The only sound after Beckett sat down again came from the defendant, giggling loudly. He was also smiling broadly, although he didn't appear to be looking at anyone, just gazing out of the high-level windows at the sky. Most of the observers stared at him in horror, and a low murmur then rippled around the courtroom. A double rap from the Judge's gavel cut that short.

Hanbury-Lee hauled himself to his feet and pulled his gown more comfortably around his shoulders.

"Ladies and gentlemen, His Lordship will no doubt address you in due course regarding the other incidents to which the defendant refers. But I am sure he will confirm what I tell you now: none of the other alleged offences mentioned should concern you in any way whatsoever.

"Today, the defendant is accused of only

one crime – the wilful murder of Mrs Adelaide Ariadne Marner. Despite the defendant's admission, I shall call witnesses to prove that matter beyond reasonable doubt."

He began his opening address to the jury, only modifying his original draft where appropriate to cover the new situation. He outlined what the key witnesses for the Crown would say. His final remarks were these: "The Crown's position is very clear. The defendant murdered Mrs Marner in cold blood, we believe because she rejected his advances. As I say, we shall adduce evidence for that. We do not for one moment accept that he did not know what he was doing at the time, nor that he did not know that it was wrong.

"That he has subsequently and conveniently forgotten what happened is also rejected. This was, in the Crown's view, a cruel and calculated act, done with what is stated in the indictment – malice aforethought. I call Henry Wilkins."

# CHAPTER 18

With clinical efficiency, the prosecution called its witnesses. Thomas Wilkins and Frances Ayers were not cross-examined, and each was in the box for only three or four minutes. Doctor Bartlett followed. After almost completing his evidence in chief, Leeming asked him if he had been called to the police station on the evening the defendant had been charged, and if so what he found and what conclusions, if any, he had drawn.

"I saw the defendant there, yes. He was being noisy – screaming and so on. As for my conclusions, well, I'm not a psychiatrist. But in my opinion, he was faking insanity."

Leeming sat down, and Perry stood. "You admit that you are not qualified to judge the defendant's mental state, Doctor Bartlett?"

"I admit nothing of the kind! What I have said is that I am not a psychiatrist – a specialist in that particular discipline. I have, however, been in general practice for twenty years, and a police surgeon for fifteen. In that time I've seen countless mental cases. I know what I saw, and I have given you my medical opinion accordingly."

"So, if the defence calls a psychiatrist, and he disagrees with your view, you would say he was in error?"

"A hypothetical question, Mr Perry. I can't answer until I hear the testimony. But – and I appreciate this isn't evidence – I have discussed the case with two other distinguished medical men who, I understand, will be called for the Crown. I agree with their views. One of those gentlemen is a professor of psychiatric medicine."

Perry, who had realised too late what Bartlett was going to say and had failed to stop him, wondered if following up with another question would make it worse. Glancing down beside him he caught a shake of the head from his leader, and the Doctor was allowed to step down.

Mr Leeming called Miss Featherstone, Mrs Pollard, and Mr Fairchild. In each case the defence asked no questions. Leeming explained to the jury the significance of a dying deposition, and proceeded to read the one made by Miss Trott. He emphasised the fact that the defendant's legal representative had been present and able to question the lady while it was being taken. He finished by saying, "Sadly, Miss Trott passed away, two weeks ago."

DCI Bryce, who as the officer in the

case was able to remain in court during the opening, had expected to be called first or second, but evidently Hanbury-Lee had decided to alter the running order in view of the revised requirements in the trial. As Leeming mentioned the death of Miss Trott, Bryce thought that might be to the Crown's advantage, given that she herself thought there was something wrong with Ferris. Her own mental faculty might also have been queried by the defence, casting doubt on her testimony. However, no earthly advocate could cross-examine her now.

Hanbury-Lee rose to take over from his junior, and called the DCI. Bryce was not asked to tell the jury much about the investigation, but he produced the two letters from the defendant which Mrs Marner had retained.

The KC took him through the interview at the police station, and how the defendant had been caught out a number of times. It was the shortest time the DCI had ever spent in the witness box. Yet again, there was no cross-examination.

It had taken under an hour and a half to hear the evidence of nine witnesses. In any trial that must constitute a record, thought Bryce, but in a murder trial it was surely unprecedented.

Hanbury-Lee again handed over to his junior, and Leeming called four of the 'bridge set'. Given that none had evidence of direct relevance to the facts, Bryce was surprised. Prentice, the two Trevelyans, and Proudlove were called in turn. However, each was only asked three questions. "For how long have you know the defendant? What interaction have you had with him? Have you ever had reason to suspect that he is insane?"

Each was then cross-examined by Beckett, who did his best to pour scorn on the testimonies of lay people attempting to deny the existence of mental illness in the defendant. This line of attack failed first with Prentice, who was highly articulate, and well able to take care of himself in the witness box. It failed even more with John Trevelyan, who came next, as Beckett hadn't evidently not realised that he was questioning another experienced doctor, as Trevelyan had used the customary surgeons' title of 'Mr' rather than 'Dr'.

Philippa Trevelyan entered the box next and Beckett was more cautious, but again failed to persuade her to produce the slightest evidence of Ferris' supposed mental frailties and failures. She described how, among a group of very competent bridge players, Ferris was as good as any, and that his 'card memory' was excellent.

By the time it was Proudlove's turn, Beckett was almost desperate to get some sort of admission. However, the artist was not only intelligent and articulate, he didn't like the way the prosecuting counsel was trying to get him to say things that he didn't believe. (Like all the earlier witnesses except Bryce, he had not been told of the 'guilty but insane' plea.) Twice, he went on the attack.

"From the questions I've been asked, it's clear that the matter of your client's sanity has been raised. Presumably by the defence. You can ask as many times as you like whether I saw any signs of incipient lunacy in Ferris, and the answer will always be the same – I did not, because there were none to see. Excellent card player. First-rate memory. Your client is as sane as I am."

Beckett tried again, and this time Proudlove really snapped. "No, Sir William. I believe your client brutally killed a close and dear friend of mine. He should just admit what he did without any more of this cowardice in trying to say he wasn't responsible for his actions. It's all rubbish."

Suspecting that Proudlove was going to say more in the same vein, the Judge intervened. After rebuking the witness, he instructed the jury to ignore the last outburst. Beckett did not attempt to continue, and Leeming didn't re-examine, feeling that the net result was already overwhelmingly positive.

The trial had fairly raced along, and the Judge decided that everyone needed an early lunch. Hanbury-Lee rose to ask if all the prosecution witnesses already called, bar the DCI, could be released. Beckett raised no objection, and this was agreed. The Judge warned all those who had already given evidence that they must not speak to anyone who was yet to do so.

***

Bryce waved to Malan across the foyer, but didn't speak. After a quick discussion with Swindley and Hanbury-Lee, he chose to eat by himself, returning to his hotel for his meal. Before eating, he made the telephone call suggested by the prosecutor.

After lunch, the Crown called the two medical witnesses mentioned by Bartlett. The prison Medical Officer was another highly experienced man. He had spoken with Ferris several times a week since his original remand, nearly four months before. He had only been expecting to give evidence regarding the defendant's fitness to plead, but was armed with ample evidence regarding his overall sanity. His uncompromising stance was that Ferris was pretending to be mad. He was adamant that Ferris currently knew what he was doing, and knew the difference between right and wrong. Similarly, that there was not the slightest evidence to show that his mental situation was any different at the time of the offence.

Try as he would, Beckett was unable to shake this view, although he spent over half an hour trying to do so.

The MO was followed into the box by a professor of psychiatry, his standing both national and international. Occupying a chair in a most prestigious university, he was the author of numerous books and papers on mental health, with four earned and eight honorary degrees to his name. This man was, as Crown counsel observed, an unimpeachable expert witness.

The Professor had conducted four lengthy meetings with Ferris over the past month. Also expecting to only rebut the 'unfit to plead' suggestion, he nevertheless entered enthusiastically into the general question of insanity. Just like the prison Medical Officer, his opinion was that Ferris was sane, not only under the M'Naghten Rules, but in ordinary parlance too.

Beckett attempted to dilute the damage of this testimony with a lengthy exchange regarding the possibility of memory loss, and whether the defendant could have committed the act of murder while being unaware of it at the time and afterwards. The Professor was having none of it, and the KC eventually sat down unsatisfied.

Since his earlier outburst of giggling, through the rest of the morning and during the testimony of the two experts after lunch, Ferris had sat in total silence. Now, he suddenly surprised the court by letting out an ear-piercing scream. That done, he sat silently again, with an inane smile on his face.

Mr Justice Salmon eyed him dispassionately, then announced that the trial would be adjourned until the following day. He asked the jury to retire, but instead of rising himself, remained in his chair. After the jurors had left the courtroom, he addressed the defence.

"Sir William, no doubt you are content for your client to display signs of abnormality in front of the jury. But there are limits to what the court is prepared to permit, when such sounds are distracting – and may even be upsetting – the jury. Any repetition in the morning, and I shall have your client returned to the cells for the remainder of the session at least. While I accept that such action would probably suit your client's case, I should say that if I have to do it you would be wise not to try to take advantage of it in your later summing up."

Beckett bowed. "As your lordship pleases." Without actually approaching the dock, he looked meaningfully at his client, who made no sign. The Judge rose to leave the court.

# CHAPTER 19

Bryce walked back to the Shirehall the following morning. He waved and smiled at Malan, sitting in the foyer and already looking very bored. The boredom wouldn't last much longer, thought Bryce. In the courtroom, he found the prosecuting solicitor talking to his Scottish Scotland Yard partner, Detective Sergeant Haig.

As Bryce had given Haig instructions the previous day, he was expecting to see him. He smiled a greeting to the DS, but sat down and didn't interrupt the conversation. After a few more words, Swindley left the court room, saying he would check on DS Malan. There was no reason why the two Yard officers shouldn't converse now.

"Never been to Norwich before, sir," remarked Haig.

"Nor I, Sergeant," replied the DCI. "You got the information, then?"

"Oh aye, no trouble at all. The War Office clerk remembered Mr Lessing had been there looking at the same file a few months ago, and probably thought the Yard was incompetent. Anyway, I got it late yesterday, but rather than travelling here last night I opted for the early train this morning."

"Well done. I think it will only be you and Malan this morning, and then the defence will presumably produce one or two medical men. Unless you have to dash back to London, I suggest we three have lunch together."

Swindley returned at this point, followed by the defence team who took their seats opposite. "Better wait in the witness box ready, Sergeant," instructed Leeming, "you're on next. I assume you have given evidence in an Assize court before?" Haig assured him that he had and took his place in the box.

Almost immediately, the archaic incantation about 'Oyer and Terminer' was heard outside, and shortly afterwards the jurors were escorted into their box. The Judge entered the courtroom with the usual pomp and looked at both sets of counsel, expecting some sort of application. When nobody moved and all four barristers looked back at him expressionlessly, he almost smiled, and gave orders for the prisoner to be brought up.

As the courtroom finally settled and became silent, Leeming rose and asked for his witness to be sworn. That done, Haig identified himself to the court.

"Where did you go yesterday afternoon,

Sergeant?" enquired the barrister.

"I went to the records department of the War Office."

"What did you do there?"

"Acting on instructions, sir, I retrieved the file of Guy Franklyn Alwyn Ferris. I read the file in its entirety, and I made notes of salient points."

"That was of course the defendant's file. When did he enter the Army?"

"January 11th 1918."

"And what was the highest rank he reached?"

"Second Lieutenant, sir."

"When was he discharged?"

"October 4th 1918."

"At a time when the Great War was still raging. Why was he discharged?"

"He was court-martialled for assaulting a senior officer a few weeks earlier. On conviction, the order was dismissal with disgrace from His Majesty's service."

"Thank you, Sergeant. Now, in the few months between his arrival in the Army, and his being cashiered, can you tell the court where he was stationed?"

"He spent six weeks doing basic training in Catterick, and was sent to Aldershot – where the assault occurred."

"Did he at any time see active service anywhere?"

"He did not."

"Thank you, Sergeant. Please wait there – my learned friends may have some questions for you."

The defence had no questions, and Haig went to sit at the back of the court. As he left the witness box he glanced at the dock and saw Ferris staring down at his feet.

Bryce was watching Sir William Beckett during Haig's evidence and could see that the KC was not at all happy. He assumed Beckett was wishing that he hadn't already read Ferris' statement to the jury – he could have excised the lie about seeing active service and being mentally damaged by the experience.

Hanbury-Lee got to his feet. "I call Detective Sergeant Malan."

Malan came into the courtroom with a carrier bag. This he set down on the floor beside him in the witness box before taking the oath. By now, inevitably, the news about the plea and yesterday's happenings were common knowledge – that much had been reported in the morning's edition of the local newspaper. The huge barrister asked no questions about the early stages of the investigation, and immediately homed in on the search of Ferris's house.

"What did you do on Sunday, May 1$^{st}$, Sergeant?"

On the instructions of Detective Chief Inspector Bryce, and in possession of a warrant issued by a King's Lynn magistrate, I searched the home of the defendant."

"What were the principal items that you found?"

"I found and seized a partly-written letter. I have the original, here, and a transcript. The letter complains that the intended recipient has ignored two previous letters, and goes on to make remarks which can only be construed as declarations of love."

"Thank you, Sergeant. To whom do you deduce that this letter was to have been sent?"

"To Mrs Adelaide Marner, sir, the murdered woman; and no deduction was necessary as the letter begins 'My Dearest Adelaide."

"Yes – a woman, who we have heard was married, and considerably younger than the writer. It will of course be open to the defence to state that the intended recipient was not the victim – we shall see. Perhaps the usher will hand the original to his lordship, and when that is done you may read from your transcript."

Beckett rose, his tone aggrieved. "It is the first the defence has heard about this letter, my lord. I should like to see the document myself before it is read out. I don't dispute that it was obtained lawfully, but it may be that I shall object to its being put into evidence."

"It goes towards motive, my lord," interposed Hanbury-Lee.

The Judge read the unfinished letter and gave it to the usher to pass to Sir William. Beckett and Perry perused it together and held a muttered conversation. With a word of apology to the Judge, Perry moved over to the dock, and exchanged a few words with Ferris. On his return, he made a slight 'nothing doing' gesture towards his leader. Beckett in his turn looked at the Judge and shook his head.

"Please read the letter, Sergeant," said the Judge. Malan read the dozen or so sentences in the letter. From his seat almost beneath their box, Bryce was unable to observe the jury, but he could see expressions of distaste among several members of the public.

"Did you find any other items at the defendant's house?"

"I did, sir." Malan picked up the carrier bag from the floor and took out the three tomes, which he placed on the shelf in front of him. "I found these modern text books. One legal, one medical, and one a combination of the two fields. All three books had been purchased within the previous two months, from Foyles in London. I made enquiries of the bookseller. They were ordered by post, paid for by cheque, and sent to Mr Guy Ferris at his Hunstanton address."

"And on opening these instructional volumes, what did you notice?"

"In all three, there are various annotations. Sentences underlined or ringed around in pencil or sometimes in ink. Notes handwritten in margins."

"I see. And can you tell the court anything about the positioning of these annotations?"

"Yes, sir. Every single one was in a section which dealt with insanity – either as a medical problem, or as to how it is treated in criminal proceedings. There were no annotations in any of the books apart from those on this topic."

"Thank you, Sergeant. My lord, it really isn't possible to describe orally each annotation and the original wording to which it is attached. I suggest these volumes can in due course be perused by you, by the defence, and by the jury. The relevant pages in each volume have been tabbed.

"In the unlikely event that's the defence argues that these notes were not made by the defendant, I should say that we can, if necessary, provide evidence from both fingerprint and handwriting experts that they are his.

"The Crown could have invited the two eminent medical experts we called earlier to comment on these annotations – and of course two barristers and a solicitor have also viewed them. However, we don't think either medical or legal expert evidence is at all necessary. We believe that anyone of reasonable education reading these will come to the inevitable conclusion that they were written solely because the defendant intended to feign insanity."

Beckett shot to his feet again. "My lord, I really must object. We have had no prior notice of this evidence."

The Judge wasn't inclined to be impressed by this complaint. "I rather think, Sir William, that the Crown will say that the books were never part of the requirement to prove your client's guilt; that they have only been produced now because of your recent change of tack, and the fact that you have made an issue of insanity. In any case, I am quite happy to grant you time to peruse them."

He smiled down at the defence KC in a benign and indulgent manner. "Let's see – it is now almost half past eleven. I shall retire with the books for half an hour now. By noon at the latest, I shall have them transferred to your care. You may have them until two o'clock, when the jury will get them for an hour."

Turning towards the twelve men and women he said. "Members of the jury, you will soon be able to see what this is all about, but you must not worry too much about trying to take everything in during that hour. When you eventually retire to consider your verdict, you will have the books – and the various letters – in your room throughout your deliberations. The court will adjourn until three o'clock – two o'clock for the jurors, of course.

"Mr Usher, please bring the books into my chambers now."

***

Bryce gathered Malan and Haig together. "Well done to both of you," he said. Let's go and eat. My hotel is adequate, and I really don't know where else to go.

Over the meal, the DCI described the previous day's events, particularly the plea and the 'statement', and outlined what the doctors had said that morning. He explained that nobody could identify a precedent in a capital case for someone coupling a guilty plea with one of insanity. For Malan's benefit he outlined the evidence that Haig had produced, which directly challenged Ferris's assertion that terrible sights in the Great War had caused him to become unhinged.

"All the jurors really have to decide is his state of mind?" asked Haig.

"In effect, yes. Life in Broadmoor, or the gallows."

"Where are you putting your money, sir?" asked Malan with a grin, knowing of the DCI's oft-repeated claim that he was 'not a betting man'.

"I'd keep my wallet firmly closed here. Practically every scrap of evidence suggests the man is clinically sane. Unless Beckett puts his client in the witness box and he appears incontrovertibly mad, or the defence produces some star alienist who is able to persuade the jury that everyone else is wrong, what we've so far levelled against Ferris will weigh heavily.

"That's my view, but it's the twelve who have to decide. Ferris's screams, giggling, and so on might well be ascribed to deliberate faking of insanity. But could any of the three of us, hand on heart, say that a 'normal' person would have deliberately tried to mislead the police in a number of serious cases? Jurors might find that hard to believe.

"The Judge will no doubt repeat the warning given by the Crown yesterday – the jury must not consider that confession; nor must they take into account the other three murders to which the man has confessed, as there is no evidence for any of them. Nevertheless, that statement is in the jurors' minds. They will almost certainly think, even if sub-consciously, 'only a madman commits four murders, all of people he knows well and allegedly loved'.

"It wouldn't surprise me in the least if the jury ignores everything else, and finds him insane. Who can say they would be wrong? Anyway, we'll see."

Returning to the Shirehall after their lengthy and relaxing lunch, the first person they met was Connor Proudlove. Despite being told he could leave, he had decided to stay, "To see out the rest of this farce and report to our friends. Good material you brought along, Sergeant," he remarked to Haig, when introduced. "That put paid to the nonsense I hear he tried to say about being exposed to terrible sights."

"Indeed," replied Bryce. "However…" and he repeated to Proudlove what he had just said to his colleagues.

"Mmph. See your point, of course. That's the trouble with juries, I suppose. Especially if there's one outspoken man who is able to manipulate the weaker ones who might have the right notion but don't have the guts or the ability to make their argument."

While in some trials there might well be some truth in this theory, Bryce didn't comment. He did briefly wonder whether the old system of 23-man inquest juries might actually have something in its favour – as many as 11 could dissent and still allow the remaining 12 to give a verdict. Not much chance of a vociferous minority overwhelming the others in that set-up. However, in a trial, one could hardly allow a man to be hanged when 11 people thought him innocent!

"Let's go in," he suggested. His original position had been rather restricted, and now he came to sit with the others in the seats reserved for witnesses who had completed their testimonies.

By twenty minutes to three, the public gallery was again packed. At ten to three, the lawyers arrived, more-or-less together. At five to three, the defendant was led back into the dock, and within seconds the jury returned too. The usher went out of the rear door on the dot of three by the courtroom clock, and returned with the Judge a minute later.

"What is your position, Sir William?"

Beckett rose, seemingly with some reluctance. Certainly he did not appear happy.

"My unambiguous instructions are to ignore the evidence adduced by the last witness, my lord. Also, my client will not go into the witness box. I waive my right to make an opening address, relying on my client's statement and my next witness. I call Doctor Frederick Voss."

Dr Voss was a man of about forty. He had a good head of black hair, with a black bushy beard. He wore heavy, black-rimmed spectacles, and was formally dressed in black jacket and striped trousers. Only a bright blue tie provided any colour. He gave the court his qualifications, and his occupation as senior psychiatrist at a well-known London asylum.

He had paid two visits to Norwich Prison to examine Ferris. Each visit had lasted about an hour. Beckett took his expert through his report. Voss testified, in essence, that in his opinion Ferris was clinically insane. In explaining his findings, the doctor went into considerable detail, which the KC seemed to encourage.

When Beckett had finished with his witness, Hanbury-Lee rose. He looked almost pityingly at the doctor.

"When did you last examine the defendant, Doctor?"

"I saw him last on the 3$^{rd}$ of June."

"That was over two months ago. You have not seen him since?"

"No."

"Since that time, the situation has changed, has it not?"

"I really don't understand your question."

"Well, the defendant has provided his legal advisors with a detailed written statement, which was read to the court yesterday. You were not, I think, in court to hear it – have you been shown a copy?"

"I only arrived in the city two hours ago; I have been shown a copy but have had little time to analyse it."

"I see. Forgetting the detail of the content for a moment, would you agree that it is coherent, cogent, even?"

"I can't deny that, but the content demonstrates an illness of the mind – schizophrenia, in fact – as I said a few minutes ago."

"Really. We heard yesterday from two very experienced doctors called by the Crown. You may have been told that both of them believe the defendant is feigning insanity. Would you care to comment?"

Voss hesitated. "I have not heard their

testimony. It is not unusual for medical people to disagree regarding a diagnosis, particularly with diseases of the mind."

"Perhaps. However, both of these experts" – he emphasised the last word – "saw the defendant much more than you – and more recently.

"This morning, we heard about three modern textbooks found at the defendant's home. Have you heard about these books, and about the notes written inside them?"

"Yes; and I had a chance to examine them briefly soon after my arrival."

"For some reason Sir William didn't mention these books in your examination-in-chief, but I'll put a question to you now. Do you accept that the handwritten annotations indicate very clearly that the defendant was preparing a defence of insanity?"

Voss flushed, and hesitated. "I suppose the notes might be interpreted in that way."

"Would you care to advance an alternative interpretation, Doctor?"

"I should need to examine the books in much more detail before I could do that."

"I see. You have told the court, in no uncertain terms, that the defendant is insane in law. Yet you accept that this evidence could suggest otherwise."

Voss was silent.

"You work in one of the largest asylums in

Europe, do you not, Doctor?"

"That is correct."

"By the time a patient arrives at your door, he or she has already been seen by other practitioners, and has been sent to your hospital after some sort of positive diagnosis of mental illness, presumably?"

"I suppose that is so."

"Yes. So how many people arrive at your facility, who in your opinion are only feigning insanity?"

"I cannot say. Not many, I think."

"Not many. Yes. Remember you are under oath. Very roughly, how many have you yourself seen in the last five years? A thousand? A hundred? Ten? One? None?"

"I cannot give a figure."

"I see. The jury will draw its own conclusions, but I myself conclude that your experience in spotting a fraudulent mental case is very, very limited. I put it to you that you have been fooled.

Again Voss didn't reply.

"I think that to ask you any further questions would be pointless."

Hanbury-Lee crashed back into his seat. As a prosecutor facing the witness box had his back to the jury, no juror had been able to observe the disbelieving expression on his face during the cross-examination, nor see the roll of his eyes to heaven as he sat down – but they might have been able to surmise both actions.

Beckett and Perry were in animated discussion. The men at the prosecution table, although only a matter of feet away, couldn't catch every word. However, it was clear that one man thought the disastrous witness should be abandoned. The other, while agreeing it was a disaster, felt that something must be done to repair the situation.

After a full minute had passed, the Judge spoke. "Do you intend to re-examine, Sir William?"

"No, my lord."

"Beckett's pulled rank," whispered Leeming to his own leader. "I wonder how Ferris will take it?"

He had hardly completed the sentence when the defendant suddenly stood up and started to scream again.

"Not very well, it would seem," whispered Hanbury-Lee in reply.

"Take the defendant back to the cells," the Judge ordered the prison officers. "The court will adjourn now until tomorrow, so he won't be required again today." Ferris, still screeching intermittently and struggling violently, was pulled out of the dock. When he had gone, the Judge continued.

"I shall adjourn until ten thirty tomorrow morning. Both sides can make their closing speeches, and my own summing up will not take long. Ladies and gentlemen of the jury, I expect that the matter will be handed to you well before lunch."

# CHAPTER 20

Malan had travelled from King's Lynn each morning, rather than staying in the city overnight. As he said, he only needed to leave home at eight o'clock to arrive at the court in good time. However, he rather regretted this now, as it would have been nice to spend an evening with the DCI again. Bryce himself alluded to this, but had insisted that the Sergeant should drive home and get an early night.

Haig had no possible excuse for remaining in Norwich. As soon as the court rose he accompanied the DCI back to his hotel, where Bryce deposited his briefcase. The two colleagues then walked down Prince of Wales Road to the railway station. On the Foundry Bridge, crossing the River Wensum just outside the station, the two men shook hands, and Haig continued to the trains. Bryce stood for a few seconds admiring the attractive station facade, a comparatively late piece of railway architecture, dating only from 1886 when the station was rebuilt. He had also read about the bridge, and how it too was a replacement at about the same time. Apparently it had been assembled in the station forecourt and then rolled into position. He went down steps beside a public house onto a footpath beside the river, and after going along for a few paces turned and looked back at the fine lines of the bridge.

Continuing along beside the sluggish river, he turned left by the old Pull's Ferry, the building recently restored and still recognisable from the dozens of paintings made of it in previous centuries. He knew, from his little pamphlet, that this was also the starting point of a short canal, dug from the river some eight hundred years before to convey stone for the construction of the cathedral – particularly the Caen limestone used for facing the basic flint and mortar. Following the line of the long-filled-in canal, he reached the great building. Bryce walked around the cloisters, looking at the old bosses, miraculous survivors from earlier iconoclastic times. He saw a one depicting a 'green man', and was much taken by another showing Death as the fourth horseman, riding out of the mouth of hell. Completing the circuit of the cloister, he entered the cathedral itself. He didn't know it, but the door he used was the Prior's door – as opposed to the Monks' Door at the next corner of the cloisters. He walked around, getting a bit of a crick in his neck as he tried to look up at the numerous bosses and the vaulting of the high roof.

His desire to look at church architecture sated for the moment, he left by the West Door, and returned via the Ethelbert Gate to his hotel and a much-needed dinner.

***

The next morning he returned to the Shirehall for what he hoped was the last time. Malan had already arrived, having left his home in Snettisham a little earlier than he had on the previous day. Hanbury-Lee was also in the courtroom, and he lumbered over to talk to the two policemen. "You gave your evidence very well, Sergeant," he remarked, to Malan's great pleasure. "Well, we'll soon see what the jury thinks. The evidence is all in our favour, but lay people considering the question of insanity are often devoid of logic, and God knows by what process this jury will make its decision." This was, of course, exactly the opinion expressed by the DCI the day before.

"My closing will take ten minutes at most. I don't envy Beckett his job – don't know what I'd say if I were in his shoes this morning. As for Salmon's summing up, well that shouldn't take too long either."

"Had you expected Ferris to go into the box?" asked Bryce.

"Up to the time the books were produced, yes. I thought Beckett would have fought to get that evidence, and the part-written letter, excluded. But he didn't even try, and once the jury had seen what Ferris had written, I think he simply couldn't risk his client being cross-examined."

The court had filled up while they were speaking, and the barrister returned to his place while Bryce and Malan went to their seats as before.

The jury came in and sat down, the defendant appeared again in the dock, and the judge returned. When he had settled, Hanbury-Lee rose.

"My lord, members of the jury, in summarising the case for the Crown I shall not take up much of your time. The defendant entered a guilty plea to the charge, and even without that plea the Crown has, I suggest, provided ample evidence to confirm his guilt.

"There remains only his allegation that he was not of sound mind when committing the offence.

"Let me deal first with the defendant's 'statement', which my learned friend read out at the start of these proceedings. No evidence whatsoever has been produced to suggest that any of the offences claimed in that statement have basis in fact. Unsubstantiated confessions to other crimes – which may not have occurred at all – are not relevant. The one and only matter in that statement which concerns you is the defendant's claim that he does not know why he killed Adelaide Marner.

"But you have heard how he wrote, more than once to Mrs Marner. You have seen the partly-written letter, in which he bemoans the fact that she has not answered previous letters. You may think, having seen the sort of things he was saying to her, that she was wise not to reply. Nobody can say what passed between them when she went down to the promenade that evening. But whatever Mrs Marner said, it was very clearly not what the defendant had hoped for.

"You heard from four highly respectable citizens, who regularly play bridge with the defendant. They testified that he is a very competent player, with a good memory. They each refuted the suggestion that he has ever displayed any signs of madness.

"You have also had the benefit of hearing the professional opinions of three doctors, each with many years' experience. Two of these saw the defendant many times. All, including one of the most highly-qualified psychiatrists, agree that he is only pretending to be mad.

"The defence put up another doctor, who tried to prove that the defendant is insane. Now with all respect to Dr Voss, he completely failed to 'come up to proof', as we lawyers say. In other words, in the witness box he was unable to sustain what he had put in his statement. There were several reasons for this.

"First, as he had not seen the defendant for some months, Dr Voss was not *au fait* with the latest position. At the time he wrote his report he had not seen the remarkably sane statement produced by the defendant.

"Second, he only saw the defendant twice, and for only an hour on each occasion. The two doctors called by the Crown to testify specifically on Ferris's mental state saw him substantially more often – and much more recently. Professor Castle saw him four times, each examination lasting around two hours. Dr Rodway had some six lengthy meetings with the defendant, and also saw him more briefly several times in each of the twelve weeks the defendant was in his prison.

"Third, Dr Voss was unable to state whether he had ever met a single case of a man pretending to be insane.

"Then ladies and gentlemen, we come to the legal and medical text books. You heard that these were bought by the defendant, only a few weeks before he killed Mrs Marner. You yourselves have seen the various annotations in each book. The Crown says that these annotations were made by an educated and perfectly sane person, and that the only possibly inference that can be drawn from them is that the writer was investigating how to feign insanity in criminal proceedings.

"The defendant has asked you to return the special verdict of 'guilty but insane'. I suggest that you have heard absolutely nothing to back up such a verdict. I ask you return a simple verdict of 'guilty'."

Hanbury-Lee sat down again, and once more the bench creaked complainingly under his weight.

Sir William Beckett rose.

"Let me tackle a couple of points straight away. First, as far as the books are concerned, the fact is that my client has no memory of even ordering them, let alone writing in them. That is very important."

Hanbury-Lee started to struggle to his feet in order to object, but the Judge forestalled him. "No, Sir William. You client didn't give evidence. You cannot now tell us what he would have said if he gone into the witness box, and been subject to cross-examination."

Beckett bowed. "As your lordship pleases.

"Second, the matter of my client's reference to seeing 'shocking things' during the First War. It was wrongly inferred that he meant he had personally been involved in such events. He meant that he had read about such terrible happenings at the time, and during the next few years saw various films showing the horrors and suffering. It was these sights which may have affected his brain."

Both the Judge and Hanbury-Lee stirred,

but neither intervened, and Beckett continued.

"The mental state of a human mind is not something that anyone can ascertain casually, or superficially. It is self-evident that it can also change over time. It is hardly surprising that even experts can sometimes disagree about a diagnosis. Dr Voss, an eminent psychiatrist, says that my client did not know what he was doing at the time of the murder. You are entitled to treat his opinion with the same respect as you treat that of other witnesses.

"I hear what my learned friend says regarding my client's statement. I must disagree with him. Had the court simply been deciding guilt or innocence, the defendant would not of course have denied one murder while admitting a series of others. It would be tantamount to suicide. Those matters would not have been put into evidence at all.

"But you are not here to decide guilt – my client has admitted killing Mrs Marner, and I concede that the evidence supports that. You are here to decide whether my client knew what he was doing that evening – and if he did know what he was doing, whether he knew that it was wrong.

"My friend used the word 'cogent' to describe the content of that statement. That is a fair comment. But we need to look far more deeply than just the manner in which it is written. We need to look at the content.

## THE AMATEUR DETECTIVE

"The defendant went out and deliberately impeded the police in other murder investigations. Would a sane man really do that? And even if he did, would he tell anyone about it?

"He tells you that he killed three other people. There is no reason to doubt his word – he says that the police are aware of those matters, and the Crown has not denied that. Would a sane man kill all these people – each of whom he loved? And would a sane man admit it in a court of law? I suggest not.

"You have seen a little of the bizarre behaviour displayed in the dock. In fact, were we to recall any of the medical witnesses, or indeed the senior detective in the case, you would hear of other noisy and even more disturbing behaviour.

"Ladies and gentlemen, I know that you will have no trouble in rapidly coming to the conclusion that my client did not know what he was doing that evening in Hunstanton, and that you are perfectly entitled to bring in a verdict of guilty but insane."

\*\*\*

Beckett sat down, and a buzz ran around the courtroom. The Judge didn't need to employ his gavel, as the sound ceased completely as he looked up and began to speak.

"It is my task to summarise the evidence for you, ladies and gentlemen. This has been a remarkably short trial, and you have not been burdened with a great deal of complex evidence. However, as in many trials, some of what you have heard has been conflicting, and where that has happened, it is for you to decide.

"There is little that I can help you with. What I feel may be important points, you may think are trivial or even irrelevant. That is your right, as individuals and collectively.

"The first thing is the matter of the murder itself. The defendant admitted that at the start of this trial. You have heard evidence from the Crown witnesses, sufficient I am sure for you to confirm that part of the plea. Indeed, Sir William in his closing address did not seek to persuade you otherwise.

"So we come to the crucial matter. Is the defendant insane, such that he didn't know what he was doing at the time he killed Adelaide Marner? He says that he did not. He further says that he remembers nothing about it. Three doctors called by the Crown say that there is nothing to suggest that the defendant is insane. Indeed, they go much further, and say that he is pretending to be mad. Other witnesses testified as to his excellent memory.

"The defence called another psychiatrist. It is undeniable that this witness spent significantly less time in the defendant's presence than the two experts brought by the Crown. It is also undeniable that they examined the defendant much more recently.

"Now, the Crown says that the defence expert has no expertise in dealing with someone who is feigning madness. You may think that is a relevant factor to take into consideration.

"The next point is that of the text books, legal and medical, with handwritten notes in them. That the books were bought by the defendant has not been denied, and there is no suggestion that the writing was done by someone else.

"The Crown says that the notes are evidence of the defendant's intention, in advance of the murder, to feign insanity. You will have the books with you when considering your verdict, and the interpretation and significance of the notes is a matter for you.

"Then there is the partly-written but unsent letter. The defence does not dispute that the intended recipient was Mrs Marner. The letter was put into evidence purely as a pointer towards motive. However, you will have it with you in the jury room, and I think you are entitled to take it into account when considering the question of insanity – even though neither side has sought to raise that point. You will also have the two letters sent to Mrs Marner previously, and you may draw conclusions from those.

"Let me just go back to the defendant's original statement. In it he confesses to three other murders. There has been no evidence that any such murders occurred. The defence says the confession is evidence of insanity. I have to tell you that that, in itself, is not evidence of insanity. Within living memory, there have been a number of cases involving multiple murders. Smith, the so-called 'brides in the bath' murderer, was not insane, merely avaricious. Much more recently Haigh was convicted of six murders, and then admitted those and three more. The Crown opposed his plea of insanity – on the grounds of malice aforethought and the clear attempts to cover up the crimes. The jury did not find him insane.

"You have two choices. Guilty but insane; or simply guilty. It is a matter for you."

The jury retired to their room, the defendant letting out an ear-piercing scream as they left their box. This surprised a lady juror so much that she stumbled on the steps and would have fallen had she not been grabbed by the usher. Ferris was taken to the cells, and the Judge retired to his chambers.

Across the counsels' table, Beckett and Perry talked with Hanbury-Lee and Leeming.

"Salmon was fair, I thought," said Leeming. "Can't argue with what he said," agreed Perry, gloomily. "I thought the reference to Haigh was rather unfair," said Beckett. The parallels are not exact – unlike Haigh, Ferris did not gain any financial reward, nor did he claim to have drunk the blood of any of his victims."

"Come off it, Beckett – Salmon was only rebutting your point about a multiple murderer automatically being insane," replied Hanbury-Lee. "And, in law, he's quite correct."

Beckett grunted crossly. Like any lawyer, he didn't like to lose, and was already trying to think about possible grounds for appeal.

"You could see the jury and we couldn't," continued Hanbury-Lee. "Even addressing them from our side of the table, is very difficult, actually. How did you think they looked during the summing up?"

Beckett and Perry both looked gloomy. "Appearances can be misleading, of course," replied Beckett, "but I'd not put a penny on getting the special verdict."

Bryce, who couldn't observe the jury from his original seat, had been able to do so when he moved to sit with his colleagues. He was just saying much the same as Beckett. Proudlove moved across from where he had been sitting. "It'll be a travesty if the jury finds him insane," was his opening remark as he joined the three policemen.

"Too true," responded Malan. Bryce didn't speak. Proudlove went on to talk about Seymour Marner.

"He telephoned me on Saturday evening, out of the blue. Asked if I was going to attend the trial. I said I was, ready to refuse if he suggested travelling together or anything. But he went on to say that as he wasn't being called as a witness he thought it would be hypocritical for him to attend just as an observer, given the way he'd treated Adelaide. He sounded quite contrite, as a matter of fact. Anyway, he asked if I would sort of represent him. Like when someone can't attend a funeral. Bit unusual, but he did sound sorry. Anyway, no skin off my nose, so I agreed.

"Wanted to ask you, Chief Inspector. When you got the paper to print the old RA shot of Addy's portrait, did it produce any results?"

"Oh yes, it certainly produced a witness – Edward Fairchild, who didn't read the local newspapers. As you heard, the chap was the final key to pinning down Ferris's movements that evening."

"Oh, good. There's been a development on the portrait front. This case apparently reached the press over in the States, and the American guy who bought the picture has had a couple of reporters trying to talk to him. Well, he's getting on in years, and doesn't seem to have any close kin – or if he does he doesn't want them to inherit it. Well, he wrote to me a couple of months ago. Remember I never had with him contact originally – he bought it from a London dealer. Anyway, he is making a remarkably generous offer. If I can find an English gallery of international standing that would be prepared to display it, he will gift it immediately. I've discussed this with the National, the Tate, and the National Portrait Galleries. All three would bite the old boy's hand off. So, with a bit of luck, in a few months it'll be coming back across the Atlantic, to hang in London for everyone to see."

"That's very good news, Mr Proudlove. I saw your work at the Academy before it was sold, and have never forgotten it – which was why I thought that even a small black-and-white image of it might attract someone to read my appeal."

There was a bit of a flurry in the courtroom as a message was delivered to the Clerk of Assize from the usher whose job was to guard the jury. The Clerk in turn despatched another usher to find the barristers, and sent someone else to produce the defendant. The Judge's own clerk was waiting nearby, and he disappeared through the rear door to alert his master.

By the time the Judge entered, everyone else was back in court.

The Clerk rose and faced the jury.

"Mr Foreman, please stand. Are you agreed upon a verdict?"

"We are, my lord."

"Do you find the prisoner guilty or not guilty?"

"We find him guilty, my lord."

"Do you or do you not add a finding of insanity?"

"We do not."

"Is that the verdict of you all?"

"It is, my lord."

"Do you wish to add anything to your verdict?"

"No, my lord; we do not."

"Thank you; please sit."

Mr Justice Salmon wasted no more time. He asked Ferris if he wished to say anything before sentence was passed. Ferris, standing silently in the dock, shook his head. The square of black silk was placed on the Judge's wig. The Judge was brief. He told the defendant there was no point in giving a homily. He said the jury had reached the only possible verdict, and passed sentence of death. There was no chaplain in the courtroom, so nobody said 'amen' after the Judge finished with the usual 'and may the Lord have mercy on your soul'.

Ferris was taken away, still not making a sound, to the surprise of many of those present.

Outside, Proudlove came over and thanked the police officers. "Justice has been done," was the artist's sober observation.

After he had gone, Bryce spoke to Malan. "I'll see you again in a couple of weeks, it seems, when the other case comes to court at long last. It may be moved to the Assizes at Cambridge, though, because the session here might be finished before everything is ready."

Malan went to find his car, and the DCI returned to his hotel. He had already checked out and, needed only to collect the bag which he had lodged with the concierge. Walking down to the railway station, he bought a first-class ticket to Liverpool Street and boarded the waiting train. He fell asleep soon after passing Diss, and didn't wake until the train restarted with a jerk on leaving Chelmsford.

At Liverpool Street – still feeling exhausted – he did something he had never done before: took a taxi all the way out to his home.

***********************************

# BOOKS BY THIS AUTHOR

## The Bedroom Window Murder

It is 1949. Sir Francis Sherwood – WW1 hero, landowner, magistrate – is shot dead while standing at an open bedroom window in his country house. A rifle is found in the grounds.

The county police seek help from Scotland Yard.

Detective Chief Inspector Bryce and Detective Sergeant Haig are assigned to the case. The first difficulty for the Yard men is that nobody with even a mild dislike of Sherwood can be found.

But before that problem can be resolved, others arise...

## The Courthouse Murder

In July 1949, an unpopular and deeply unpleasant man is stabbed in the courthouse of an English city. As the murder has been committed in a room to which the general public doesn't have access, it seems probable that the culprit is someone involved with the business of the courts.

Suspects include a number of lawyers, police officers, and magistrates.

For various reasons, the local Chief Constable decides to ask Scotland Yard to investigate the murder.

Chief Inspector Philip Bryce and Sergeant Alex Haig are assigned to the case.

Theirs is a recent partnership, but the two men worked well together in another murder case a few weeks before. (See 'The Bedroom Window Murder'.)

## The Felixstowe Murder

In August 1949, Detective Chief Inspector Bryce and his new bride are holidaying in the East Anglian seaside resort of Felixstowe.

During afternoon tea in the Palm Court of their hotel, a man dies at a nearby table.

Reluctant to get directly involved, Bryce

nevertheless agrees to help the inexperienced local police inspector get to grips with his first murder case, turning his own honeymoon into a 'busman's holiday'.

## Multiples Of Murder

Three more cases for Philip Bryce. The first two are set in 1949, and follow on from The Bedroom Window Murder, The Courthouse Murder, and The Felixstowe Murder.
The third goes back to 1946, when Bryce – not long back in the police after his army service – was a mere Detective Inspector, based in Whitechapel rather than Scotland Yard.

1. In the office kitchen of a small advertising agency in London, a man falls to the floor, dead. Initially, it is believed that he had some sort of heart attack, but it soon becomes clear that he had received a fatal electric shock. A faulty kettle is then blamed. But evidence emerges showing that this was not an accident. Chief Inspector Bryce is assigned to the case.

2. Just before opening time, a body is found in the larger pool at the huge public baths in St Marylebone. The man has been shot, presumably the previous evening. It is DCI Bryce's task, aided by Detective Sergeant Haig and others, to

discover the identity of the victim, why he was killed, and who shot him.

3. For a few months in 1946, a traditional London bus was modified in an experiment to allow passengers to 'Pay-As-You-Board'. Doors were fitted, instead of having the usual open platform. The stairs rose from inside the saloon rather than directly from the platform. On the upper deck, a man is found stabbed to death. None of the passengers can shed any light on the murder, yet the design of this bus meant that no-one could have jumped off the bus unnoticed – one of them must be the murderer. Inspector Bryce, together with colleagues from Leman Street police station, solves one of his earlier cases.

## Death At Mistram Manor

In September 1949, a wake is being held at a manor house in Oxfordshire, following the burial of the chatelaine. Over a hundred mourners are present.

Within an hour, the clergyman who conducted the funeral service is taken ill himself. The local doctor, present at the wake, provisionally diagnoses appendicitis, and calls for an ambulance. However, the priest dies soon after being admitted to hospital.

An autopsy reveals that the cause of death was strychnine poisoning.

The circumstances are such that accidental ingestion and suicide are both ruled out. The rector was murdered, and the timing means that the poison must have been taken during the wake.

The local police, faced with a lengthy list of potential suspects, ask Scotland Yard to take on the investigation, and the case is assigned to Detective Chief Inspector Bryce and two colleagues.

Although most of the mourners can easily be eliminated from the enquiry, around eight of them cannot. The experienced London officers have to sift through a number of initially-promising indications, before finally being able to identify the killer.

## Machinations Of A Murderer

There are at least two reasons why Robin Whitaker wants to eliminate his wife, Dulcie. He is not allowed to drink any alcohol, nor to gamble.

Dulcie controls his life to an extent that he finds

intolerable. But she is also wealthy, so merely leaving her is not an acceptable option.

In most circumstances Dr Whitaker thinks and acts like the very intelligent and highly-educated man he is. However, he has somehow convinced himself that the action of killing his wife is justified. He is also certain that his innate brainpower will give him a significant edge over any police detectives, and allow him to outwit them with ease.

What are his thoughts? How does he make his decisions? What does he do?

Will he get away with murder?

## Suspicions Of A Parlourmaid, And The Norfolk Railway Murders

Two more cases for Philip Bryce.

1 An affluent elderly lady dies. The death certificate cites 'natural causes', but the servants are uncomfortable.

A parlourmaid decides to go to New Scotland Yard, and talk to someone there. She is fortunate, because Detective Sergeant Haig happens to pass through the foyer while she is explaining. The busy desk officer intercepts him, and asks to him to listen to the maid's story.

Haig listens politely, but is ready to dismiss the story as tittle-tattle, when he hears one thing which makes him take notice. He goes to report to his boss, DCI Bryce, who also finds the point of interest, and speaks to the maid himself.

The full might of the Metropolitan Police is then focused on the matter – and a post mortem examination reveals that the lady certainly did not die from natural causes.

In the leafy South London suburb of Dulwich Village, Bryce and Haig investigate the happenings, and sort out who is innocent, and who is guilty.

2. DCI Bryce is sent to Norfolk, where two solicitors have been killed. There are obvious connections between the crimes. First, both men were partners in the same firm. But also, both appeared to have been killed while travelling on local railway trains, and the bodies then thrown off. Over the whole existence of railways in Britain, the number of such cases could be counted on the fingers of one hand. So one such case would have been rare enough, but for there to be two – on different trains and a few days apart – was almost unbelievable.

However, shortly before these two men were found, a third body was discovered. This victim didn't seem to have any connection to the firm of solicitors – but he too was found beside a railway track.

A temporary absence of CID officers in King's Lynn causes the Chief Constable to ask Scotland Yard to take the case. DCI Bryce and two of his officers travel to West Norfolk, where they find a local Detective Constable eager to help.

Which of the three victims was the real target, and which murders were either dry runs or red herrings?

## This Village Is Cursed

A young provincial journalist receives a telephone call from a man who won't give his name. Anticipating the scoop of his career, Marcus Cunningham arranges to meet the informant at Liverpool Street station.

Subsequent events quickly draw in Scotland Yard detectives Chief Inspector Philip Bryce and his colleague Sergeant Alex Haig, as they conduct a complex murder investigation.

## Demands With Menaces

1950. Out of the blue, Philip Bryce is suddenly given two pieces of news – one domestic, the other work-related.

Within hours, he finds himself given a 'double-jump' promotion, and put in charge of a new and important department at Scotland Yard.

At the same time he learns about his promotion, he is given a new case. It's a change from the murder cases he spends a lot of time on, but it's tricky. This one involves 'demands with menaces' – blackmail. And the first three victims are high-ranking people – a rich peer, a government minister, and a bishop. In fact so important are they that the Commissioner instructs the newly appointed Detective Chief Superintendent to take charge of the case himself.

Bryce investigates, with the also-promoted Inspector Haig alongside him.

But who is the blackmailer? From where does he or she acquire the information? And just how innocent are the 'victims'?

## Death Of A Safebreaker

1937. A burglar is found shot dead in the home of Viscount Tallis, a wealthy industrialist. The man was equipped with a stethoscope, and appears to have been attempting to open a safe in the study. Tallis himself is in the middle of the Atlantic Ocean, on his way to America on Government business. Although various members of his family are present in the house, together with guests, nobody has access to the safe – nobody even knows what it might contain. It isn't even clear if the safebreaker succeeded in opening it. Detective Inspector Tommy Rees is given the case. Rees is approaching retirement, and has never had to investigate a murder in his rural county before. Initially he has little choice about taking advice from two or three people who are themselves on the suspect list. Eventually, he must rely on the goodwill – and deep pockets – of the absent Lord Tallis.

Printed in Great Britain
by Amazon